Consider the Sunflowers

Elma Schemenauer

To Kathleen,
Great to finally meet you.
God bless.
Elma Schemenauer
Sept. 2015

Canadä

The Publishers acknowledge the financial assistance of the
Government of Canada through the Book Publishing Industry
Development Program (BPIDP) for our publishing activities.

Library and Archives Canada Cataloguing in Publication
Schemenauer, Elma, author
    Consider the sunflowers / Elma Martens Schemenauer.

Issued in print and electronic formats.
ISBN 978-0-88887-575-4 (pbk.).–ISBN 978-0-88887-576-1 (epub)

    I. Title.

PS8587.C4347C65 2014   C813'.54   C2014-904419-4
                                          C2014-904420-8

ALSO AVAILABLE AS AN EBOOK ISBN 978-0-88887-576-1

Cover design: David Ross Tierney, Ottawa
Printed and bound in Canada on acid free paper.

Consider the Sunflowers

Elma Schemenauer

BOREALIS
BOOK PUBLISHERS

Borealis Press
Ottawa, Canada
2014

To Bob, my man for all seasons

Acknowledgements

I'd like to thank members of the Internet Writers Workshop and others who critiqued *Consider the Sunflowers* at various stages. When I followed their sometimes challenging suggestions, I usually felt the story growing into something clearer and deeper. I also want to thank the folks at Borealis Press in Ottawa. Frank Tierney believed in my story and invited me to join his extensive list of authors. Janet Shorten wisely and patiently edited the manuscript. David Tierney spearheaded its transformation into a finished paper book and e-book.

About the Mennonite Timeline

Several characters in this novel are Mennonites who emigrated from Russia to North America. I prepared the Timeline at the end of this book to summarize their history. The Timeline also interweaves the Russian Mennonites' story with that of Mennonites who came from Switzerland and southern Germany.

About the Study Guide

The Study Guide at the end of this novel is intended to enhance the reading experience by stimulating thought and discussion. It's aimed at readers and writers interested in narrative elements such as setting, plot, characterization, motivation, and point of view. It will be especially useful to book club members, educators, and post-secondary and secondary students, including those in homeschool settings.

Chapter 1

Municipality of Coyote, Saskatchewan, March 1940

Tina felt like liverwurst in a sandwich, trapped in the stalled truck between her dad and the man he wanted her to marry. Rich, boring Roland Fast.

From the looks of things, she might not survive to marry anyone. Freezing to death seemed more likely. All she saw through the windshield was blowing snow. Occasionally she glimpsed the fence beside the ditch they were stuck in. Beyond the fence, only a wilderness of white glittering in the afternoon light: no Saskatchewan prairie, no horizon, not even a telephone pole.

She stamped her boots, trying to warm her icy feet. She should never have agreed to come along and sketch Roland's horses. She liked horses, but getting stranded in a blizzard wasn't supposed to be part of the deal.

To be fair, she couldn't blame Roland and her dad. They weren't expecting this storm. It had howled in from the northeast with hardly a whimper of warning.

Her nostrils tingled with cold and the green-banana stench of Roland's hair oil. She pulled the collar of her jacket higher, nudging him with her elbow. "How about trying the ignition again?" If they got the truck going, they'd at least have some heat.

Roland slumped over the steering wheel, his apple-cheeked profile making him look younger than his twenty-eight years. "It's no use. This stupid truck isn't going to start."

"Don't blame the truck, Roland," Tina's dad said. "There's probably snow in the engine."

Roland's sigh puffed out white in the frigid air.

Tina almost felt sorry for him. According to Roland, his

1940 Ford was the most modern half-ton on the road. No other new model had such a powerful engine. But all that horsepower under the hood was useless without a spark to get it going. Something like her and Roland. There wasn't any spark between them.

Her dad shifted on the seat, jostling her onto Roland's wide shoulder.

She edged away. "Could we brush the snow out of the engine?" she asked, sounding more hopeful than she felt.

Roland gave her a bleak smile, his face too close to hers. "I doubt it in these conditions."

"Okay, I just thought I'd ask." She didn't know how Roland felt about her. Not knowing made her nervous. He was awkward with women, but she sometimes caught him watching her with a certain softness in his eyes.

Whether he was interested or not, she should quit letting her parents throw them together every time she came home from Vancouver. She should simply tell her folks, "Look, I don't want you interfering in my life. I'm a grown woman; I've got a job in the city. Anyway I'm in love with someone else."

She shuddered to think of the avalanche of questions her parents would ask. She wasn't ready to answer them, not yet.

The wind whooped around the truck, rattling the windows.

Roland reached behind the seat, grabbed his hat, and plunked it over his blond curls. "I think we should walk to Frank's house. It's the closest."

Tina's heart jumped at the mention of the man she loved, but she kept her expression blank. She didn't want her dad or Roland guessing how she felt about Frank. They'd be shocked. Her dad would scold and rage. He wanted her to marry a church-going Mennonite, preferably the owner of this impotent truck.

She jerked her chin toward the bottle of pills in Roland's pocket. "What about your mare? I thought she needed that medicine."

"We'll get it to her as soon as we can, but we'll want some-place to get warm along the way." His voice reminded her of a radio announcer booming out news of Hitler's war.

Her dad rummaged under the seat, crowding her against Roland.

She moved away.

Her dad sat up, his head bobbing. "Roland, do you have any blankets? I think we should stay here till the storm lets up. It's too dangerous to walk in weather like this."

Roland shot him a narrow-eyed look. "Obrom, we've got no heat in here. We could freeze to death, even with blankets. This storm could last for days."

"We could freeze outside, too." Tina's dad pulled his hand-kerchief out of his pocket and gave his nose a honk. "The snow's blowing too thick. We might get lost and wander around like drunkards."

"Not if we follow the pasture fence," Roland said. "It'll lead us right to Frank's." He raised his eyebrows at Tina. "What do you think?"

She peered out into the arctic blankness. If they stayed here, they'd probably freeze unless someone came along and helped them—not likely. If they braved the blizzard, they'd either reach shelter or die trying. "We can't be far from Frank's," she said. She remembered passing his neighbour's granaries before the storm hit.

"It's about a quarter-mile," Roland said.

Tina sucked in a chilly breath. "We can make it." It was better to face danger head-on than wait around to see what would happen, wasn't it? She reached into her pocket for her fuzzy woollen cap and tugged it down over her ears.

Her dad's brow puckered like it did when he was deep in thought. With all her heart Tina hoped she and Roland were making the right decision.

Her father sighed, then glanced from her to Roland as if

they were a couple. "I guess you young people are right." He put on his cap and lowered the earflaps. Tina helped him tie his scarf over his nose and mouth. Then he opened the passenger door and she plunged out after him.

The wind hit her hard, whistling through her cap and making her ears smart. She pulled her scarf from under her jacket. Fighting the wind, she tied it over her cap.

Her dad motioned for her to follow Roland, who was ploughing through the ditch toward the fence. She struggled along in his footsteps with her father close behind. Snow spilled into her boots, shocking her with coldness.

The drifts were shallower on the pasture side of the ditch. Strands of barbed wire appeared and disappeared between blasts of snow. God willing, that elusive fence would lead the three of them to her boyfriend's house. Tina dared to smile. The good Lord must have a sense of humour.

"We'll walk in the pasture, away from the ditch," Roland bellowed above the yowling wind. He set one boot on the lower wire of the fence, held it down, and lifted the upper one, creating a gap for Tina to climb through. She scrambled between the wires, careful not to catch her jacket on the barbs, then stepped aside as her dad and Roland ducked through.

"Come on," Roland called, heading along the fence. "Single file. Stay together."

Tina followed, admiring Roland's boldness in spite of herself. She knew why her parents wanted her to marry him. He was strong, worked hard, and came from a family who had owned an estate in the old country. Roland's ancestors had the same Dutch-German-Mennonite background as hers. According to her folks, that shared heritage would make a solid foundation for marriage and children.

But Roland was as boring as turnips compared with Frank. Her Frank was hot peppers, red cabbage, and wild mushrooms. He was adventure, music, and laughter. Some people said he didn't have the gumption to buckle down to farming, but they didn't know him like Tina did. He just needed a good woman to settle him down.

Her hands ached with cold, even in the coyote-skin mittens Frank had given her. She clenched and unclenched her fists, trying to get her circulation going, then peered over her shoulder to see how her dad was doing. His tall figure loomed through a whirling smoke of snow. The scarf over his nose and mouth was white with frost from his breath clouding into the air. She motioned for him to shift the icy patch away from his face and turned to follow Roland again.

She didn't see him. Where was Roland? She took a few steps forward, feeling like a ship without a rudder, and almost bumped into a lumpy snow-covered mound. It seemed big, wider than an outhouse though not as high.

"Tina!" Roland's shout came from ahead and to her right. "This way."

A bolt of relief shot through her as she spied Roland chugging along beyond the obstacle. She checked to make sure her father was still behind her, then followed Roland, grateful for the partial shelter offered by the mound of whatever it was.

A rock pile. Of course. Frank's father had picked tons of rocks off his land when he farmed here. This must be one of the places where he'd chosen to dump them. She fought the wind to the far side of the rocks. Once she was clear of them, she caught sight of the fence again and turned to wave to her dad.

He wasn't there.

Tina's heart fluttered like a bird caught in a fox's jaws. She drew a breath to call to Roland, then saw something long and dark slumped beside the rocks. "Roland," she shrieked, "something's wrong with Dad." She stumbled toward her father, fell, picked herself up, and hurtled forward.

Chapter 2

"Dad, what's the matter?" Tina's father lay huddled in the shelter of the rock pile. She dropped to her knees in the snow beside him.

His watery eyes flitted from her face to Roland's.

"Are you sick?" Tina asked.

"Just resting," he said, his voice muffled by the scarf over his nose and mouth.

Roland grabbed his arm. "Obrom, we can't stop here. We'll freeze."

"I'm tired."

"We're all tired," Roland said. "But we've got to keep moving."

"Now I lay me down to sleep," Tina's dad drawled in a faraway voice. "I pray the Lord . . ."

Tina didn't catch the next few words, but her memory supplied them: "I pray the Lord my soul to keep." She shuddered. Her dad had taught her that prayer when she was little. Usually she found it comforting, but now the words horrified her. People who lay down to sleep in a blizzard never woke up. Her heart tightened. Tears trickled down her cheeks. She couldn't imagine a world without her father. Dear old-fashioned irritating papa.

She and her father had their differences, but they were still pals. He couldn't die. He just couldn't.

Roland seized her father by the shoulders. "Come on, Obrom. It's not far now." He hoisted him into a sitting position and leaned him against the rocks.

A flurry of snow swirled around the rock pile and erupted in her dad's face.

He slumped sideways, his eyelids drooping.

Tina threw Roland a frantic glance. "What'll we do? Can we carry him to Frank's?"

Roland shook his head. "It's better if he walks. Keep his circulation going."

That was easy for Roland to say. The cold hardly seemed to bother him. His forehead wasn't mottled with red like her dad's. Roland had his bulk to insulate him, and younger blood to warm him.

She bent to her father's ear. "I'm afraid you'll have to walk." Frank might find a better way if he was here, but he wasn't.

Her dad's eyes flickered open.

She leaned closer. "I don't think God wants you to give up." It was the sort of thing her father would say to her.

He lifted his head.

Tina squared her face to his. "You want to live to see your grandchildren, don't you?"

Something glinted in her father's eyes. Determination? Stubbornness? Probably visions of blond babies, hers and Roland's.

"Tina," Roland bellowed in that radio-announcer's voice of his, "let's go." He shoved his hands under her father's armpits and lugged him into a standing position. "I've gotta get these pills to my mare."

Tina scrambled to her feet, arms flailing. "How can you *kvetch* about your mare at a time like this? What about my dad?"

"He's tougher than he looks." Roland took one of her father's arms and hung it around his neck, then motioned for Tina to do the same on the other side. "Okay, Obrom, stir those stumps." Roland took a step forward, half-lifting, half-dragging her dad along.

Her father's right knee buckled, but he managed one shambling step.

"That's it," Roland roared. "Forward march." Tina helped

Roland propel her dad ahead, and he took another step, his face grim behind a veil of wind-driven snow.

"Dad, you're doing great," Tina shouted. She leaned into the wind, her shoulders straining against her father's weight. He staggered a few times, then hit a stride that kept him plodding forward like a plough horse. Tina prayed his energy would last till they got to Frank's house.

She pictured herself in her boyfriend's kitchen, warming her hands over his cook-stove, hearing his kettle steam, his voice rumble. His beautiful eyes swirled up in her memory, pools of dark chocolate in his swarthy face.

A whirlwind of snow billowed around her. She could hardly see the fence any more, just an occasional post or strand of wire when the wind slowed. Roland had better not lose track of that fence. He was the one walking closest to it.

Something caught at her jacket. She turned and saw the shrivelled heads of sunflowers. They looked sad with their summer glory gone. How had they survived the cold and wind?

"Tina!" Roland bellowed. "Come on."

She trudged forward, her father's arm heavy on her shoulders, her mind back with the sunflowers and that magical August afternoon when she and Frank had watched bees browse through their blossoms, pollen bright on their bodies.

Would she ever see her sweetheart again? She and Roland and her dad might never make it to his house. Her mind floated away from her body, drifting off with the snow. Spots danced at the edges of her vision.

"There it is," Roland shouted, pulling Tina and her dad to a halt. "Frank's house." Its peaked roof jutted into view and Tina's mind snapped back into her body, her heart kicking like a colt.

"We'll leave the fence here," Roland blared. He bent over it, stretched the wires apart, and helped Tina and her dad climb through. "Now," he said, vaulting over the top wire, "all we gotta do is get across that driveway to the house."

Chapter 3

Frank watched through narrowed eyes as his unexpected guests huddled around his cook-stove warming their hands. What was Tina doing here with Roland Fast? She didn't fancy the snob, surely.

Her dad swayed on his feet. The old man must be exhausted. Frank pulled a chair up to the stove and helped him seat himself.

Obrom was shaking with cold, his teeth chattering.

"I'll be right back," Frank said. He ran upstairs and pulled patchwork quilts from a closet. Back in the kitchen, he tossed a quilt on the table for Roland, handed one to Tina, and hung another around her dad's shoulders. "Here, Obrom, put your feet on the oven door. It's warmer than the floor." Frank opened the door, wincing as its hinges screeched. He should oil those hinges.

He reached for the old man's feet. "Let's get your overshoes off."

Obrom pulled his feet away. "I'll manage." He groped the metal fasteners, his hands red and swollen.

Frank sighed. Stubborn old coot. He wouldn't pull his feet away from his golden boy, Roland. But if Obrom hoped to get Tina and Roland hitched, he was wasting his time.

Or maybe not. Was she fluttering her eyelashes at the snob?

Frank pulled the ladder-back chair up to the stove for her. She nodded her thanks, smoothed her grey trousers under her well-rounded bottom, and seated herself, elegant as a czarina.

Frank jerked his head at Roland. "What were you thinking of, driving with Tina and her dad in this weather?"

Roland stamped clods of snow off his boots. "The sun was shining when we left. The storm came out of nowhere."

"All storms come from somewhere." Frank's fists tingled like they often did when Roland gave him that stuck-up smirk.

Tina fumbled with her scarf, her hair drooping from her cap like trickles of molasses.

Obrom cleared his throat. "Roland, you could help her untie that scarf."

Roland shuffled his feet and stared at the floor.

Frank elbowed him aside and went to her. "Allow me, *Fräulein*."

Tina glanced at her father, then gave Frank a prim little smile. "I may be cold but I'm not helpless." She slid the knot from under her chin, lifted the scarf over her face, and removed it along with her cap.

Roland brushed melting snow off his jacket. "I'll leave as soon as I get warm."

Frank barked out a laugh. "Where would you go in this weather?"

"To my uncle's place." Roland patted his jacket pocket. "I've got pills for that mare he's keeping for me. I can't take a chance on her getting any sicker."

"You can't go back out in that storm," Frank said. He wasn't fond of Roland but he wouldn't want the guy dying either.

"I've got to go. It's only half a mile along the pasture fence."

"The best thing for that mare is bran mash with powdered aspirin," Frank said. "I told Isaac yesterday."

Roland shook his head. "The veterinarian said bran and aspirin wouldn't work for her."

"Why?" Frank asked. "Is she too high-class for it?"

Roland sneered at Frank like he was manure, stalked over to the north window, and stared out into the storm.

Tina turned in her chair, draping her wet scarf over the back of it.

"Here," Frank said, "I'll hang that up for you."
She handed him the scarf along with her cap, her blue eyes
telegraphing a warning. What did she mean? *Don't let Dad and
Roland suspect there's anything between you and me.* Or maybe
she was saying, *You'd better propose to me soon or you could lose
me. You're not the only coyote on this prairie, you know.*
He should propose to Tina, Frank thought, hanging her
scarf and cap on the clothesline near the pantry. He really
should. But what would happen then? Once she settled on this
farm with him, she'd expect them to stay, put down roots, have
babies. Was he ready for that? There were places he wanted to
see before he married, things he wanted to do.
Roland turned from the north window. "Come on, Frank.
You'd better drive me to my uncle's place."
The wind whistled down the chimney. "In what?" Frank
asked, irritation crisping his voice. "A tank?"
Roland rolled his eyes. "In a sleigh, of course."
Obrom cranked his head around and frowned at them.
"You boys better stay put. The snow's blowing too thick. You'll
get lost."
"Not if we follow the pasture fence," Roland said.
Tina shook her head. "Do you expect Frank to risk his
horses for the sake of yours? That doesn't seem right."
Frank flashed her a grin, glad to hear her stick up for him.
"I can't let anything happen to that mare," Roland said.
"She's worth fifty dollars, maybe more."
Frank snorted. "Money won't help you if you're frozen to
death." Money was one of Roland's main interests.
The golden boy glanced at the coffee pot on the shelf. "I'll
walk if I have to. I just need coffee first."
Frank hooked his thumbs into his suspenders. "Where do
you figure on getting coffee?"
Tina glared at him.
"Okay, okay. I guess I can make some." As Frank poured

hot water into the coffee pot, Roland sauntered over to the bookcase and picked up the photograph of Frank's Gypsy mama. She
looked as proper as any Mennonite in that photo, her dark eyes
modest under her fringe of black hair, a ruffle of lace trimming
her high-necked dress. Roland squinted at her like she was a
beetle in a bowl of mashed potatoes.

Frank tossed a handful of coffee into the pot, his mind
flashing back to himself as a fourteen-year-old cowering in the
bushes behind the school barn. He could still hear Roland yell
as he and his buddies came racing around the corner of the
barn. "You can't hide from us, Gypsy Boy. Not with that weasel-
brown skin."

Frank set the pot on the stove, his heart sickening at the
memory of Roland and his friends dragging him out of the
bushes. Frank had tried to fight back, but even his long arms
and legs couldn't do much against so many. Corny Braun had
pinned Frank's fists against his sides. Then Roland had pushed
him to the ground, leering into his face. "My grandpa lived in
the same village in Russia as your family. He said your mama
couldn't keep her legs together like the Mennonite women. She
was willing, more than willing."

"Shut up," Frank had yelled, his adolescent voice breaking.
He loved his mama. His dad had married her over the other
Mennonites' objections, and Frank would fight for her no mat-
ter what.

Frank wrenched his fist out of Corny's grasp and swung it
at Roland. But before it connected, the bully and his friends
flipped him over and pushed his face into the dirt.

Frank gagged, coughed, and fumbled for his handkerchief.
After all these years he could still taste dirt and bugs in his
mouth. He grabbed his mama's photo from Roland and set it
on the shelf. He was tempted to beat the guy to a pulp. Roland
didn't have any buddy-thugs to help him this time, and Frank
was taller and quicker. Smarter, too.

Chapter 4

Frank's anger swelled till his chest heaved with it. He longed to slug Roland, to feel his knuckles connect with that stuck-up nose and see the blood spurt. He hauled in a breath, forced his fists to relax, and took a step backwards. He'd get even with Roland someday. But not here, not in front of Tina and her dad.

Tina tossed her quilt aside and rose from her chair. "Frank, how's that coffee coming?"

"What? Oh, yeah." He grabbed a pot-holder, took the pot off the stove, and handed it to her.

As she served the coffee, Frank remembered the half-price chocolates he'd bought in Dayspring. He fetched the box from the bookcase and passed it around.

"No, thanks," Roland said. He blew on his coffee. "I prefer German chocolates. They're better quality."

Frank's forehead prickled with irritation. Roland figured Germans were the top people in the world: the hardest-working, the best organized, and the most reliable. The golden boy talked like he was pure German himself, though he had mixed roots like most Mennonites from Russia. Many of them stressed their Dutch or Polish backgrounds now that half the world was at war with Germany. But not proud, stubborn, stupid Roland.

Frank selected a chocolate sunflower, his favourite. "You should ask your Uncle Adolf to send you a case of chocolates."

Roland stiffened. "I don't have any Uncle Adolf."

"That's odd." Frank bit into the chocolate, crunching sunflower seeds. "Isn't that your Uncle Adolf I keep hearing about on the radio?"

"Hitler's no relative of mine." Roland swung his fist up, aiming an uppercut at Frank's chin.

Frank dodged, stumbling against a chair. Roland's love of Germans didn't seem to extend to the *Führer*. Or maybe it did but he didn't want to admit it.

"You boys should try to get along together," Obrom said.

Frank sighed, sorry he'd goaded Roland into trying to start a fight. He was the host around here; he should try to keep things peaceful. He didn't want anybody's blood on his linoleum, not tonight anyway.

Roland rattled the bottle of pills in his pocket. "I'm going to my uncle's place now. I've gotta get this medicine to my mare."

"You'd better wait till the storm dies down," Frank said. He paused, considering the possibilities. "All three of you can stay overnight if you need to. I've got space. Obrom, you and Roland can take the spare bedroom. Tina can sleep in my room."

Her dad bolted out of his chair, his face as pink as beet borscht.

Frank held up a restraining hand. "Don't get excited, Obrom. I'm not suggesting anything unseemly."

"What *are* you suggesting?"

"I've only got two bedrooms. I figure the lady should have the warmer one." Frank glanced into the living room. "I'll sleep on the couch. Would that be far enough away from Tina?"

"I guess so." Obrom sank back onto his chair, the colour in his face receding.

Frank saw Tina's hand tremble as she refilled his coffee cup. Did the prospect of sleeping in his bed make her heart thump like it did his? He hoped so. "We better make supper," he said, glancing around at his guests. "I've got some leftover roast goose."

"I'm going to my uncle's now," Roland bleated. "I can't let that mare die. I've got too much money tied up in her."

"Money isn't worth risking your life for," Frank said.
"It's not just the money. It's poor Schatzie. I hate to think
of her suffering."
"Of course," Frank said. "Nobody wants an animal to suffer, but you'd better stay here under the circumstances."
"I've been through worse storms." Roland set his hat on his
greasy blond head, turned down the earflaps, and opened the
door to the lean-to.

A cold draught swirled in. That little anteroom was always
like an icebox in the winter. Frank caught the gleam of frost on
its rough-timber walls.

Roland stood in the doorway putting on his mitts, squinting
around like he was daring someone to stop him.

Frank could if he wanted to. Just knock the guy out and tie
him up with his own suspenders. He'd love to. But that would
be too violent to suit Tina and her dad. Anyway Roland was a
grown man responsible for his own stupid decisions.

Whether Roland stayed or not, the leftover goose needed
to be thawed. "Excuse me," Frank said. He pushed past Roland
and hurried into the lean-to. He fetched the pan of goose from
the cupboard and headed back to the kitchen with it, squeezing
around the golden boy.

"I'm going now," Roland announced to nobody in particular.
"Please don't," Tina said. "It's too dangerous."

Obrom laid a fatherly hand on Roland's shoulder. "Your
uncle will do his best with that mare. And we'll pray for her. If
it's God's will—"

"I won't let her die," Roland said through clenched
teeth. "It's only half a mile." He lurched through the lean-to
and opened the door to the blizzard. Through a whirl of blowing snow, he barged outside and slammed the door behind
him.

Tina's eyes clouded with anxiety. "I didn't think Roland
would actually go."

"He's out of touch with reality," Frank said, shutting the lean-to door. "A lot of rich Mennonites are like that."

Obrom scowled at him. "That's not fair. Roland is just doing what he believes is right."

"I'm not sure about that," Frank said, carrying the pan of goose to the kitchen table. "I think he's just stubborn. He planned to go to his uncle's place so he's going, storm or no storm."

Tina paced the floor, wringing her hands. "Frank, can't you do something? Roland's a decent person at heart." She paused. "He's changed since you went to school with him."

Frank studied her cameo-like face. Was that all Roland was to her, a decent person? Or was he something more?

He went to the north window, scraped some frost off it, and looked out. Roland was standing on the porch fiddling with the guide-rope Frank had strung between the house and the barn. Maybe he was still hoping for a sleigh ride. Well, let him hope.

Obrom came and peered over Frank's shoulder. "Do you think he'll make it to his uncle's?"

"I don't know. The guide-rope should get him to the barn, but I doubt that he'll risk slogging through the north pasture on foot. My guess is, he'll take one of my horses."

"Are they reliable?" Obrom asked.

Frank felt the anger vein twitching in his neck. "Reliable? Do I strike you as a guy that wouldn't have reliable horses?"

"No, no. I just meant, do you have a horse that'll head into a blizzard for a stranger?"

"Maybe, if he picks the right one."

Tina sucked in her breath. "What do you mean?"

"Knowing Roland, he'll pick Maynard because he's bigger and classier looking than Reyna. But Maynard can be ornery with people he doesn't know."

"Could you go with Roland?" Tina asked, her voice quiet and careful.

"I'm not crazy about that idea." Frank went to the table and opened the pan, revealing the remains of the goose. "We could get lost and freeze as stiff as this bird. Is that what you want?"

"Of course not," Tina said. "But Roland . . . he needs help." Frank felt her eyes bore into him. What if Roland died in the storm? She might blame him for the rest of their lives. Tina laid her hand on his arm. "Frank, could you try, please? You could take both Maynard and Reyna. Use your closed-in sleigh so you'd have shelter. Take some blankets."

Frank turned away from her. How much did she really care about him, her supposed boyfriend? Maybe she was just trying to use him to save Roland's skin. Well, he wouldn't take the bait. He was nobody's fool, not even Tina's.

Frank fetched a knife from the pantry and pried at the frozen goose, lifting the wings so it would thaw faster. He should just let Roland go and suffer the consequences of his own stubbornness.

But that would be cowardly, and Frank Herbert Warkentin was no coward. He set the lid on the goose. "Obrom, could you keep an eye on the fire? I'll go and see if I can take that clown to his precious mare."

Chapter 5

Frank woke to sunlight streaming in around the window blinds. The storm must have blown itself out, thank goodness. He stretched his legs, grimacing as his feet bumped against the arm of the couch. They'd been half-frozen when he'd stumbled into the house after taking Roland to his uncle's place. What a jerk, that Roland. Tina wasn't interested in him, was she?

He smiled, picturing her soft and warm in his bed upstairs. Was she awake yet? All he heard was her dad snoring like a threshing machine.

Frank sat up, pulling down the sleeves of his long under-wear. He'd forgotten to grab his pajamas when he'd shown Tina to his bedroom last night. Later, when he'd remembered, he hadn't wanted to disturb her, though he'd like to have seen her in bed with her wonderful hair spilling over his pillows like a waterfall. He'd never seen Tina with her hair down, never seen her bare shoulders, not outside of his imagination anyway. He'd never even seen her arms above the elbows. That was all forbidden territory unless he married her.

He threw back the quilt and swung his legs off the couch. His frost-swollen toes hit the floor and he muttered a curse.

He got dressed, put on his slippers, and limped into the kitchen, his right foot pulsing with every step. He dipped water from the stove reservoir and rinsed his mouth, then poured water into the basin and washed his face. As he added coal to the fire and stirred it into a blaze, he heard Tina's light step on the stairs. He turned to watch her come down, her chest curving like a young pigeon's in her grey sweater.

Frank grinned. "It's high time you got up."

"I've been awake for ages," Tina said, coming to the stove,

"but I didn't want to disturb you." She warmed her hands over the fire, her shoulder brushing his arm.

Was that accidental? She must know how crazy it made him. She sidled away from him. "How do you feel this morning?" Frank shut the stove lid. "Great if you don't count feet. I've got chilblains again." He pulled a chair to the stove, sat down, and eased his slippers off.

Tina bent over his feet. "Poor Frank." Her long smooth fingers stroked his toes. "Do you have some ointment to put on your feet?"

"No, but you could do a Mary Magdalene impersonation." He gave her a crooked grin. "Wash them with your tears and dry them with your hair."

"That's sacrilegious." Tina's eyes grew round with disapproval.

"Sorry."

Her eyes narrowed. "You're really sorry?"

"Sure." Frank smiled and patted his knee. "Come sit on my lap and I'll show you how sorry I am." He glanced up the stairs. "While your dad's still snoring."

Tina threw him a teasing glance and darted into the living room.

Frank lurched to his feet and hobbled after her. "Just one little kiss." He caught her around the waist and held her till she quit squirming, then pulled her down onto the couch. Shifting to hide his rising passion, he turned Tina's face to his. The lingering kiss warmed him from the top of his head right down to his chilblains.

She quivered and bolted away from him.

Frank slumped back on the couch, throbbing with frustration.

When he'd calmed himself enough to look up, Tina was standing in the kitchen doorway, her face crimson. With passion? Embarrassment? Anger? Mostly guilt, if he knew Tina.

He shouldn't have gone so far, shouldn't have made her feel guilty. She believed God was with her every minute of the day, and would know immediately whether she behaved herself or not. He should try harder to respect her faith even though he didn't share it. On the other hand, he wished she'd let him get a little closer to her, just a little. It might help push him over the brink of holy matrimony.

Frank followed Tina into the kitchen, dragging his aching foot. He watched her dip water into the dishpan and set it on the table. She shook soap powder into the pan, then added the plates from the supper she'd cooked last night. Her forehead creased into a frown as she scrubbed at smears of goose, cabbage, and potatoes. Even when she frowned, Tina was gorgeous, her face like an ivory cameo, round and creamy. He saw something of Mama in her. Tilt of the head? Curve of the shoulder?

Maybe Tina could fill the empty space he'd carried in his heart since Mama had left.

Maybe. But if he married Tina, Obrom Janz would be his father-in-law, imagine. Frank got a bitter taste in his mouth, dreading the moment when the old man trotted down the stairs with that watchdog look on his face, guarding his daughter from the not-good-enough Gypsy. Frank limped to the door of the lean-to, grabbed his mackinaw jacket off the hook, and put it on. He'd go out and do his milking, feed the cattle and horses, feed the chickens. He'd show Obrom he could at least get his chores done before breakfast like a regular Mennonite.

"Where are you going?" Tina asked, her voice small against the clatter of dishes.

"Out. Gotta do my chores." He pulled his boots on.

Tina came to him like a scolded child, her hands dripping dishwater. "Are you mad at me?"

He shook his head no.

"Are you sure?" She laid her wet hands on his shoulders.

Frank growled and pretended to bite her hand. "I'd like you better if your hands weren't so wet."

Tina laughed and wiped them on his mackinaw. "How's that?"

"Some better." He bowed over her right hand and kissed it like a knight bidding farewell to his lady. Then he grabbed the shovel from the lean-to and headed out into the snow, pulling the door shut behind him.

Sunlight was spilling across the snowdrifts like broken egg yolks. Frank plunged his shovel in, hoisted a load of snow, and threw it aside. Plunge, hoist, throw, again and again. When he'd cleared the porch, he started shovelling a path to the barn. The farther he got from the house, the colder the wind felt. It bit into his nostrils and made his lungs burn.

It had been a cold morning like this when Mama had left him, maybe colder. That was twenty years ago, half a world away on a treeless Russian steppe. He was seven years old.

Frank shivered, remembering himself darting after Mama, his boots skidding on the porch of his parents' little yellow house. Mama had kissed him goodbye, smelling of wool scarf and coriander. He felt her arms around him, saw her cheeks shine with tears.

A moment later she turned and hurried toward the khaki-clad soldier who sat on his horse, tapping his whip against his boot. The soldier smiled at Mama, his teeth flashing, his hair crisp and curly under his hat with the red star on it. He reached down, put his arms around Mama, and swung her onto the horse.

Terror seized Frank's heart. "Mama, please don't go," he screamed as the soldier spurred his horse forward. "I love you."

What would Papa say when he came home from church? Could he get Mama back? "Please, please, please," Frank prayed as she disappeared in the fog of his tears.

He leaned against his shovel, wiping his eyes on his sleeve.

A hand touched his arm and he jumped. "Tina, what're you doing here?" Her coat hung open. "Button up," he barked, embarrassed to be caught crying. "You'll catch pneumonia."

Tina buttoned her coat and put on her mittens. "What's the matter? Your eyes—"

"My eyes are fine. They're just watering from the sun on the snow. It gives me a headache."

"Poor darling." Tina reached up and massaged his forehead, her mittened hands as nimble as kittens' feet. "You'll feel better after you eat. I'm frying potatoes and sausages. And I just put a pan of raisin *schnetki* in the oven."

Mmm, raisin scones. Mama had made those when Frank was a boy: puffy golden rectangles smelling of wheat and cream.

Mama had fed him well. She'd embroidered his shirts, dried his tears, put healing herbs on his scrapes and bruises. She'd loved him, so why had she left? He didn't know. After twenty years he still didn't know.

Maybe Tina would leave him, too. If he gave her his heart, she'd probably break it. She was a classy dame, too classy to stay with a guy like him.

She leaned closer to him, her breath pluming out white in the air. He could steal another kiss; she was in the mood. No, better not, he decided, glancing at the house. Her dad was probably watching them, trotting from one window to the other to get a better view. Frank backed away from Tina. "You and your dad go ahead and eat." He felt his voice harden. "I gotta do my chores."

"Frank, please don't be like this. I was hoping the three of us could eat breakfast together." She paused. "You must realize Dad was impressed with you last night. It was so brave and unselfish of you, taking Roland to his uncle's place."

Frank rammed his shovel into the snow. "That Roland is a jerk."

She glanced across the pasture toward Isaac Epp's house, where the golden boy was probably eating breakfast right now. "Roland has his good points."

"He sure does. He's rich, he's not half-Gypsy, he works hard. Goes to church every Sunday. But he's a jerk all the same."

"Roland's nicer when you're not around. You don't bring out the best in him."

"So why don't you go after Roland instead of me? Your dad likes him. They're two of a kind. Both snobs."

Tina's eyes flashed blue as a gas flame. "How dare you insult my father?"

Frank scowled at her. "Why shouldn't I? He sure insults me, frowning at me like I'm a weevil in a wheat bin. Forcing me to sneak around like a criminal, just for the privilege of spending a few hours with his precious daughter."

Tina tossed her head. "If his precious daughter isn't worth your time, maybe you shouldn't bother with her."

"I didn't mean it like that. You know I didn't."

"So why don't you tell Dad about us?" Tina's cheeks reddened. "Ask him for my hand in marriage."

Frank's next words crept out cautiously, like a barn cat. "What would your dad do if I asked?"

Tina gave him a thin smile. "He'd get mad and forbid us to see each other."

"That's what I figured."

"But he'd soften once he realized how we feel about each other. He's not really prejudiced, just slow to accept new ideas."

"I'm not sure about that. You love your dad, and love blinds you to what he's really like."

Tears shone in her eyes. "I think you're just using Dad as an excuse. You're either a coward or you don't love me."

Frank opened his mouth to reply, then closed it. He had no answer for Tina, none that either of them could accept. "You better get to the house," he said, his voice thick. "Put those *schnetki* on the table for your dad. Then we'll figure out how to get you and him home."

Frank watched Tina turn and trudge toward the house, her shoulders shaking with sobs. He started to follow, then stopped. He should probably break up with that woman. She was dangerous. If he let her fill the void in his heart, she could easily empty it. Then he'd be worse off than before. Anyway he and Tina weren't that good together. Too many rules, angry words, accusations.

But he couldn't break up with Tina face to face. It would hurt too much. He'd better wait till she went back to Vancouver, then write her a letter. It was a coward's way out, but he'd rather be a coward than get hitched and realize he'd made a horrible mistake.

Chapter 6

The harrumph of a foghorn greeted Tina as she hurried across the veranda to her uncle and aunt's mailbox. Would there be a letter from her sweetheart today? Probably not. This would probably be another dreary day without a word from Frank.

Delaying the disappointment, she pulled the *Vancouver Sun* out of the box and scanned the headlines: *Hitler still threatens to invade Norway. Germany and Italy to form alliance against UK. America remains neutral but for how long?* She thrust the newspaper under her arm and dug the smaller pieces of mail out of the box. Aunt Irmie's music magazine was here. So was the doctors' newsletter for Uncle Yash. The ice bill slid out from under a Baptist missions bulletin. But there was nothing from Frank.

Her footsteps dragging, she carried the mail into the house. Why didn't he write? She'd sent him two letters since she'd returned from Dayspring. He hadn't answered either of them. She'd tried phoning but his line was dead, probably still down from the snowstorm.

Tina dropped the mail on the hall table and wandered up the stairs to her office. Frank didn't like her office. Whenever he visited her, he complained about the walnut panelling. It made him feel trapped. Too dark. The lily-patterned carpet made him feel like he was wading through a swamp. Frank wasn't fond of Vancouver in general. Too crowded. Too many buildings, cars, streetcars, trees.

Frank was like the coyotes that ran through his pastures, wild and free. That was probably why he fascinated her. She loved the bravado in his eyes, the brash exterior hiding his warm heart. If only he'd open it to her.

Tina sank onto the chair at her desk. Thank God she had work to do. It might ease her mind. She pulled the cover off her typewriter, cranked in two sheets of paper with a carbon between, and began typing the report she was compiling for her Uncle Yash.

March 19, 1940
Ebenezer Baptist Activities Report

As Tina typed she paused frequently to consult letters and memos from Baptist volunteers working in missions, soup kitchens, hospitals, and orphanages.

"Drat it," she muttered half an hour later. "How could I have typed the wrong figures?" She flicked the lever to release the papers, yanked them out, and cranked in a fresh pair. Usually she enjoyed typing reports for her uncle's charity projects. She took pride in her neatness and accuracy. But she'd been fighting a war of nerves lately, wondering when she'd hear from Frank.

Victor Graf had never made her wait and wonder like this. From the day she'd met him, she'd been able to read him like a Baptist missions bulletin. During the year she and Victor had gone together—before she'd fallen in love with Frank—she'd been number one on Victor's list, first in his heart. After God of course.

"Missus!" Eduarda called, knocking on the door.

Tina sighed. How many times did she have to tell the maid not to call her Missus? She wasn't a Missus. She'd probably never be if she kept waiting for Frank to propose.

"Missus Tina." Eduarda's voice rose. "*Almuerzo!* Lunch!"

"Could you please bring it up here?" Tina called through the door. She was too nervous to go downstairs and chat with Eduarda.

Tina ate her salmon salad at her desk, gazing out over the grey waters of English Bay. A yellow tugboat steamed toward the mill. The lighthouse jutted up against the sky. She'd miss this view if she moved back to Dayspring. She'd miss a lot of things about Vancouver, especially her work.

But Dayspring was in her blood, in her bones. She'd grown up there. She'd be only too happy to move back if only Frank would propose.

By four in the afternoon, Tina had finished the Activities Report. She leaned back in her chair, her mind drifting to Victor. He'd be twenty-two years old now, no longer the fresh-faced boy who'd courted her three years ago. Was he still doing carpentry? Maybe she should drop him a note and ask, just for curiosity's sake.

She shook her head. No, she shouldn't write to another man when she was in love with Frank Warkentin.

But did Frank love her? The big lug was probably just wasting her time. She might wait years for a proposal, growing old and grey at her typewriter.

Tina opened the bottom drawer of her desk. All right, Lord, she prayed, if I find the blue-hyacinth notepaper Victor gave me, I'll take it as a sign it's okay to write to him. Tina flipped through a pile of old photos. Peeking out from under a snapshot of Uncle Yash at Vancouver General Hospital were several sheets of notepaper decorated with blue hyacinths, Victor's favourite flowers.

Tina's heartbeat quickened as she pulled out a sheet of hyacinth paper and laid it on her blotter. "Silly girl," she murmured, "it's just a note." She filled her pen from the ink bottle and began to write.

March 19, 1940
Dear Victor,
How's life in Chilliwack? You'll be surprised to hear from me after so long. How's your dad's heart now? Do you and your cousin still have your carpentry shop?

As you may know, there's going to be a missionary conference at First Baptist Church in Chilliwack next month. Uncle Yash plans to send me since I'm his secretary for charity projects now. How about that? You probably didn't think I was smart enough to be a secretary, ha ha. If you attend the conference, maybe we could meet for a cup of tea.

How should she sign off? Not *Love, Tatiameana.* Victor's silly nickname for her was too personal for a note to a man she hadn't seen in years. What about *Your old friend, Tina?* No, still too personal, and why call attention to the fact that she was three years older than Victor? Maybe just Tina Janz. Yes, that was it. She signed the letter and sealed it into a hyacinth-patterned envelope.

Tina's boots beat a nervous tattoo as she hurried along the street to the mailbox. Should she really mail her note? Victor was such an earnest fellow. He'd taken her at face value when she'd insisted they break up because he was too young to commit himself. She hadn't had the heart to tell him the real reason— she was in love with someone else. What if Victor had just been biding his time, waiting till she considered him old enough?

No, that was ridiculous. Victor wouldn't keep pining for her; he'd have another girlfriend by now. Maybe he was even married. There'd be nothing wrong with meeting him at the conference. She could play the older sister, giving sage advice. It would be fun. She ran the last few steps to the mailbox and tossed the envelope through the slot.

The next afternoon, as she returned from taking the deposits to the bank, Uncle Yash met her in the hallway, his face as round and affable as a cherry pie. "Telegram for you, Tina." He held up a brown envelope, squinting at the light through it. "Looks like it's from Dayspring."

"I wonder who'd send me a telegram." Tina tried to sound casual but her hand trembled as she took the envelope. It was probably from Frank, or about him. She removed her coat, passing the telegram from hand to hand, and waited for Uncle Yash to step aside so she could escape to her office.

Her uncle regarded her with hazel eyes as curious as a village matchmaker's. "I hope it's nothing serious."

"I hope not." She slipped the telegram into the pocket of her dress.

Uncle Yash stooped to remove his shoes, and Tina caught a whiff of ether.

"Were you doing surgeries today?" she asked.

"Four," he said, putting on his slippers. "One leg amputation, one tuberculoma, and two appendectomies."

"You must be tired." Why didn't he go into the living room and read his newspaper?

Tina fingered the telegram in her pocket. "I finished typing that article for you. I'll run upstairs and get it."

Finally her uncle stepped aside and Tina fled up the steps. Safely behind the door of her office, she leaned against the walnut panelling and tore open the envelope.

Caught a chill driving home from Sigurd's place. Sick for three weeks. Some better now. Love you, Frank.

Frank loved her! Tina's heart thundered; the whole house must hear it. Frank Warkentin still loved her. She hugged her arms around herself and danced across the lily-patterned carpet, feeling as if nothing could ever be too hard for her again, as long as Frank loved her.

She reread his telegram. Poor darling. She'd better phone Sigurd or some other friend of Frank's whose phone worked. She'd ask them to make sure Frank was okay.

"Tina?" Uncle Yash called from downstairs. "If you've got that article, I'll read it before dinner."

"Coming." She snatched the article off her desk and hurried

down the stairs with it, her feet hardly touching the steps. Halfway down she stumbled. What about her note to Victor? She should never have mailed it. What a selfish, short-sighted thing to do. If only she could get it back.

Chapter 7

Saturday morning dawned grey and rainy. Tina stood at the easel in her office, peering at the portrait she was painting. Was that the right shade of black for Frank's hair? Maybe a touch more brown. As she picked up her paintbrush, a vehicle rumbled into the driveway.

Who could that be? She wasn't expecting anyone and nobody else was home. She peered out the window and saw a yellow taxi park near the rock garden. A barrel-chested man in a leather coat ducked out and sprinted toward the veranda, his red hair flaming up at her through the rain. Tina dropped the brush, her hands flying to the collar of her painting smock. Victor! What was he doing here? Why hadn't he written or phoned first?

She groaned. He must have come because of her note. She should never have mailed it.

The doorbell rang, its piano-like notes echoing up the stairs. Tina backed away from the window. She'd enjoy seeing Victor again. She liked him; everybody did. But what would she say to him?

She tiptoed back to the window, looked out, and saw the driver lean out of the taxi, the brim of his hat low on his forehead. Maybe he and Victor would simply leave if nobody answered the doorbell.

No, that wasn't fair. Victor had probably come all the way from Chilliwack. She watched him plod back toward the taxi, his leather-coated shoulders sagging. It was cruel to let him go without at least saying hello. She opened the window and leaned out. "Victor!"

His head bobbed up.

She steadied herself against the window frame. "Don't go. I'll come down." Tina pulled off her painting smock, threw it on a chair, and hurried down to the front door. Behind it, she took a trembling breath and turned the knob.

Victor stood on the veranda grinning, his blue-grey eyes as eager as a child's on Christmas morning. "Hello, Tatiameana." His teeth were as wide apart as ever, his freckles like nutmeg sprinkled across his ruddy cheeks. "I sure surprised you, *nicht?*"

"You sure did." She'd almost forgotten Victor's habit of adding the German *not* to the ends of his sentences. It made him sound so homey, like some long-lost cousin you'd throw your arms around. She steeled herself against the impulse.

Victor waved the taxi away. As it growled out of the driveway, his eyes searched her face. "You're even more beautiful than I remembered."

Oh, no. That sounded dangerous.

"Is that a new hairdo?" Victor asked. "I don't remember your hair looking so fancy before."

Tina adjusted the celluloid comb above her left temple. "I'm wearing more combs now. They help keep my hair off my face when I type."

"So you're a big-shot secretary now. Don't secretaries usually invite visitors in?"

"Yes. Yes. Of course." She led her visitor into the hallway, her legs shaking with apprehension. He removed his leather coat and she took it from him. "So how are you?" she asked, hanging the coat in the closet. "Are you still doing carpentry?"

"Yup, still fighting nails and sawdust." Victor straightened his grey-blue tie and Tina noticed it was almost the same colour as his eyes. "My cousin and I just landed a contract to build cupboards for the biggest restaurant in Chilliwack," he said, following her along the hallway. "But I'm thinking about moving back to Vancouver."

She almost tripped on the roses in the carpet. "What for?"

He gave her a gap-toothed grin. "Vancouver General Hospital offered me my old job back. Isn't that great? They say the maintenance department isn't the same since I left. The hospital phoned the day after I got your letter, so I took it as a sign that God was leading me back here."

Tina prayed it was no such sign. Having Victor working at Vancouver General again would be complicated, more than complicated. Uncle Yash would start bringing Vic home again, getting him involved in the charity projects. She wouldn't be able to avoid seeing her former boyfriend. What would she say to him? How would she act?

She led Victor into the living room. "Sit down, please." He chose the leather loveseat and she sat on the yellow sofa across from him. "Why would you move back to Vancouver?" she asked, straightening the pile of medical journals on the coffee table. "It sounds like your business is doing great in Chilliwack."

"Yeah, but I miss the big city." Victor leaned across the coffee table, his eyes holding hers. "And I miss you." His voice dropped to a whisper. "A lot."

Tina couldn't suppress a thrill of excitement. Victor had always been direct; she liked that about him.

His face flushed, his freckles almost disappearing into it. "You and I broke up because I was too young. But I'm twenty-two years old now, old enough to know my own mind." He paused as if waiting for a response.

When she said nothing, he rose, stepped around the coffee table, and sat on the sofa beside her. "What would you think of you and me getting back together?"

A window opened in what Tina had previously seen as a blank wall. Why couldn't she get back together with Victor? She'd been happy with him before she'd met Frank. She'd been a better Christian then, too. She and Vic had prayed together, read the Bible, worked in soup kitchens and orphanages together.

But Frank—Tina felt like Frank had tied a rope to her heart and was pulling on the other end. "I'm sorry. I don't think I could."

His face turned as pale as cream under his freckles.

Poor Victor. Tina reached out to take his hand, then pulled hers back. Why tempt herself and torture him?

Some colour returned to his face. "I shouldn't have asked so soon. Is that it? You need time to get reacquainted with me."

"No, that's not it," she blurted, bolting off the sofa. "I don't want to get reacquainted with you."

Victor gasped. "But I thought—when I got your letter, I figured you wanted to—"

"Oh, that little note." She dismissed it with a wave of her hand. "I just dashed that off. I thought it might be nice to meet if you happened to attend the conference. I didn't expect you to come all the way to Vancouver." She hated herself for the half-truth.

"You mean—" Victor's face crumpled.

"I wouldn't have written if I'd known you'd take it so seriously."

Her own cruelty shocked her. Victor deserved better. But she couldn't very well throw herself into his arms, could she? Not when she was in love with Frank.

Victor stared at her, his Adam's apple bobbing. He swallowed once, twice. Then he rose and barged out of the living room, knocking over a chair on the way.

Tina followed him into the hallway. "I'm sorry, Victor."

He stopped under the photo of Uncle Yash and Aunt Irmie's wedding. "Are you in love with somebody else? Is that it?"

Tina didn't know what to say. Victor wouldn't approve of her sweetheart if he knew him. Vic wouldn't consider Frank a Christian, though he was, deep down. She was pretty sure of that. Her sweetheart had told Preacher Schellenberg he was a believer.

"I asked if you're in love with somebody else?" Victor's voice had a sandpapery edge to it. "Are you engaged to him?"

Tears welled in her eyes. She wasn't engaged. Maybe she never would be.

"Okay, don't tell me if you don't want to tell me." Victor stomped down the hallway. A moment later Tina heard the closet door open.

"Wait!" She hurried after him. "I'll call you a taxi."

"Don't bother." Victor put on his coat. "I'll take the street-car. My train doesn't leave till this evening." He opened the door and Tina noticed that the rain had stopped. The air smelled fresh, washed clean.

"Goodbye, Tina." Victor's eyes looked old, like they'd been buried for years. The streetcar rattled up the hill and he ran to catch it. A moment later the iceman's truck roared onto the street, blocking him from view.

Chapter 8

Tina wandered along Vancouver's busy Hastings Street, as aimless as the fog that swirled off the bay. Where was she going? Anywhere. Nowhere. It didn't matter. Her heart ached for Victor Graf. He didn't deserve what had happened today.

But she couldn't help feeling the way she did. Frank was the man she wanted. She'd known ever since she'd met him on the train platform in Dayspring. That was three years ago, but it seemed like yesterday.

* * *

She'd arrived home from Vancouver, elegant in a pink spring coat. The wind off the Dayspring flatlands had smelled of melting snow and damp earth. Tina had scanned the parking lot for her father and noticed a swarthy young man lounging against the fender of a black DeSoto. The young man's shoulders were broad in his red mackinaw jacket, his legs long in his denim trousers. Sunlight glinted off his dark glasses. He grinned at her, his wide sweet mouth almost stopping her heart.

Tina forced herself to look away. She shouldn't show a strange man how she felt; she was a lady. She set her suitcase on the platform and turned to the station house, pretending to study its squat yellow-brown architecture.

Calm yourself, the familiar old building seemed to say. *This is Dayspring. It's no place for extravagant emotion.*

Calm yourself. How could she calm herself when her heart kicked like it wanted to run across the platform and throw itself at the stranger's feet?

She needed to get hold of herself. She already had a sweetheart, Victor Graf in Vancouver. The blue hyacinth Victor had given her was pressed between the pages of her Bible. Victor's picture was in her wallet.

She heard boots crunch across the platform and glanced over her shoulder. The stranger was sauntering toward her. "Tina?"

She wheeled around, almost tripping over her suitcase. How did he know her name?

He extended a big square hand. "Remember me? Frank Warkentin."

"Frank?" Tina's voice came out high, like a child's. "Warkentin?" She remembered a kid by that name, years ago. The half-Gypsy boy she'd seen in the Mennonite church, following his dad around like a bony shadow. The kid had looked as nervous as a grasshopper, gnawing his fingernails till they bled and not meeting anyone's eyes. Could this really be the same person? He seemed so confident, so jaunty.

Tina took the hand Frank offered. His thick fingers curved around hers and her knees turned to mashed potatoes. She steadied herself against her suitcase, picturing herself holding Frank's hand for an hour, a day, a lifetime.

What a rash thought. She'd just met the guy, or re-met him. She hardly knew a thing about him. Tina managed a shaky smile and withdrew her hand. "You don't live around Dayspring anymore, do you?"

"No, I'm mostly on the road nowadays."

"Doing what?"

Frank grimaced.

She shouldn't have asked. Too nosy. She racked her brain for something else to say.

Frank shifted from one foot to the other. "I've done some rodeo-riding. And I worked on a farm near Grande Prairie last winter. But I'm out of a job at the moment."

Tina nodded. "It's not easy to find work nowadays." At least Frank was trying, not just living on the dole like some people.

"I've done some logging, too. I sure enjoyed that."

"Whereabouts?"

Frank shrugged. "Here and there. Mostly the BC interior." He squinted down the train track. "I'm home helping my folks on the farm for awhile. I'm supposed to pick up my sister, Fania. Her train should be in soon."

"If it's running on time." Obviously. What a stupid thing to say.

"It better be. I just picked up a carton of baby chicks for my stepmother." He glanced at the black DeSoto. "I'm afraid they'll get cold in my car."

"Did you put a blanket over them?" Tina asked.

"Yeah, I laid an old quilt over the carton, away from the air holes."

"That should be enough, with the sun coming through the windows."

Frank quirked an eyebrow at her. "Do you know anything about chicks?"

"I used to help Mom. Do you want me to take a look?" Tina gulped, shocked at her own boldness. Nice girls didn't follow strange men to their cars.

"I'd love your opinion." Frank sounded as eager as Tina felt. He removed his sunglasses and she sucked in a sharp breath. She hadn't remembered Frank's eyes being so . . . brown. She could lose herself in those eyes, follow their promises to the ends of the earth.

He touched her arm. "Are you okay?"

"Of course not." She clapped her hand over her mouth. "I mean of course I am."

Frank gave her a crooked grin and reached for her suitcase. "Come on. I'll carry that."

As she handed him her suitcase, someone called from the parking lot. "Tina!"

She jumped. "Dad!" She hadn't noticed her father's car

pulling up. He climbed out and hurried toward her. "How's my little girl? It's great to see you."

Tina hurried to meet him. "It's great to be home."

Her dad kissed her, his leathery face smelling of shaving soap and tooth powder. "I'm sorry I'm late. I had a flat tire."

Frank strolled toward them. "Good afternoon, Obrom. Did you get your flat fixed okay?"

"Yes, thank you." His eyes narrowed. "What are you doing with my daughter's suitcase?"

"I'm kidnapping her," Frank said, straight-faced. "Gonna hold her for ransom. Her and the carton of blonde chicks I've got in my car."

Tina laughed. Victor never said anything that funny.

Her dad stared at Frank like he was a cabbage worm.

Frank's eyes glittered with—what? Pain? Anger? Maybe scorn.

Tina's father took her arm. "Come on, let's go home and have coffee. Your mother baked those walnut buns you like so much."

Frank cocked his head, his lips curving into a lazy grin. "Maybe Tina could stay till Fania's train comes in. Fania would love to see her."

Joy bubbled up from Tina's stomach. Seeing Frank's sister suddenly seemed like the most exciting thing in the world. She hardly remembered Fania, but what did that matter? Frank wanted her to stay. That was the important thing.

Her dad tightened his grip on her elbow. "Tina needs to come home. Now. Her mother's waiting."

Tina sighed. "I'll be there in a minute, Dad. I, um, just need to talk to Frank about those chicks first."

"You're a chick expert now?"

"I used to help Mom, remember?" She gestured toward her suitcase. "I wonder, could you take that to the car?"

He frowned.

She gave him her little-girl smile. "Please? I'll be right there."

Her dad shook his head, but took the suitcase from Frank. As he carried it to his car, Tina turned to Frank. "Do you have a lantern in your car?"

"Yeah, I figured I could warm the chicks with that."

She nodded. "That should work."

His voice dropped to a whisper. "Fania and I are meeting some friends at the Chinese café tomorrow. Around two o'clock. Maybe we'll see you there."

"Maybe." Tina forced a doubtful note into her voice. "If not, I may see you somewhere else." She gave him a jaunty wave and strolled toward her father's car, trying not to look like a girl who'd fallen shoulders over ears in love. But her heart was shouting, *Tomorrow. I'll see Frank tomorrow. Two o'clock. Chinese café.*

The smell of leather and liniment greeted her as she slid into the passenger seat of her dad's Model T.

Her father stepped on the starter. "I suppose you realize Frank's mother was a Gypsy dancing girl."

"What about it?" A Gypsy mother sounded exciting, exotic.

Her father shifted into reverse, released the clutch, and backed out of his parking spot. "Those Russian Gypsies were a bunch of thieves," he said, jolting the Ford along the main street. "They stole one of our horses, remember? He was a grey stallion with—"

"Dad, we're not in Russia anymore."

Her dad navigated the car onto the street that ran past the grain elevators. "The Gypsies never stayed in one place, just lived on the road all the time, like Frank does."

"Frank isn't on the road now. He's home helping his dad and stepmother."

"For how long?"

"I don't know, but he'll settle down eventually. Won't he?" She fiddled with a button on her coat. "His dad's a Mennonite."

"*Na yo*, but Frank's a wind chaser like his mother. It's in his blood. He can't help it."

Tina turned away, trying to ignore her father's words. *Tomorrow*, her heart whispered. *Tomorrow. I'll see Frank tomorrow. Two o'clock. Chinese café.*

* * *

Tina squinted through the fog at the sign that blinked Saltwater Saloon—on, off, on, off. Where was she? Vancouver obviously, but she'd never seen this street. Music blared from the saloon. A vehicle growled up beside her. A horn tooted and somebody whistled. "How ya doin', Babe? Wanna ride to paradise?"

Tina cast a terrified glance over her shoulder and scurried into a nearby doorway. It smelled of rotting wood and mouse droppings. She shouldn't be here. This was dangerous.

A tall figure loomed through the fog, approaching with a rolling gait like a sailor's. The stranger's black coat flapped around his shins.

Tina shrank deeper into the doorway.

"Miss, are you all right?" The man spoke with an accent she couldn't place. Australian maybe. "This neighbourhood is no place for a lady, if I may say so."

"S-s-sorry," Tina stammered. Sorry—what a stupid thing to say. "I-I-guess I lost my way."

"We all lose our way from time to time." The stranger peered into her face and Tina caught the gleam of a backwards white collar. A priest? What was he doing here?

The door of the saloon opened and a burly figure staggered out. The man vomited onto the sidewalk, swayed on his feet, and fell into the stinking mess.

Tina's stomach heaved.

The priest took her arm and led her to where the street grew wider and brighter. "I've got work to do back there." He jerked his head toward the man lying on the sidewalk. "But I'll hail you a taxi first, shall I?"

"Yes, if you would, please," Tina said. "I'll pray for you," she blurted. "For your work, I mean."

He nodded, stuck two fingers into his mouth, and whistled for a cab.

Chapter 9

A few grimy snowdrifts still lurked on the north side of Frank's machine shed. But on the south side, where he was cleaning his seed wheat, dark-green rosettes of chickweed poked through the damp earth. Frank dumped a shovel-full of wheat into the hopper of the fanning mill, his mind churning over the work that needed doing. He had to get his machinery ready for seeding, order baby chicks from the hatchery, plough the potato field, plough the garden, fix the loose shutters on the house.

Things would go easier if Tina was here. She could help him. Even just having her around would fuel his ambition, give him more of a reason for working.

Frank started turning the handle of the fanning mill, taking care to keep the speed steady, just right to sieve the weed seeds out of the wheat. He smiled, picturing himself waking up beside Tina every morning. That would sure give a man ambition. Her breasts would be like grapefruits under a lacy pink nightgown. The two of them would make love, she'd cook breakfast, and he'd face the day roaring like a tiger.

He should propose to her, just go ahead and do it. She was beautiful and smart—probably smarter than he was. She was someone a man could talk to about almost anything—farming, baseball, the war, history, music.

Frank stirred the wheat in the hopper, then began turning the handle again. Tina was an orderly woman, too, always sure of what was right and wrong. She'd make a good mother. He pictured tall strong sons working this farm with him, taking it over when he got old.

The sun pounded down on his head. His collar was damp

with sweat. As he unbuttoned it, he heard hoof-beats clopping along the road. He looked up and saw Dorrie Harms turn her bay mare into his driveway, her blonde curls flying like a flag against the sky.

What was Dorrie doing here? She'd dropped in last week, too, selling tickets for the school raffle. He'd thought it was odd, considering she was past school age. She must be twenty years old already, maybe twenty-one.

"Whoa, Bambi." Dorrie drew her mare to a halt near the clotheslines. She swung herself out of the saddle, her pert little derriere like an apricot in her orange trousers.

"Good morning," Frank called as Dorrie tied Bambi to a clothesline pole.

His visitor smiled, her small face flushed with the freshness of spring. She reached into her saddlebag and pulled out a bunch of dried wildflowers. Sunflowers, purple fireweed, a few blue flowers, some red ones. She held the bouquet in front of her like a bride and sashayed toward Frank. "Would you like to buy one of my flower arrangements?"

What kind of a question was that? Frank had seen Dorrie selling bunches of dried flowers around town, but it was mostly women who bought them. Why would she expect a bachelor to want one?

Dorrie's eyes widened; she was waiting for an answer. Frank noticed that her eyes were the same blue as Tina's. No, Dorrie's were lighter, more like flax flowers. Her eyebrows were lighter than Tina's, too. She almost looked like she didn't have eyebrows, they were so blonde.

"I had one flower arrangement left from last year," Dorrie said. "So I thought to myself, Frank Warkentin needs this to cheer him up, now that his folks have moved away."

Frank patted the pockets of his overalls. "Sorry, I don't have my wallet on me."

Dorrie pursed her orange lips.

Orange? Did her mother know she wore lipstick? Nice Mennonite girls didn't.

Dorrie studied her flower arrangement, then repositioned one of the purple fireweeds. "This arrangement would go good with your brown couch," she said, glancing toward the house. "Do you still have that couch or did your folks take it to Calgary?"

She was trying to get him to invite her inside. That was brassy of her. Frank shovelled more wheat into his fanning mill. "Listen, Dorrie, I'm kind of busy here. Why don't you go peddle your weeds to Adeline Epp?"

Dorrie wrinkled her nose. "Adeline doesn't like me."

Frank snorted. "She doesn't like me neither. I'm not clean-blooded enough for her."

Dorrie's eyes combed over him. "Adeline's just jealous because you're better-looking than her boys. In fact, you're one of the handsomest men in this whole municipality."

"Whoa, Dorrie. You could get in trouble saying things like that." Was she teasing him? Didn't sound like it. She probably wanted something. Maybe her mom had sent her to flatter him into fixing the Harms's clotheslines or rousting a skunk out from under their porch. Well, whatever it was Dorrie wanted, let her come right out and say it.

Frank emptied the weed seeds into a pail.

Dorrie reached for it. "Shall I take these seeds to your chickens?"

"No, thanks."

She watched him in silence for a few moments. Finally she said, "If you don't want to buy my flowers, I could give them to you."

Frank concentrated on turning the handle of his fanning mill, wondering what Tina would think of this conversation if she could hear it. She'd probably be jealous. Dorrie wasn't bad-looking, and she was at least five years younger than Tina. Quite a bit slimmer, too.

When the silence had lengthened into minutes, Dorrie gave Frank a sidelong look and laid her flowers on his seed box.

He said nothing.

She shrugged, minced back to her horse, and swung her apricot derriere into the saddle. She and Bambi trotted away, leaving Frank scratching the stubble on his chin.

Chapter 10

Three days later Frank was in the chicken coop gathering the eggs when he heard footsteps in the chicken yard. He peered out, shading his eyes against the late-afternoon sun, and saw Dorrie Harms picking her way through the chicken muck in high-heeled boots. She wore a red coat, too small for her. Probably she'd grown out of it but it looked nice anyway. It showed off her neat figure.

"You're sure dressed up," Frank called. "What's the occasion?"

"I just came back from Saskatoon." Dorrie stepped around a couple of Barred Rock hens who were squabbling over a worm. "Leif Lindberg dropped me at the school corner. I walked from there."

Frank nodded, glad she hadn't asked Leif to drop her off here. He'd get the wrong impression.

Dorrie teetered on her high heels. "I wanted to tell you something."

"Yeah?" Frank stepped out of the chicken house and set the egg basket on the feed barrel.

A smile lit Dorrie's childlike face. "I've always wanted to be a hairdresser so I went to the hairdressing school for an interview. And guess what? They might have a place for me."

"That's great. When are you leaving?" Presumably Dorrie's surprise visits would stop once she moved to the city.

Dorrie tossed her blonde curls. "Oh, they haven't accepted me yet. They want some character references. I wonder, could you write me one?"

Frank frowned. "Shouldn't you ask somebody who knows you better?"

Dorrie pulled a brown envelope from her coat pocket. "It's not that hard. All you need to do is fill out this form. I'll tell you what to write."

"I don't have a pen on me."

Dorrie glanced toward the house. "You must have a pen inside."

She sure wanted to get into that house. But it didn't seem right to invite her. He was a bachelor living alone. What would the neighbours say if they knew? What would Tina say? Frank retreated into the chicken house.

Dorrie stood in the doorway watching him gather the rest of the eggs. "The Mennonites around here treat me like a black sheep because my dad messed with me when I was a kid." She said this as casually as if she were announcing egg prices on the radio.

Frank's face grew warm with embarrassment. "They should-n't hold that against you." He retrieved a cracked egg from a nest box near the door. "It wasn't your fault." He brushed a bit of straw off the egg and set it in the pail he kept for the cracked ones.

Dorrie shrugged and put the envelope back in her pocket. "They don't like getting chummy with somebody who's not respectable. *What will people think?* That's their motto."

"Yeah, some folks can be mean-minded." He knew how Dorrie felt. He and Dorrie were the same that way, both dis-criminated against for reasons beyond their control. Frank checked the last nest. Poor Dorrie. She'd had some tough breaks in life, but she'd made her share of mistakes, too. Running off with a travelling salesman hadn't been her best idea. The guy wasn't even good-looking. A pockmarked Fuller Brush man with eyes the colour of mud. On the other hand, maybe the way Dorrie's dad had—used—her had compromised her character, so to speak. Lowered her barriers.

"I wish people could forget about that travelling salesman," Dorrie said like she'd read Frank's mind. "I've grown up a lot since then."

"I'm sure you have." Frank stepped out of the chicken house. "But it's hard to escape your past in a little fishbowl community like Dayspring."

"That's why I'd like to move somewhere bigger like Saskatoon."

"Sounds reasonable to me." Would it be so terrible to invite Dorrie inside, show her a little human kindness? Frank scratched his chin, considering, then handed her the pail of cracked eggs to carry. "Listen, do you want to come inside and we'll take a look at your paperwork?"

The neighbours would gossip if they knew. But they didn't know. Anyway, he intended to behave—keep his hands to himself, his thoughts clean.

The kitchen smelled of the sausages Frank had left simmering on the stove. He stirred the pot, then turned to watch Dorrie remove her coat. She was wearing a mauve dress too tight under the arms. "Mom would be mad if she knew I was here," she said, plunking herself down in the rocking chair. "She's over-protective."

"Well, maybe you need protecting."

Dorrie looked like Goldilocks in the children's story, her little feet swinging inches above the floor. "Actually I get a kick out of the way the Mennonites treat me. They all expect me to get pregnant and marry some good-for-nothing. I can hardly wait to tell them I'm leaving for hairdressing school. In Saskatoon yet."

"That'll surprise 'em all right." Frank's stomach rumbled. "Listen, Dorrie, I'm kinda hungry. Maybe we should eat first, then do your paperwork." He speared a couple of sausages, dipped them in water to cool them, and passed one to Dorrie. "You might want to make pancakes," he said, putting the other sausage in his mouth. If Dorrie was like most girls—women— she'd enjoy showing off her cooking skills.

She wrinkled her nose.

Frank wiped his hands on the kitchen towel. "I've got a recipe book around here somewhere." He went to the bookcase.

Dorrie took a bite of her sausage. "I don't know how to make pancakes, even with a recipe. Mom always makes them at our place."

Frank found the book and flipped through it. "What about scones? You could put raisins in them." He winced, remembering the raisin scones Tina had made for him last winter. She'd be mad if she knew Dorrie was here in his kitchen. But he was just trying to give the poor kid some guidance. That was the Christian thing to do, wasn't it?

Dorrie crossed her legs, slipping one foot under her derriere. "I can't cook at all. I'm more the artistic type."

Frank shrugged. "I guess that's okay as long as your mother's taking care of you." He headed for the cellar. "I'll go get a jar of corn and some applesauce if there's any left."

Dorrie took another bite of her sausage. "I hope there's applesauce."

Frank fetched the corn and applesauce from the cellar, dumped them into two saucepans, and put them on the stove to heat. As he set the table, Dorrie watched from the rocking chair like a spectator at a baseball game. She sure was different from Tina. Tina would have at least set the table. In fact, Tina would have taken over the whole meal by now. But why compare the two women—girls? There was no comparison. Dorrie was a lost little puppy. And Tina was—what? She was either the long-distance sweetheart he should break up with, or the woman he intended to marry. Frank sighed and went to the pantry for some buns. The buns were a bit hard but not mouldy anyway. He put them on the table, then the rest of the food. "Okay, Goldilocks. Pull up a chair."

When Dorrie had seated herself, Frank waited to see if she'd say grace like Tina always did.

Nothing.

Frank didn't know whether to feel relieved or disappointed.

Dorrie took a bun and tore it in half. "I wish I could get to church more often."

Oh, okay. Maybe Dorrie was more religious than he'd thought.

She spooned applesauce onto her bun. "It's too far to walk, and Mom and I don't have a car. Dad took it when he left."

Frank speared three sausages onto his plate. "You could ask the Epps to pick you up."

"Adeline doesn't like me."

"Right. That's what you said. But Adeline never lets feelings stand in the way of doing God's work. She's always telling people that."

Dorrie shuddered. "I'd rather stay home than accept her snobby charity."

Frank split a bun and lined his sausages up in it.

"Do you go to church much?" Dorrie asked.

"I go once in a while," he said cautiously, "mostly just to see people." Dorrie was obviously leading up to something.

She chewed a bite of bun and swallowed. "You must miss your parents."

"Yeah, I miss my dad. My stepmother and I don't get along, but she's a pretty fair cook. I don't know what I'll do when her canned stuff is all gone."

Dorrie turned and fixed her flax-blue eyes on Frank. "My mom's a good cook," she said, her lips puckering on the words good and cook.

For a second he pictured himself kissing those lips.

No, he wouldn't do that. It would be wrong to take advantage of the girl. Anyway he was practically engaged to Tina. He scraped his chair back from the table. "I'll make some tea." As he rose, Dorrie reached for his hand. Hers felt as soft as warm meringue. Frank melted into it for a moment, then pulled away.

She grabbed his arm. "I've got an idea," she said, her fingers pleating his shirt sleeve. "You could take Mom and me to church next Sunday, then come to our house for dinner."

"What would the neighbours think?"

Dorrie laughed. "Don't be such an old fogey. People will be thrilled to see the prodigals in church."

Chapter 11

Frank felt contented and full as he manoeuvred his DeSoto out of the Harms's driveway. Dorrie's mother had outdone herself with those cabbage rolls today. He'd eaten dinner at the Harms's five Sundays in a row now. Every meal Dorrie's mom had cooked had been great. Ham and fried potatoes the first Sunday, meatballs and mashed potatoes the second Sunday, then chicken noodle soup, then smoked sausages with dumplings. And today cabbage rolls with sour cream, boiled potatoes, and chives from the garden.

As for Dorrie, that girl was as pretty as a palomino pony. Now that the days were getting longer, she was developing a nice suntan. It made her blonde eyebrows show up better. And that apricot derriere of hers—ripe for the picking.

Frank's fingers tightened on the steering wheel. He'd better keep his hands to himself. A girl like Dorrie wouldn't put on the brakes like Tina did. He wouldn't want to get Dorrie pregnant. That would sure give the Dayspring Mennonites something to gossip about. He could just hear them: *Shame on Dorrie. We thought she was on the straight and narrow. The question is, will Frank marry her? How honourable is he, really? His mother left him and his dad, you know. What kind of a wife and mother would run off with a Red Army soldier? Frank is like his mother, flighty.*

He shook his head. No, he wouldn't take Dorrie to bed, not unless they were married. Somehow marrying Dorrie didn't seem as scary as marrying Tina. He could relax with Dorrie. She didn't try to improve him like Tina did. And Dorrie got so much fun out of even the simplest things. Frank chuckled, remembering that silly game of Snakes and Ladders this afternoon.

Dorrie was crazy about him no matter what he did. If he crossed his eyes, she thought he was clever. If he wiggled his ears, she considered him a genius. Of course she couldn't cook; she couldn't even make coffee. But what did that matter? If he and Dorrie got married, her mom could live with them and do the cooking and housework. Cleora's health might get better at his house, too. Her arthritis might ease up once she got out of that draughty shack she and Dorrie lived in.

But if he married Dorrie, they'd be together for the rest of their lives. What if they got tired of each other? What if Dorrie's mom died? Who'd do the cooking and housework?

Frank sighed as he passed the Coyote Junction School with its sagging green roof. If he had his papa's courage, he'd quit dithering and propose to Dorrie. He'd heard his parents' story a hundred times, but it always kicked him in the gut.

The other Mennonites had warned Papa about marrying Mama. *Morga's flighty. She won't make a reliable wife.*

But Papa had wanted Mama, and he'd married Mama, and he'd never been sorry. The guy was a real *mensch*. He'd ignored other people's prejudices, risen above them, and followed his heart. And he'd taken responsibility for the decision he'd made. No regrets, few complaints.

Frank steered the car into his driveway. Even after Mama had left, Papa hadn't believed what the village gossips said— that she'd run away because she wanted a younger man. Papa had saddled his gelding and ridden from village to village searching for Mama, asking questions, hungry for any crumb of news. The poor man hadn't found anything. He'd mourned for months, years.

Frank parked his car near the porch, shuddering at the memory of Papa crying in the attic, great wrenching sobs. Love was a dangerous thing.

He clumped into the kitchen and winced at the sight of Tina's letter propped against the salt shaker: *Darling, I could come for a visit once you finish seeding. Uncle Yash said he'd give me a couple weeks off.*

He'd had that letter for three weeks and still hadn't answered it. What could he say? *I'm dating Dorrie Harms, and I don't know if I love you or her.* Tina wouldn't understand something like that. What if he wrote *I love both you and Dorrie, just in different ways?*

He shook his head. No, that was worse, far worse.

Chapter 12

Tina slumped into a chair on her uncle and aunt's veranda. No letter from Frank again today. Was he just busy seeding? Maybe he was too depressed to write. Maybe some Dayspring busybody had looked the wrong way at him, or remarked on how much browner his skin got from working in the sun all day. Anything could set Frank off when he got into one of his sensitive moods.

The wind sighed through the spruce tree beside the veranda. *Tomorrow*, its branches seemed to whisper. *Maybe tomorrow there'll be a letter from Frank.*

Tina grimaced. Those sappy branches had said the same thing yesterday and the day before. Frank still didn't write. Maybe he didn't love her anymore. She could phone and ask, but he'd think she was being pushy. He might freeze on the phone, go all cold and distant. She hated it when he did that. Better not to hear his voice at all.

Tears trickled down her cheeks, their salty taste seeping into the corners of her mouth. She reached for her handkerchief and felt something slip off her lap. The letter from her mother. She'd almost forgotten it. Tina picked up the pink envelope and tore it open.

Box G
Dayspring, Saskatchewan
June 7, 1940
Dear Tina,

How are you? We're fine. I planted a lilac bush on the east side of the house.

Leif Lindberg's mother has tuberculosis. She's in the sanatorium in Qu'Appelle. Leif says

she's not doing too good. He and Katie just came
back from there.

Frank Warkentin's bachelor friend Thor
bought the old ranchers' cabin near Frank's place.
It's in poor shape. Crows are nesting in the chimney. Their friend Sigurd says it's a waste of money.

Frank brings Dorrie Harms and her mom to
church every Sunday, and goes to the Harms's
house for dinner afterwards. Dorrie tried to plant
a garden at Frank's place, but it's not coming up
too well. She's not much of a gardener or a housekeeper. Her mother spoils her, you know. You
should have seen Frank and Dorrie at the ball game
in the schoolyard. He hit a home run and she kissed
him in front of everybody.

"Dorrie!" Tina exploded. "That little minx." Was she turning Frank's head? No, couldn't be. Dorrie was too silly for Frank
and too young. Maybe he was just humouring the girl. But that
shouldn't involve eating Sunday dinners at her house. And he
definitely shouldn't have let her kiss him, even for a joke.

Tina bit her lower lip. She'd probably been stupid to stay in
Vancouver, expecting Frank not to notice other girls while he
made up his turtle-slow mind whether to propose to her. She
should move back to Dayspring, where she could fight for her man
if she had to. But that would mean giving up her job. What if she
moved and Frank still didn't marry her? What would she do then?

She bowed her head. Dear God, please show me what to
do. You know how much I love Frank.

The Lord didn't seem to answer her one way or another.
But as Tina continued to pray, a plan formed in her mind. She
rose to her feet. She'd phone Roland right away, discuss the situation with him, and ask if he'd help her. Roland wasn't a really
imaginative guy, but he might do okay with her coaching him.

Chapter 13

Frank parked his car beside the Friesens' garden and sat scowling at their house. "I wonder when the Mennonites are going to get a proper church building."

Dorrie patted his arm, her fingers light as a doll's. "I like having church in people's houses. It's fun to see their colour schemes." She opened the passenger door and hopped out of the car.

The fringes of her cowgirl dress swirling past her little rosebud breasts, she helped her mom out of the back seat.

"Dorrie, Cleora," Nettie Friesen called from the porch, "come and help me pick flowers for the table."

Good old Nettie, Frank thought, following them toward the house. She made an honest effort to befriend the not-quite-respectable Harms women.

When they reached the porch, he left Dorrie and her mom with Nettie and went in through the kitchen door. The Friesens' kitchen smelled of floor polish and the geraniums on the windowsills, red as tomatoes. Frank would have enjoyed a cup of coffee, but nobody seemed to have made any. He shrugged and continued into the living room.

The benches and chairs were already set up for church. Preacher Schellenberg met him near the Boston fern, under the picture of *The Last Supper*. The preacher extended a bony hand. "It's good to see you, Frank. Did you hear the news? Tina Janz is moving back to Dayspring."

Frank's heart reared like a startled horse. Tina? Moving back here? She hadn't said a word to him about it. He glanced at the gaggle of women gossiping near the east window. He could just imagine what they were saying: *What will Frank do now? Will he go back to Tina or stick with Dorrie? Dorrie suits him better. Tina's too classy for him.*

Frank nodded at the preacher. "Excuse me." His mouth felt so dry, he could hardly say the words. He retreated to the kitchen. He felt like running away—heading out the door and going straight home. But if he did, people would gossip about him even worse. Besides, Dorrie and Cleora needed a ride home after church. He found a cup in the cupboard and filled it from the dipper in the Friesens' water pail. The water went down cool and fresh. He helped himself to another cupful, chugged it down, and returned to the living room feeling steadier.

He slid onto a bench near the back of the men's side. More Mennonites were arriving, crowding through the door laughing and talking.

Frank's heart jumped. Was that Tina behind Bill Schmidt in his wheelchair? Frank hardly recognized her. She looked like a fashion model in that blue suit. And she must have done something to her hair. It had never looked so puffy before. He rose from his bench and sauntered toward her.

She turned away, checking the seams in the backs of her stockings. Apparently satisfied that they were straight, she turned and headed to the front of the women's side, slipped into a bench, and bowed her head in prayer.

What was going on here? Why hadn't Tina even said hello? She must have seen him. Maybe she figured talking to God was more important than greeting the long-distance sweetheart she hadn't seen for months. It probably was, at least from Tina's point of view. But she could talk to God any time day or night. Why right now?

He took a hymn book off one of the chairs and strolled toward the bench Tina was sitting on. He stood near it, paging through the book, waiting for her to finish praying. He still loved her; he must. Otherwise his heart wouldn't be kicking like a bronco. He should have written to her more often; he should have phoned. As soon as she looked up, he'd apologize.

She didn't move, didn't raise her head, though she must sense him standing just a few steps away. Maybe she was mad because she'd heard he was dating Dorrie.

Dorrie—the name skittered across Frank's conscience. What if she came in right now and saw him watching Tina like a cat stalking a robin? What would his little Goldilocks think?

What was everybody thinking? People were throwing glances his way as they seated themselves. Men on the men's side, women on the women's, couples across the aisle from each other, passing babies back and forth. Frank left the women's side and strolled back to the men's. As he sat down beside Benno Fehr, a few stragglers hurried in from the kitchen, Nettie Friesen among them. She carried a low vase of wildflowers to the front and set it on the lace-covered table that Preacher Schellenberg used for a pulpit.

When Nettie had retreated to a bench near the back, the preacher took his place behind the table and opened his hymn book. "*Nummer 48,*" he announced in High German, the language of church. "*Komm, du quelle alles segens.*" Come, thou fount of every blessing.

Frank heard a mouse-like scurrying in the aisle and turned to see Dorrie slide into the bench across from him, a sprig of scarlet mallow caught in her hair. He reached over and handed her his hymn book.

Dear scatterbrained Dorrie. She loved him. She needed him. Dorrie and her mom both needed him. But Frank was pretty sure he loved and needed Tina Janz. So what was he going to do?

When the last notes of the hymn had died away, Dave Friesen rose, read a psalm, and led in prayer. As Dave seated himself, Preacher Schellenberg returned to the table, his bulgy eyes scanning the congregation. He cleared his throat. "It is an honour to have Sister Tina Janz back in our midst. Sister Janz has just returned from Vancouver, where she served as a secretary for her uncle, Dr. Yash Siemens."

Wow, Frank thought, star treatment.

"I believe some of you know Dr. Siemens," Preacher Schellenberg continued. "Sister Janz ably assisted the doctor in serving on the boards of several charitable organizations. According to a letter I recently received from Dr. Siemens, Sister Janz showed outstanding skill and dedication in the fulfilment of her duties."

Frank's eyes widened. Tina must be some kind of a celebrity now. Preacher Schellenberg had never announced Frank in church like that. What might the preacher have said if he had? *It is an honour to have Brother Frank Warkentin back in our midst. He has just returned from several areas of Canada and the USA, where he served in a variety of jobs—rodeo-rider, farm-hand, dishwasher, logger. After being laid off from his position as a manure shoveller, he remained unemployed for several months, for which reason he was forced to return to Dayspring.*

Tina rose and stepped into the aisle, interrupting Frank's musings. "What's happening?" he whispered to Benno.

"Tina's going to give a report," Benno whispered. "About the charity work she did with her uncle."

How about that? Tina had never been asked to speak in church before. She was nervous. Frank could tell by the way her head bobbed as she arranged her notes on the table beside her Bible.

He glanced across the aisle at Dorrie. What was Goldilocks thinking? Her eyes looked cloudy. Frank gave her a half-smile and turned back to Tina. But he couldn't concentrate on her report and Tina didn't look at him, even when he faked a coughing fit. As she returned to her seat, Frank leaned into the aisle, trying to catch her eye.

Tina's gaze slid over him and came to rest on Roland Fast with that ridiculous red handkerchief puff in his pocket. What was going on here? Tina loved him, Frank Herbert Warkentin. Her love wouldn't have evaporated so fast. Frank hardly heard Preacher Schellenberg announce the closing hymn. He hardly heard the congregation singing. The closing prayer passed in a blur, and then people were milling out into the Friesens' yard. A crowd gathered around Tina, who stood near the lilac hedge clutching her Bible under her blue-suited arm.

"Imagine that," Frank heard a female voice say. "We've got a famous doctor's secretary right here in our church. Just wait'll I tell my cousin in Fresno."

Another voice. Nettie's: "Tina, how could you ever type all those reports? It must be terrible hard, keeping all those figures straight. But what do you plan to do in Dayspring? There aren't many jobs for secretaries around here."

Preacher Schellenberg raised a bony hand. "Just a minute. I'll get my camera. I want to get a picture of Tina for the church paper."

As the preacher hurried to his car, Frank left Dorrie with Benno Fehr and ambled over to Tina. "Welcome home," he said in what he hoped was a casual voice. "Your report was great."

Tina glanced up as if trying to connect a name to his face. "Oh, Frank. Nice to see you again." She extended a white-gloved hand.

Why so formal? She was acting like she was the Queen of England and he was a shoeshine boy. Of course Tina must be mad at him for dating Dorrie, but—

"Tina!" Preacher Schellenberg called, waving his camera at her. "You'd look good in front of that white lilac bush."

She moved to the white lilac and posed like a model, one foot ahead of the other. The preacher peered through his eyepiece and clicked the shutter. "Very nice." He took another snap, then glanced around at the crowd. "Let's get a picture of Tina with some of our other young people. Roland, good. You stand beside Tina. Greta, beside Roland. Susie, on the other side of Greta. Back a bit. That's great. Bill in the front row — Corny, you could help him with the wheelchair. Frank, Dorrie, Benno."

Benno straightened his tie and hurried to stand beside Susie. Dorrie stayed where she was.

Frank went to her. "Come on, Goldilocks." He tried to smile. "You might as well be famous, too."

"I don't want to."

"Why not?"

"I don't feel like it, that's all."

Frank considered saying *Don't worry, I won't go back to Tina.* But he couldn't say those words, especially not with so many people listening. Frank wished they'd stop staring at him like he was a fly in a water pail. They were waiting for him to decide. Would he stay on the sidelines with Dorrie, or go and get himself photographed with Tina and the others? Whatever he did, people would read something into it.

Frank raised his eyebrows at Tina, hoping for a smile or some other sign that she still loved him.

She turned away, looping her arm through Roland's.

Something stabbed Frank's ribs, sharp as a sword. Surely Tina wasn't really interested in the golden boy.

Or maybe she was. Stranger things had happened. Well, Roland couldn't have her. Frank brushed a bit of lint off his lapel and strode toward the group in front of the white lilac bush. Benno moved over to make space for him. Frank nodded his thanks but circled around to the back of the group. He stood behind Tina and Roland, inserting his head so it would appear between theirs in the picture.

Preacher Schellenberg jerked his chin at Dorrie. "There's room for you beside Benno."

Dorrie shook her head and retreated across the lawn to where her mother sat on the Friesens' porch.

The preacher sighed, raised his camera, and took a few more snaps. "All right," he said, "that's it."

After the preacher had left, Frank laid his hand on Tina's arm. "Sister Janz, could I offer you a ride home?" Dorrie and her mother needed a ride, too, but maybe Benno would like to take them. Dorrie was chatting with Benno on the Friesens' porch, smoothing her dress over her slender hips. What was she saying to him to make him laugh and toss his head like that?

Long cool fingers closed around Frank's hand. Tina's fingers. She lifted his hand off her arm. "I believe I already have a ride," she said, turning to Roland. "Are you ready to go, Rolly?"

"Rolly!" Frank exploded. "What kind of a stupid name is that?"

"It was Tina's idea," Roland said in his blaring radio-announcer voice. "It's a more modern name than Roland. She suggested it while we were walking beside the lake last night."

Frank's stomach shrivelled with disgust. "Walking—beside the lake—you and Tina. What for?"

Roland lifted his fedora and smoothed his greasy hair off his forehead. "It was a nice night. The moon was out." He replaced the hat.

Frank wheeled around to face Tina. "What are you trying to prove?"

She patted her puffy hairdo. "Why are you getting so excited? You didn't write to me; you didn't phone. You were too busy kissing D-d-dorrie Harms." Her voice wobbled. "Rolly and I are old friends so it seemed only logical to—"

"Maybe you and Rolly are friends," Frank growled. "But Roland and I ain't." He lunged at the golden boy, pushing him into the lilac bush.

Roland swung a fist at Frank, his fedora spiralling off his head into the lilacs.

People turned and stared.

Tina grabbed Frank's arm. "Please don't fight, especially not right after church." She retrieved Roland's fedora and set it on his greasy head.

"Tina, please—" Frank said.

She took the golden boy's arm. Frank almost vomited at the sight of them standing there like a married couple.

"Tina, dear," Roland said, straightening his fedora. "We should get going. We don't want to be late."

Late for what? Frank didn't have the stomach to ask.

He watched in silence as Roland led Tina to his black Studebaker and opened the door for her.

Chapter 14

Frank tried to ignore the mosquito that was whining around the pictures above his bed. It was one-thirty in the morning. He needed to sleep. He had haying to do in the morning; the brome-grass was ready. "Forget the mosquito," he muttered. "Just pretend it's not there."

Moments later he sprang up with a curse and swatted at it.

Silence, precious silence.

Frank lay down again.

Whine, yammer, whine.

"Aaaaah!" Frank roared into the darkness. That stupid mosquito was as maddening as Roland Fast buzzing around Tina. The guy had been at it for three weeks now—taking Tina to church, buying her dinners at the Chinese café, escorting her to community picnics.

Frank heard a whine like a tiny fighter plane. Then something feathered past his ear. "Ha!" he yelled, smacking the side of his head.

Silence. He'd either deafened himself or broken every bone in that wretched mosquito's body. Too bad it wasn't so easy to get rid of Roland.

Frank lay down and pulled the covers up. He was too riled to sleep, but maybe he'd rest his eyes anyway. He closed them. Moments later he felt himself drifting over a field of brome-grass and clover, beige and green, rippling in the wind. Rippling, swaying. Rippling, swaying.

A bird screeched outside his window.

Frank jumped, waking with a start. He peered at the clock. Four-thirty already? He'd actually slept, but now he was wider awake than a pig the day before a sausage-making festival. He sighed and threw back the covers.

Down in the kitchen he got the fire going and started some coffee. No fake java for him this morning. That was okay on good days, but today he needed the real thing. He was hungry, too. Maybe he'd fry some ham and eggs. He could fry some left-over potatoes too. As he lifted the frying pan off its hook, his elbow knocked against the bouquet of yellow coneflowers that Dorrie had arranged in his teapot.

Frank set the frying pan on the counter and stared at the teapot full of flowers. His mind drifted to Dorrie picking them in her mauve sundress, hitching up the sleeve that kept sliding off her pretty shoulder.

What would she do if he went back to Tina? He'd need to tell her it was all over between them. Could he do that?

Frank poured himself a mug of coffee. The sun was rising, purple and orange on the horizon. Maybe he should saddle his mare and ride over to Dorrie's house right now. He could take a thermos of coffee, some bread, ham, cheese, a few raisins. He'd tap on Dorrie's window and when she appeared—eyes full of sleep, hair tangled over her shoulders—he'd invite her out for a breakfast picnic. They'd gallop through the pasture, her arms around his waist, her small body pressed against his, breasts warm and soft. Then they'd stop and eat, and he'd ask her to marry him.

Frank clenched his hands around his coffee mug. Of course, as soon as he and Dorrie announced their engagement, people would start giving him well-meaning advice:

"You know what Dorrie's dad was like. That kind of thing runs in the blood, you know."

"You'll end up supporting Dorrie's whole family. Brothers, cousins, uncles, aunts—they'll all want handouts."

On and on it would go:

"Your dad and stepmother want you to make something of the farm. That wouldn't be easy, married to Dorrie. A farmer needs an organized woman, a woman that can cook, wash clothes, take care of kids, clean the house. There's enough for a guy to do outside without worrying about inside work, too."

"Why don't you go back to Tina Janz? Now there's an organized woman. But you'd better not waste any more time. It looks like Roland Fast is moving in on her."

Frank sighed and trundled down to the cellar for ham and eggs. He wouldn't bother with the potatoes. He wasn't that hungry anymore.

Chapter 15

Frank eased his DeSoto along Dayspring's main street, his eyes watering in the morning light. The red door of Mah's Café opened and the usual gang of farmers filed out. They'd finished their morning coffee, eight o'clock on the dot. Frank raised a finger in greeting, too tired to wave. His whole body felt stale with fatigue. But his mind was clear, so clear his nose hurt. That was one thing about fatigue. It focused a man on what he needed to do.

Frank turned left at the train station, then jolted his car over the railway tracks and past the Lutheran graveyard with its high iron gate. Beyond the graveyard he caught a glimpse of dark-blue water. Knutson Lake, where Roland and Tina had gone walking. What had they talked about? Had he kissed her? She wouldn't let him, would she? The thought of Tina mouth to mouth with "Rolly" was too disgusting to consider.

A few bleary moments later, Frank steered his car into her parents' driveway. It was straight and narrow. Their front porch was swept clean, its boards bleached by years of sun and wind.

"Frank, what's the matter?" Tina asked when she answered the door. She stepped out onto the porch, looking crisp and fresh in her green-striped dress. "How come your eyes are so red? Are you sick?"

Frank blinked, so tired his eyes felt like they were full of sand. "How come you're dating Roland Fast? Do you think you're too good for me all of a sudden, going after a rich guy?"

She planted her hands on her hips. "How can you scold me about Roland when you're practically engaged to Dorrie Harms?" Tina's voice had a sharp edge to it, but Frank thought he saw pain in her eyes.

A tide of fatigue dragged at his legs. He leaned against the door frame. "What makes you think I'd get myself engaged to Dorrie?"

"Adeline Epp says you'll be married to her before freeze-up."

"I should wash that Adeline's mouth out with soap."

Tina's shoulders sagged, the stripes of her dress drooping with her. "Why? Everybody knows how fascinated you are with Dorrie." Tears pooled in her eyes.

Something broke inside Frank, like an elastic band. He'd been a fool, letting Tina suffer while he dithered over Dorrie. Tina was the woman for him, wasn't she? She still loved him, didn't she? He squared his shoulders. "Would you do me the honour of accompanying me to the wiener roast tomorrow evening?"

Tina adjusted one of the combs in her hair. "Sorry. Roland already asked me."

Frank imitated a smile. "I wouldn't go with Roland if I was you. He puts lard on his hair."

"No, he doesn't."

"Of course he does. That's why the mosquitoes follow him around like they do."

Tina laughed. "Frank, you're crazy."

"Yeah, I know." He paused. "That's why you're in love with me." He studied her face, searching for evidence.

Her expression was as blank as vanilla pudding.

He cleared his throat. "So we'll go to the wiener roast, right?"

Tina tucked a stray curl behind her ear. Was her hand shaking or was that his imagination? "What about Dorrie?"

"I'm not asking Dorrie. I'm asking you."

Tina scrunched her mouth to one side. "I guess I could break my date with Roland."

"Okay, good. I'll quit haying early and pick you up about five."

"Or I could catch a ride with the Lindbergs. It would save you some time and gas."

That was considerate of Tina but kind of awkward. "You'll be at my place too early if you get the Lindbergs to drop you off. I'll still be out in the field." He really did need to get that hay in.

"I don't mind," Tina said. "I can take a walk, do some sketching."

Frank grinned. "You can pull weeds in my garden if you want. Feel free. There are lots of them."

Chapter 16

Tina hurried up the driveway into Frank's yard, her heart dancing with anticipation. In a couple hours he'd come in from the hayfield and they'd go to the wiener roast, she and her sweetheart together again.

Tina's denim skirt brushed against her legs as she stepped off the driveway and headed for the garden. At the edge of the garden she stopped short. Who was that crouching over the corn plants like she owned them?

The little blonde figure turned and frowned at her.

Dorrie Harms. What was she doing here? Frank wouldn't have invited her. Not when he had a date with another woman.

Dorrie yanked a weed from between a couple of corn plants, her pigtails swinging past her shoulders.

Tina's heart lurched. Was that Frank's green shirt Dorrie was wearing? Of course it was. What was Dorrie doing with it? Frank wouldn't have loaned it to her. The little minx had probably swiped it off his clothesline. That was the sort of thing she'd do.

Tina plunged into the garden, her shoes sinking into the soft earth. She trudged toward Dorrie.

Dorrie flounced over to the carrot patch near the fence.

Tina followed, grimacing as she watched the tails of the shirt swing across Dorrie's neat derriere. She herself had never been that slim. She never would be, no matter how much cake and pie she denied herself. She pictured Dorrie visiting here in the past, planting Frank's garden for him, weeding it, watering it, offering him her supple young body. Had he taken it? No, of course not. Frank was a Christian; he had principles.

Tina faked a smile. "Dorothea," she said, using the schoolgirl name she knew Dorrie hated. "What a surprise, seeing you here."

Dorrie pulled a couple of stray beet plants from among the carrots and tossed them into the air. They fluttered in the breeze and landed near Tina's feet.

"You can go home now," Tina said, trying to maintain her smile. "Frank asked me to weed his garden." She stooped and picked up the strays Dorrie had discarded. "I'll plant these with the other beets. There's no point wasting them."

Dorrie ran at Tina, snatched the beets from her, and threw them on the ground. "I planted this garden," she muttered, trampling the plants under the heel of her cowboy boot. "And I'll run it my own way."

"This isn't your garden," Tina snapped, "even if you did plant it." Dorrie had done a sloppy job: crooked rows, bare spots where the seeds hadn't come up. "It's Frank's garden." Someday it would be Tina's too, if he ever proposed to her.

Dorrie spat on the ground. "Frank loves me."

The words stung like a wasp, though they weren't true of course. "No, he doesn't. You misunderstood. I realize he dated you for a while, but that doesn't mean . . ."

Dorrie hugged his shirt more tightly around herself. "He loves me."

"Does he?" Tina planted her hands on her hips. "So how come he's taking me to the wiener roast?"

Doubt crept into Dorrie's blue eyes. "Frank isn't going to the wiener roast. He's too busy."

Tina couldn't suppress a smile, a real one this time. "No, he's quitting early so he and I can go."

Dorrie twisted a button on Frank's shirt. "How come he's going with you when he's marrying me?"

Tina's heart almost stopped. "Marrying? You?" One of the combs in her hair slipped from its moorings. She jabbed it back, wincing as its teeth poked her scalp. "What gives you that idea?"

"Frank hasn't proposed yet, but I just—" Dorrie hiccupped. Or was that a sob? "I just know in my heart he'll—"

"You're imagining things, Dorothea. Anyway, how can he marry you when you're not even going to be here? You're heading for hairdressing school in Saskatoon, aren't you?"

Dorrie tossed one of her pigtails over her shoulder. "I decided not to go."

"Oh, but you should," Tina said, feeling like a hypocrite. "You're artistic, pretty, talented. You'd make a great hairdresser."

"I know and I'd love it, but I couldn't stand being so far away from Frank."

Anger smouldered in Tina's stomach. "You've got no future with Frank. He's determined to make something of this farm. You'd be no help. You can't even cook. You can't—"

"He loves me," Dorrie wailed.

"No, he doesn't." Tina grasped Dorrie's shoulder and steered her toward the driveway. "Go home to your mother."

Dorrie leapt out of Tina's grasp, lithe as a cat. A pair of hairdressing scissors bounced from the pocket of the green shirt. They hurtled to the ground, their slim blades flashing.

Dorrie snatched them up.

"What are you doing with those?" Tina demanded.

"Going to give Frank a haircut."

Tina grabbed at them. Missed. "No, you're not. I'll cut Frank's hair if it needs cutting."

Dorrie clacked the scissors in front of Tina's nose, open and shut, open and shut. "That hairdo looks terrible on you. Do you know that? It makes you look like a mushroom. I don't know why Frank wants to date an old maid who looks like a mushroom."

Tina's confidence wavered. She wasn't an old maid. She was only twenty-five. And she was proud of her hairdo. It—

She caught a flash of steel as Dorrie lunged toward her, scissors pointed at her hairdo. Tina dodged, too late. Dorrie seized a handful of Tina's hair, yanked it free of its combs, and sliced the scissors through it. Molasses-brown curls tumbled onto Tina's shoulders and slithered to the ground.

Tina stared down at her amputated locks. "Dorrie, you vicious—"

Dorrie lunged at her again, scissors poised.

Tina snatched them, wrenching them out of her hand. "Get away from here, Dorothea." She pointed the scissors like a sword. "Go." She jabbed the scissors at Dorrie's arm, hoping to scare the girl off.

"Ouch." Dorrie clutched her arm.

Tina was horrified, then glad, to see a trickle of red staining the green fabric. "Go!"

Dorrie scampered away. "Okay, I'm going. I'll come back when Frank's home." She hurried to the fence where her mare waited, untied the horse, and swung herself into the saddle. Her pigtails bounced across the back of the green shirt as she galloped away.

Tina reached up with trembling hands, removed the rest of her combs, and ran her fingers through her mutilated hair. She'd look terrible at the wiener roast, if she even went. Maybe she should just ask Frank to take her home.

Her heart tightened. What a two-timer that Frank was, stringing both her and Dorrie along.

Or maybe he had broken up with Dorrie and the little minx just hadn't accepted it. Tina put her combs in her pocket and headed for the hayfield. She needed to talk to him.

* * *

"Dorrie's just a lost little puppy," Frank said when Tina had told him about the encounter in the garden. She and Frank were sitting on a big rock near a clump of wildflowers. Rows of new-mown hay curved through the field around them, sweet as a baby's breath.

Tina ran a hand over her new-mown hair. "Look at this. It's awful."

He tilted his head to one side. "It's not bad. Actually, it's cute in a way."

"It's a mess. I'll need to get it all cut now, thanks to your floozy."

"Dorrie's not a floozy." Irritation edged Frank's voice. "She's like a sister to me."

Tina shook her head. "That's not the way she sees it. She claims you're going to marry her."

Frank was silent for so long, Tina thought he wouldn't answer. He shifted on the rock, then examined a black beetle that was crawling over his shirtsleeve. When he finally spoke, his voice was so quiet, Tina hardly heard him. "How could I marry Dorrie when I love you?"

"What did you say?" Hope stirred in Tina's heart.

Frank slid off the rock, knelt on the ground, and steepled his hands like he was praying. "Tina Alice Janz, will you marry me?"

Tina stared down at him, astounded. She hadn't expected this. Well, she had. She'd dreamed of this moment, longed for it, but—

"You wouldn't marry Roland, would you?" Frank's voice cracked on the name. "He's a jerk."

She gave him a teasing smile. "So are you. A jerk."

"Of course." Frank swayed on his knees. "And I'm restless and I'm grouchy at breakfast. You'll find that out soon enough, probably the morning after we get hitched." He reached up, curving his arm around Tina. She dodged and he lost his balance, toppling to the ground.

Tina scrambled down after him. "Oh, poor Frank. I didn't mean to make you fall. Are you hurt?"

"No, I'm fine. There's nothing wrong with me that a good kissing won't cure."

Chapter 17

Tina paced the floor of her parents' kitchen, her white satin gown swirling around her high-heeled shoes. Where could Frank be? It was twenty minutes to three already. The wedding was supposed to start at three. She went to the screen door and peered out for what seemed like the fiftieth time. There was no sign of his car.

Almost everybody else was here. She scanned the parking area near the pasture and saw the Friesens' truck pull up. Dave and Nettie Friesen got out and hurried toward the machine shed.

That old shed looked almost like a church with the steeple Tina's dad had built. The inside looked good too, with the machinery gone, and chairs and benches arranged in rows for the guests. Frank and his friends had even carried in an organ.

But there wouldn't be any wedding without a bridegroom. Maybe Frank had had an accident. No, the thought was too horrible. Tina pushed it from her mind. Maybe he was sick. But if he was, he'd have sent somebody to tell her, surely.

Frank had seemed nervous yesterday, helping her dad nail the steeple in place. Was he having second thoughts about marrying her? Dear God, please no.

A black car approached the parking area. Tina jumped, her pearl-embroidered coronet wobbling on her head. Was that Frank's DeSoto? No, it looked like a newer model. Must be Sigurd's.

Her coronet slipped toward her left ear. She wished she had more hair to hold it in place. Thanks to Dorrie's handiwork, she'd needed to get most of her hair cut off.

Tina retreated to her bedroom. Peering into the mirror, she anchored the coronet with bobby pins. Thank God Frank didn't mind the new hairdo. He said it made her look young and modern.

"Tina?" a voice rumbled from the porch. "Are you in there?"

"Frank!" She darted into the kitchen. "Where were you?" She opened the screen door. "Are you okay? Did you have car trouble?"

"The car's fine." He stepped inside. "Everything's fine, Sweetheart. I'm sorry I'm late. I had to park behind the caragana hedge. There was no room left in the—"

Frank let out a low whistle. "You look amazing." His voice turned husky. "That dress. Your hair."

Tina's heart melted like a snowball on a hot stove. "You look amazing, too." She picked a bit of thread off the lapel of his charcoal-striped suit. "I'm so glad you came." What a stupid thing to say.

Frank kissed her, his wide sweet mouth laughing against hers. "I wouldn't miss it for all the salt in Siberia." He hooked his arm into Tina's and led her out onto the porch. "I'd have been here an hour ago," he said, escorting her along the path toward the machine shed. "But I had to get these pants altered."

"Your suit pants? What was wrong with them?" She and Frank passed the end of the caragana hedge, and Tina skidded to a halt, teetering on her high heels. Who was that hopping out of Frank's car? Tina blinked and looked again. Dorrie? She whirled around to face Frank. "What's Dorrie Harms doing here?"

Frank sucked in a breath that whistled through his nostrils. "I told Dorrie to go into the machine shed with her mom, but she must have—"

Tina crossed her arms over her pearl-embroidered bodice. "First you arrive late, making me crazy wondering where you are. Worried something happened to you. Then you show up with D-d-dorrie." She winced, watching Dorrie smooth the peplum of her white suit over her slender hips.

Frank took Tina's arm. "Darling, I can explain."

She pulled away from him, tears clouding her eyes as Dorrie headed for the machine shed, hips swaying. "I thought we were rid of her. Isn't she's supposed to be at the hairdressing school in Saskatoon?"

"Sweetheart, please. She was in Saskatoon. But this morning when I went to ask her mom to alter these pants, Dorrie happened to be home and—"

"Dorrie happened to be home?" Tina's voice squeaked. "Maybe you knew your—your little Goldilocks was home. Maybe your suit pants were just an excuse to see her."

"Why would I want to see Dorrie on my wedding day?"

"You tell me."

Frank fingered the silver clip that held his necktie in place. "Look, Tina, I really needed help with these pants. They fit fine when I bought them, but this morning when I put them on, I could hardly pull up the zipper." He gave her a weak grin. "I guess you and your mom have been feeding me too good."

Tina sighed. "I can understand your pants might need altering. But why ask Dorrie's mother to do it when your stepmother was right there in the house with you?"

"There's no sewing machine at the house anymore. You know that. Anyway, my stepmother was too busy cleaning the place."

"What, this morning?"

Frank rolled his eyes. "She figured the ceilings weren't spotless enough for my new bride."

Tina gazed into his eyes, trying to read his mind, his soul. Frank had called her his bride. She wanted to be his bride. She wanted it more than anything in the world. But could she trust him enough to bet her life on him?

"Come on." He took her arm again. "Let's go get hitched before everybody gives up on us."

Tina jerked away from him. "Not till you tell me why you brought Dorrie Harms to our wedding."

"It's simple." He ran his finger around the inside of his shirt collar. "Dorrie's mom had trouble fixing these pants. She had to take out the whole zipper and put it back, twice. By the time she got done, she'd missed her ride to the wedding." He shrugged. "So I had to bring her."

"That explains Cleora, but what about Dorrie? Frank, it's our wedding day. Is nothing sacred to you?"

What was that she saw in his eyes? Embarrassment? Shame?

"Aw, Honey. You know what Dorrie's like. She's just a silly little girl. She jumped into my car and wouldn't get out so—"

"So what?"

"I didn't want to waste time arguing when the woman I love was waiting to make me the happiest man in the world."

Tina's shoulders tensed. Did Frank mean that? Could she really believe—

"Darling, please." He slipped his finger under her chin and lifted it, his eyes searching hers. "I chose you, not Dorrie. You and I chose each other. I could have married Dorrie, and you could have married Roland Fast. But we didn't."

Tina's shoulders relaxed a little. Frank wanted her, Tina Alice Janz. He'd chosen her. As far as rivals for their affection went, she and Frank were even. Actually they were more than even, she realized with a guilty start. Frank didn't know about Victor Graf, and she didn't plan to tell him.

She took her bridegroom's arm.

He grinned. "That's my girl."

As they followed the path to the machine shed, Tina felt like she was walking a tightrope, a tightrope of hope that her marriage would turn out okay despite its rocky start. She prayed it would. She and Frank stepped over the threshold and Hilda Wiens, at the organ, launched into Handel's "Wedding Hymn."

Proceeding up the aisle with her bridegroom, Tina felt as if the floor of the machine shed was swaying under her feet. She tried to steady herself, concentrating on the marigolds she and her friends had arranged in vases and set on the windowsills. Such cheerful shades of orange and yellow. Just as good as anything a Vancouver florist could do. Well, maybe not. But they were nice anyway.

By the time Tina and Frank reached the lace-covered table Preacher Schellenberg used as a pulpit, the floor felt firmer under her feet. The preacher gave the signal, and she and Frank seated themselves on the chairs her mom had tied together with yellow ribbons.

Preacher Schellenberg faced them across the table, his frog-like eyes darting around them to the congregation. "*Liebe Geschwister*," he began in High German. Dear brothers and sisters. Tina glanced at Frank and noticed a tiny cut on his chin. He must have cut himself shaving. Imagine, tomorrow she and Frank would wake up together. She could watch him shave. Watch him take off his pajamas. She shivered with anticipation.

Preacher Schellenberg paced back and forth behind the table. "Marriage takes courage and endurance." The preacher scanned the congregation, and then fixed his gaze on Tina and Frank. "You two could face many problems. Drought, grasshoppers, crop failure, accidents, sickness. You could disagree about where to go coffee-drinking on a Sunday afternoon, or where to plant the potatoes, or where to build a new backhouse." He laughed.

That backhouse remark must be Preacher Schellenberg's idea of a joke. Some people in Vancouver wouldn't even know what he was talking about.

"Other folks may try to come between you," the preacher continued. "But God can keep you true to each other. You need to pray for that."

Tina glanced at Frank. Did he pray, or did he just go through the motions in church or when somebody said grace at the table? She'd never had the courage to come right out and ask. She hoped they could pray together.

"Please kneel," Preacher Schellenberg said.

Frank and Tina knelt in front of their chairs and Preacher Schellenberg laid his hands on their heads. As he asked the Lord to bless their union, joy flooded Tina's heart.

Chapter 18

Tina kicked off her shoes. "Whew, my feet are killing me. I'm glad I don't have to help with the food today." She sat with Frank near the back of the machine shed, enjoying the breeze from the door. His Norwegian friends Sigurd and Thor sat on a quilt-covered bench opposite them.

Sigurd's head bobbed up from the guitar he was tuning for the singing games that would follow the wedding supper. "That's quite a spread," he said, nodding at the sawhorse tables where the women were setting out the supper. Buns, sausage, cheese, pickles, jellied salads, potato salads, pies, puffed wheat cakes, chocolate cakes. "You Mennonites sure know how to—"

He swivelled his head around as Dorrie Harms burst through the door wearing a sprig of purple fireweed in her hair. She darted over to the circle of chairs where Roland Fast sat with his friends, gave a high-pitched giggle, and snatched the red handkerchief puff out of Roland's pocket.

He popped up like a gopher from its hole and sprinted after Dorrie, grinning at his friends as he rounded their circle of chairs. In and out among the benches and chairs he ran, gaining on Dorrie until she flopped down on a bench near Frank and Tina. "Roland, please stop. I can't—run—anymore. I'm—no match for you."

Thor twitched his bushy eyebrows at Sigurd. "Looks like Dorrie's startin' the games early."

Sigurd snorted. "She's gotta take her mind off Frank not marrying her, don't she."

Frank said nothing but Tina could see from the dark-red colour flushing his face that he was embarrassed. He should be. He shouldn't have gotten mixed up with Dorrie in the first place. The little minx had almost spoiled the wedding and now she was—

"Tina!" Adeline Epp squawked from the gift table near the west wall. "Don't you want these blue dishes on the head table? I asked your mom and she said no, but they look so wonderful nice."

Tina stepped into her shoes and hurried to the table where Adeline had set out the wedding gifts, including the blue-hyacinth china. The dishes had arrived on the train in two cardboard cartons. Plates, nests of cups and saucers, a cream and sugar set, a wonderful teapot. The card read *Congratulations and best wishes, Tina and Frank.* It was signed *Love and prayers from your friends in Vancouver.* The handwriting was Victor Graf's and Tina knew he must have chosen the china pattern because blue hyacinths were his favourite flowers.

Adeline lifted the edge of her hairnet and tucked a stray curl under it. "So Tina, what do you think? Shall I put these blue dishes on the head table or shall I leave the white ones?

Why couldn't Adeline leave well enough alone? The last thing Tina needed was her former boyfriend's hyacinths staring at her every minute of the wedding supper, and the speeches, and Preacher Schellenberg's second sermon—he was sure to have one.

"Well?" Adeline glanced out the window at the women bringing the coffee pots from the house.

Tina opened her mouth to tell Adeline to use the white dishes. Then Dorrie Harms let out a shrieking giggle and Tina changed her mind. "Yes, Adeline. Please put the blue dishes on the head table. They'll remind me of my friends in Vancouver. Too bad none of them could be here." So what if the dishes reminded her of Victor? Frank had more than a reminder of his former sweetheart here.

Chapter 19

The bleak light of a winter dawn slanted through the kitchen windows, glinting on the porridge pot as Tina passed it to Frank with a trembling hand. She had a touchy subject to discuss with her husband, and she couldn't delay much longer. She gulped and plunged in. "I met Dad at the hardware store yesterday."

Frank ladled porridge into his bowl. "Oh, yeah? What was the old man up to?"

"He was looking at linoleum."

Frank said nothing, just dropped the ladle back into the porridge pot.

Tina forged ahead. "Dad says our house near town needs new linoleum."

"Does he now?" Frank spoke in a neutral tone of voice, but Tina saw the anger-vein pulsing in his neck.

Her insides quivered like a jellied salad. She'd been married to Frank for six months, and she still didn't know how to handle his anger. Would she ever know? She took a bite of bread, hoping the nourishment would steady her. The bread felt dry in her mouth, but she forced herself to chew and swallow. "Dad's just trying to help us. The renters are heading to the coast for a few weeks. It'll give us a chance to fix the place up." Nausea swirled up from her stomach, and she put the slice of bread down.

Frank got the cinnamon tin from the pantry and shook it over his porridge. "It's our house, ain't it? I thought your dad gave it to us." He set the tin on the table, banging it down harder than necessary. "What does your old man think I'm made of? Fifty-dollar bills? Once that baby comes—"

"Dad says he'll buy us new linoleum. Wallpaper too, if we want it."

A muscle twitched in Frank's jaw. "Why would he do that? It's not like we're going to move into the place."

Irritation prickled Tina's forehead. Them moving into the house north of Dayspring had been her dad's plan all along; Frank knew that. "It was generous of Dad to give us the place, especially with all that land."

"Especially since he don't care for me." Frank sloshed milk onto his porridge. Some of it splattered onto the red flowered oilcloth.

"Dad likes you. He's just—"

"Trying to control me."

"Of course not. He just wants what's best for us all. Think how handy it would be, living close to town and my folks." It would be less scary, too, Tina had to admit. Her mom knew everything about taking care of babies.

Frank scraped his chair back from the table, clumped into the pantry, and returned with the dishrag. "I never promised your dad I'd move into that place."

"Then why'd you let him transfer the title to us? You knew he expected us to live there."

Frank wiped the spilled milk off the oilcloth. "He can transfer the title back anytime he wants."

"How can you say such a stupid thing? Try to be reasonable."

He dropped the dishcloth. "Me, reasonable? You're telling me to be reasonable. You're the one who wants to force me off this farm just when I'm settling down here. I thought that was what everybody wanted me to do. Isn't that what Preacher Schellenberg and all those old Mennonite biddies used to pray for?" He adjusted an imaginary hairnet and struck his palm against his forehead. "*Lieeeeber Gott*," he squawked in a voice like rusty wheels turning. "Deeeeear God, please let the Warkentins' prodigal son stay home and make something of himself already."

Tina couldn't help laughing, though she didn't like to hear

Frank make fun of praying. "Even if we move, you'll still be farming. What's the difference?"

Frank's nostrils flared with anger. "You expect me to *schlep* all my livestock to that broken-down barn by town, that lousy chicken coop—"

"Don't get so excited. Those buildings can be fixed up. Dad would help you."

Frank grunted. "I'm sure he would."

Tina realized she was asking a lot, but her feelings were important too, weren't they? She took a sip of coffee. "I get too lonesome here with nothing but fields and pastures all around me."

Frank pulled his chair closer to hers, the lines around his eyes softening. "I know it's not easy for you," he said, putting his arm around her. "But you haven't given this place a fair chance yet. You haven't even lived here around the seasons." He glanced out the window. "I picture our baby when he gets bigger, running through the wildflowers with his pretty mama. Her hair flying in the wind." Frank gave her the crooked smile that almost always made her heart melt.

Tina shrank away from him. She wouldn't weaken, not this time. "It's a nice picture, but we have wind and wildflowers on our farm by town, too."

"It's not the same. Some of our land here is virgin prairie. It's never been touched by a plough."

"It's running with coyotes."

"Coyotes are okay. They help keep the rabbits down."

Tina shivered. "They scare me, howling at night. They sound like lost souls." Sometimes she felt like a lost soul herself.

Frank lifted his arm off her shoulders. "I told you, Tina, I can't live near town. I can't stand being so close to other people. They crowd me. I feel like I'm not myself anymore. And that house—it's creepy. Too low and dark. Too many trees around it."

"I love those trees, especially the blue spruce."

"I'd chop it down, first thing. I've gotta be able to see the sky, the whole thing from one end to the other. You can't lock me in a cage. Please don't try." Frank rose and clomped out to the lean-to.

Tina followed. She slumped against the lean-to doorway, watching him put on his overshoes. "I love you," she blurted. She couldn't let him go without telling him that.

He came to her like a bee to a flower. "I'm sorry I was grouchy," he said, stroking her hair.

Tina leaned against her husband, wishing she could absorb some of his warmth and strength. Frank squeezed her tight, then released her with a pat on the behind. "Why don't you go lie down? You look kind of poorly."

She felt poorly. "Couldn't you stay in the house for a change? There must be something you can do inside, like mend harness. I could make popcorn this afternoon. We could cuddle on the couch and listen to the radio."

"I'm tempted," he said with a smile. "But I promised Thor I'd help him clean up that old ranch house of his."

Tina sighed, feeling like a Mennonite dissident abandoned in the wastelands of Siberia.

Frank put on his mackinaw jacket. "I won't be late. I promise."

After he'd gone, Tina carried her mending basket into the living room and sank down on the couch near the coal heater. This was probably the nicest room in Frank's house. She loved the picture window with its carved frame—Dutch-white against the blue petunias on the wallpaper. Too bad all she could see through that window was Frank's west pasture. Not a building in sight, not a tree or even a bush, just flat snow-covered prairie. So empty. It made her feel like a fish in a bowl with no visible edge to her world.

Tina turned from the window and patted her stomach, trying to picture the little sweetheart growing inside. Maybe she wouldn't feel so lonesome once the baby was born. She picked up her mending basket, found her darning needle, and started darning one of Frank's socks.

The hole in the sock seemed huge, yawning. Her fingers were tired. Her arms were tired. Everything was tired. She dropped the sock into the basket. Why hadn't somebody told her that being pregnant was so exhausting? She kicked off her slippers and stretched out on the couch, pulling the green and orange quilt over her.

Tina woke with a start. It was almost noon according to the clock on the wall. She hadn't washed the breakfast dishes, hadn't fed the dog. She got up, scraped the leftovers together, put on a coat, and took them out for Slim, the grey mongrel Frank had brought home a few days ago. "Slim!" she called. He bounded toward her, wagging his tail.

Tina patted his rough head and emptied the leftovers into the dog dish. Slim woofed and lowered his muzzle, his pink tongue siphoning up the leftover porridge, the half egg, the bread. She nudged him in the ribs. "It doesn't take much to make you happy, does it. A few leftovers, a mouse, a rabbit. A kind word from Frank." Tears welled in her eyes. "But I can't live in this hinterland. I just can't do it." She sank to her knees, burying her face in Slim's wiry coat. "I can't stay stranded here, day in and day out."

The dog whined and turned his yellow-brown eyes on her.

She hung her arm around his neck. "I married the man of my dreams and now I'm miserable." She rolled her eyes toward heaven. "Dear God, what shall I do?"

Chapter 20

Monday was laundry day. Frank stood at the stove dipping hot water out of the boiler, his bass voice rumbling something from Tchaikovsky. He seemed to be in a good mood. Maybe this was the time to ask him. "Frank?"

"Yeah?"

"I've been thinking." Tina dropped a flannel sheet into the washtub and rubbed a bar of laundry soap over it. "We haven't invited the Fehrs or Brauns over since we got married. Or the Friesens or any of our other Mennonite neighbours."

"So?" Frank's expression was as blank as dough.

"We could ask some of them to come for coffee, maybe Sunday afternoon."

He dumped a pail of hot water into the washtub and swirled it around, mixing it with the cooler water. "What makes you think the Fehrs and Brauns and them want to visit with us?"

"Why wouldn't they?"

"Come on, Tina. You know as well as I do. I don't fit in with the Mennonites. They didn't even invite me to the men's breakfast."

"That's because we don't attend church regularly."

He snorted. "Don't fool yourself. They think I'm not good enough for them."

"How can you say that?" Tina scrubbed the sheet on the washboard. "They practically begged you to play your guitar at the Christmas concert."

"Sure, but you know what they were thinking: 'Gypsies are great entertainers. You've got to admit that. In Russia they played and sang like angels. But you didn't dare turn your back on them. First thing you knew, they'd pick your pocket or steal your horse.'"

Tina rolled her eyes. How could Frank keep harping on the few stories he'd heard about Russian Gypsies? There were worse characters in Russia, far worse. She dropped the sheet into the rinse water and jerked her chin at it. "You could rinse that sheet now."

Frank swirled it through the water. "I'd rather visit with Scandinavians or British people any day. They don't carry all that Russian baggage."

Tina sighed and dropped his suit of long underwear into the washtub. As she swished its blue-striped arms and legs through the water, fatigue dragged at her own arms and legs. If only she could lie down for a few minutes.

No, she'd better not. If she quit working, Frank would too. Laundry was her job. He was only helping.

He wrung the sheet out and dropped it into the basket of laundry to be hung on the line. "You must remember how Roland and Corny cheated me on that hay deal."

"I wish you'd quit bringing that up. It was a misunderstanding, that's all." Sometimes Tina felt like chopped liver in a sandwich, caught between Frank and the Mennonites who supposedly treated him so badly.

"Misunderstanding! They short-changed me on purpose. They figured I wouldn't stick up for myself because I'm only the son of a Gypsy dancing girl. Roland and Corny are hypocrites just like a lot of other Mennonites."

"You don't mean that." Tina dropped his underwear into the rinse water, where it swirled like a headless water ghost.

"Sure I do. They are hypocrites." Frank swished his underwear through the rinse water. "I'm not surprised some people turn away from religion." He wrung out his suit of underwear, twisted it into a soggy pretzel, and over-handed it into the basket.

She studied his face. "You haven't, have you?"

"Haven't what?"

"Turned away from Jesus?" She grabbed Frank's arm. "You're a Christian, aren't you, deep down? You led me to believe you were."

Frank pulled away from her. "There's lots of things we led each other to believe."

She felt the blood drain from her face. "What do you mean?"

He picked up the laundry basket. "Forget it, okay. Just forget I said that. I'd better hang out this washing before the snow flies again."

Chapter 21

Frank fought the wind to the clothesline, then yanked his suit of underwear from the basket. As he hung it over the line, the wind wrapped its soggy arms around his neck. If he'd been superstitious, he'd have thought they were trying to choke him, punish him for what he'd told Tina. He should have let her keep thinking he was a Christian. He discouraged her enough already, making fun of praying and the Scriptures. Joking about the pictures she painted, each one featuring a Bible verse.

He unwrapped the blue-striped arms from around his neck and grabbed a handful of clothespins from the basket. He anchored his suit of underwear to the line, then pulled a sheet out of the basket. But when he tried to hang it, the wind billowed it out, flapping it into his face. More punishment.

Frank jerked the sheet off his face and hurled it over the clothesline. He hated doing laundry. He shouldn't have agreed to help. Why couldn't Tina at least manage the housework? Of course being pregnant sapped her energy, but most farm women helped with the outside work too, even when they were expecting a baby. Anyway Tina wasn't that tired. She wasted her energy painting pictures, then asked him to help with her chores besides his own. That was the sort of foolery he might have expected from Dorrie Harms. But if he'd married Dorrie, it wouldn't have mattered so much because her mom would have lived with them and done the laundry, cooked the meals, darned his socks.

Roland Fast didn't seem to care whether Dorrie was a good housekeeper or not. She had Roland mooing after her like a sick calf. They were an odd pair, Dorrie scatter-brained and charming, Roland boring and money-grubbing.

Frank pulled another sheet out of the basket. What about him and Tina? They didn't have much in common. But they'd chosen each other. They'd entered into matrimony with their eyes wide open, and they needed to make this work. Tina was sweet, really. And good in bed. Better than he'd expected. He smiled, recalling their wedding night. Tina had had zero experience, but she was crazy about him and her passion had ignited his.

His wife was a prize. She was classy, respectable, smart, and getting more beautiful by the day as her tummy swelled. Frank pictured his baby growing inside her and returned to the kitchen with a smile on his face.

Tina wasn't there. The washtubs sat on the bench beside the table, looking forlorn. The living-room door was closed. "Tina?" Frank called through the door. "Shall I make some coffee?"

Silence.

"Cocoa?" He put his ear to the door.

Nothing.

He tried the door. It was locked.

He rattled the knob. "Do we have any calcimine?" He needed to get Tina talking. "Thor wants to slap a couple coats of calcimine on the walls of his ranch house."

"In the cellar." Tina's voice was muffled. "Near my crock of sour cream."

Frank allowed himself a half-smile. He was making progress. "Listen, do you wanna come along to Thor's house tomorrow?"

No answer.

He rapped on the door—three louds and two softs followed by a drum roll—their secret knock. "Thor would love to show you what we've done with the place."

Nothing.

"He and I got that old stove going pretty good. It worked better once we pulled the dead crows out of the chimney. You shoulda smelled—"

The living-room floor creaked and Frank sighed, hearing Tina retreat to the lean-to off the living room. Why had he mentioned the crows? Tina was probably retching into the chamber pot even now. "Sorry, Sweetheart," he called when he heard her return to the living room. "Are you okay in there? Look, why don't you come out? I'll make tea. I'll rub your back."

The key rattled in the lock.

Frank turned the knob and eased the door open an inch. "I found that Acts 16:31 picture you painted."

Tina peered around the door, her face red and puffy.

He fetched the picture from the pantry, where he'd noticed it propped behind the shelves. "It's too nice to hide." He tilted the painting toward the light. "I like the fence post. The sunflowers are good, too. You got them just the right shade of yellow."

Tina's eyes narrowed. Was she taking him seriously? Actually the picture wasn't bad. It was the Bible verse that bothered him. "We could hang this picture somewhere," he said. "Maybe in the kitchen." It would mean staring at those words—'Believe on the Lord Jesus Christ'—every time he ate. But he supposed he'd get used to it. It was a small price to pay for peace with Tina.

A candle of hope flickered in her eyes.

He pushed the door open another inch. "Can we work this out? Please, Honey?"

She fiddled with a loose button on her sweater. "Frank, why did you let me think you were a Christian if you're not?"

Frank cleared his throat. "You never asked me outright. So I never said."

"But Preacher Schellenberg said you got saved and baptized at a lumber camp where you worked. That's what you told him, isn't it?"

Frank stared down at the floor. "Yeah, I believe that's what I told Schellenberg."

"But it's not true?"

Frank remained silent.

"How could you lie about something so important?"

"What else could I do?" Frank slouched against the door-frame. "Shelling-Peas wanted to baptize me with Roland and Corny and them. After the hell those guys put me through when we were in school."

"I wish you wouldn't call him Shelling-Peas. It's not respectful."

"Okay, but you gotta understand something. I just couldn't wade into Knutson Lake with Roland and Corny and them, and smile, and hear them thank Jesus for coming into their hearts, and nod and agree, knowing what a sham it was."

"Maybe it wasn't a sham. God can change people, you know."

"Yeah, well, I don't think he changed Roland and Corny. Not enough anyway."

"God can change you," Tina said softly, "if you give him a chance."

Frank grunted. "Seems to me I've heard a lot about change since we got hitched." He set the picture on the floor, leaning it against the wall. "Why did you marry me if you didn't like me the way I was?"

Tina gulped. "I didn't mean it like that. You know I didn't."

"Sorry. Look, why don't you come out of there? I'm not a monster. I'm still your same old Frank. Come on, I'll make cocoa. I'll finish the laundry." He attempted a smile. "I'll do it single-handed. You can relax in the rocking chair and supervise."

Chapter 22

Frank felt as calm as wool, steering his tractor along the crumbly brown furrow. It was good to be out on the land again after the long winter. There was something almost holy about sowing seeds in his own soil and getting food off it. He felt closer to God here than he ever had in church. He wished Tina could understand that.

The sun was almost straight overhead: hardly any shadows. It must be noon. Time to go in for dinner. He silenced the tractor and got off. Tramping across the field toward the house, he wondered how much of the garden Tina had managed to plant this morning. It was a great day for gardening—not too hot, not too windy. Frank grimaced, remembering the garden Dorrie Harms had planted for him last spring, while Tina was still in Vancouver. Crooked rows, seeds so shallow they blew away. Dorrie sure wasn't a smart, organized woman like Tina. He had picked the right wife, no question about that.

He opened the kitchen door, and the earthy aroma of cabbage and tomatoes filled his nostrils. "Tina," he called, "your hungry man is here."

He stopped short in the doorway. What was this? Tina was crouching over her sewing table stuffing a flurry of paper and paints under a pair of overalls he'd been waiting for her to mend. He scowled at her. "What were you doing painting in the middle of the day when the garden needs planting?"

Tina clutched her belly like she was trying to protect the baby inside. "I made a nice borscht for your dinner, Frank. I put in lots of cabbage and tomatoes, just the way you like it."

"But why were you wasting time painting when the weather's so nice?" Frank went to the stove reservoir, dipped warm water into a basin, and washed the dust off his face. "I hope you managed to plant the peas at least."

"Sorry, I didn't start the garden yet."

"Didn't start? At all?" he barked, the towel muffling his voice. "For Pete's sake, why not? We won't get any vegetables this year if you don't hurry up and plant some."

"I told you," Tina said, heading toward the stove, "the sun is too strong." She ladled soup into two bowls and carried them to the table. "My eyes hurt when I work outside."

Frank sat down at the table, trying to curb his anger as he waited for Tina to say grace.

"Come Lord Jesus," she said in her careful lemon-flavoured voice. "Be our guest. And let this food to us be blessed. Amen."

Frank picked up his spoon, wondering what the Lord Jesus thought of Tina sitting around the house all day when the garden needed planting. Before he'd married her, he'd admired her strong character. But that character seemed to be crumbling. Of course she was tired, being pregnant. But she found the energy to do things she enjoyed, like painting pictures and going to town with the neighbours. Dorrie had at least gotten some of the garden planted when she was in charge of it.

He buttered a slice of bread. "Tina, you really need to get that garden going. It won't take long. Just do a couple rows at a time. Wear a hat to keep the sun off your face."

She wrinkled her nose. "My hat doesn't help enough."

"Find a better hat. Make a better one. Figure something out. What kind of a farmer's wife are you?"

"A bad one, I guess." Her voice sounded sullen.

Frank reached across the table and took her hand. "That's not what I meant. You're a wonderful soup-maker and you're good at looking after chicks. I never had much patience with them—hungry all the time, cheeping in those demented little voices of theirs."

Tina pulled her hand out of his. "I enjoy cooking and taking care of chicks."

"That's great, but we can't just do what we enjoy, can we? I don't enjoy shovelling manure but I do it anyway. Marriage is supposed to be a partnership. Isn't that what Preacher Schellenberg said?"

Tina banged her spoon down on the table. "If this marriage is a partnership, why don't I have more say in it?"

The headache-vein in Frank's temple started to pulse. He massaged it, waiting for Tina to launch into her 'let's move closer to town' speech.

She sat up straighter. "You refuse to move closer to town; I got that point. But if you won't move, why can't we improve this place a bit? For one thing, we could plant some trees so the sun doesn't blind me every time I step outside."

"This isn't Vancouver," Frank said. "It's not even Dayspring. Trees won't grow here without a lot of watering. I don't have time for that."

"I'd water them," she snapped. "At least I would once the baby is born."

"The pails would still be too heavy for you."

"I wouldn't use the big pails, just the garden ones."

Frank choked on a spoonful of borscht. "You can't even plant peas. How are you going to grow your trees?"

"Okay, okay, I'll start the garden this evening when the sun's not so strong. The mosquitoes will eat me alive, baby and all, but I'll do it."

Frank heaved a weary sigh. "I guess I could help you." Not that he had the time. He had the milking to do plus a dozen other things. But he probably needed to try harder if he and Tina were ever going to get this marriage working like it should.

Chapter 23

Frank steered his half-ton along the road toward home, enjoying the rattle of the new tractor hitch in the truck-bed behind him. Soon he'd have a son to talk to about tractor hitches and trucks and crops.

A son would ease his loneliness. He'd carried loneliness like a basket of snakes on his head ever since his mama had abandoned him when he was seven. Tina tried to relieve the pain, but a wife can only do so much. Frank longed to start over, without the snakes. A son would give him that chance. The boy would be like a new Frank Herbert Warkentin.

Frank passed the Coyote Junction School with its sagging green roof, picturing little Herbert starting grade one. The boy would probably have a high intelligent forehead like Tina's. Long legs like his dad's, good for kicking a football.

Frank knew the baby was a boy. Tina was carrying the infant low in her belly and her hips had widened right out. All the neighbour women said that was a sure sign of a boy. Their prophecies made Frank feel like fate was in his favour for a change.

He steered the truck into the driveway and slowed past the garden, expecting to see Tina and her mom picking the pole beans. There was no sign of the women. Maybe they were finished. He parked beside the house and headed inside for coffee, wondering if his mother-in-law would stay for the corn harvest, too. He hoped so. The house felt homier with Rachel around. She baked cookies, picked wildflowers for the table, darned his socks, and sang hymns while she and Tina worked in the garden.

Frank hurried into the kitchen and was surprised to hear a squeaking like a kitten's but louder. A baby? Crying? Upstairs? He bolted to the stairway. "Hello?"

No answer. He bounded up the stairs. Little Herbert wouldn't have arrived already, would he? He wasn't due for a month according to Doc Muirhead.

Rachel met him at the top of the steps. She was holding a flannel-wrapped bundle in her arms. "Congratulations, Frank." Her pie-round face was flushed. "You have a beautiful daughter."

Frank grabbed the stair railing, catching his balance. "A daughter?"

"Yes, a lovely little girl."

Frank felt like his head was floating off his body. Where was his son? Frank had felt him kicking in Tina's belly. Strong fast kicks like a football player's.

Rachel held the bundle out to him. "Do you want to hold her?"

He backed away. "I'd better not. My hands aren't clean." That was an excuse, and his mother-in-law must know it.

"Your hands look fine to me."

"But—" Frank's voice gave out. He cleared his throat. "You said we were having a boy."

"That's what I thought. It's what everybody thought. But God has a way of surprising us."

"I guess so." Actually God had a way of disappointing Frank, if there was such a thing as God.

"Frank?" a wavery voice called from the spare room.

Tina. He hurried into the room.

His wife lay on the bed under a washed-out seersucker quilt. Frank's heart slipped a gear when he saw her face. It was almost as pale as the quilt. "Sweetheart, are you okay?"

"I think so."

"How did the birth go? Did it hurt much?" Part of him wished he'd been here heating water, pacing the floor, doing whatever expectant fathers did. Part of him was glad he'd been in town out of the women's way.

"It wasn't too bad," Tina said. "It went fast but I'm exhausted now."

"That's normal," Rachel said, bringing the baby into the room. "But we should get Doc Muirhead to come and check you over anyway. You and Klara."

Klara. The name gave Frank a jolt, though Klara was the name he and Tina had decided on, in case the baby was a girl. It was hard to picture a little girl around the place, wearing dresses instead of overalls. Playing with dolls instead of toy trucks.

Tina squeezed his hand. "Isn't she beautiful?" Her voice was hushed, like they were in church.

Frank cranked out a smile. "I haven't had much chance to look at her." Tina must realize he was disappointed, but this wasn't the time to discuss it.

"Here, Frank." Rachel held the baby out to him. "Why don't you hold her?" She laid the infant in his arms. "Prop her head up like this." She bent his arm and settled Klara's head into the crook of his elbow.

Frank peered down at the newcomer. Her face was red and wrinkled, but he saw she had a wide mouth like his mama's. Her chin was like his mama's too, with that little dent in the middle.

What was that on Klara's throat? He peered at it and almost dropped her. She had a birthmark like his mama's, purple and shaped like a rose.

He stroked it and felt tears chase each other down his cheeks. He didn't have his son, not yet. But he had this tiny new person, Klara, connecting him with his lost mama. He touched one of the baby's little hands and she curled it around his finger, holding tight.

Chapter 24

Frank stood at the top of the hill watching the snow diamonds sparkle on his pasture. The air felt as brisk and cold as peppermints. What a great afternoon for sliding with his best girl.

He sat down on the toboggan, and three-year-old Klara plopped her solid little body into his lap. She turned her head, her red bonnet brushing his cheek. "Daddy?"

"Yeah?"

"When is Mommy getting the baby?"

"Soon. Grandma Janz says I'll have to go for Doc Muirhead any day now." Frank put his arm around his daughter and pushed with one foot to start the toboggan sliding.

It swooped down the hill, skidded to the left, twirled, and dumped them into a snowdrift. Klara jumped to her feet, whooping with delight. "Get up, Daddy!" She yanked at his arm. "I wanna slide down again."

"I'm too tired." He lolled back in the snow, grinning up at her. "We musta slid down twenty times already."

"Please, Daddy." She tilted her head, her smile digging dimples into her honey-brown cheeks. Frank's mama had done that, the exact same way. It was a hard gesture to resist.

He hauled himself to his feet. "Okay, we'll take a couple more runs down the hill. Then we'll go in for supper. Mommy and Grandma are making cottage-cheese dumplings."

"Oh." Klara plunked herself down on the toboggan. "I hope Mommy gets a baby girl."

"I hope it's a boy myself. I already have the nicest little girl in the world."

* * *

Klara snuggled under the purple quilt in Daddy's rocking chair, hearing the lamp hiss on the hook above the kitchen table. Drops of hot water jumped out of the boiler that sat on the stove. The water sizzled like the sausages Mommy had fried for supper.

Klara wished Mommy was here, or Daddy or Grandma. If they were, they'd tell her a story or sing her a song. But nobody was in the kitchen with her. Just Lois, the rag dolly she and Grandma had made.

Daddy was in town getting the doctor. Grandma and Mommy were in the living room. The door was shut but Klara knew Mommy was lying on the bed near the coal heater. Daddy had carried the bed down from upstairs because the living room was warmer than upstairs.

Mommy was making a crying sound, like the kitty that got its paw caught in the fence. Klara heard a window blind roll up. Then Grandma said, "What's taking Frank so long?" She sounded scared. "Maybe the doctor wasn't home."

Klara hugged the dolly to her chest. "Come on, Lois, let's go watch for Daddy." She dragged a kitchen chair over to the window. Then she and Lois climbed onto the chair and looked out. But they couldn't see Daddy's horses and sleigh, just snowdrifts. The drifts looked like coyotes in the moonlight. Lois was afraid of coyotes so Klara turned the dolly's face away. She showed Lois the pictures that Jack Frost had painted on the bottom of the window. They were pictures of streets with trees and houses. A church with pointy windows. Maybe it was Daddy's village in Russia, far away from here.

Grandma came out of the living room shaking her head. Grandma was wide and she smelled like honey. Her feet were big in her everyday stockings and slippers.

Klara scrambled down off the chair. "Can I have some bread and milk?" Her mother always made it for her, every evening.

Grandma warmed milk on the stove, soaked bread in it, and poured it into a blue bowl. She put it on the table and Klara sat down to eat. Then Mommy's crying started again. This time it sounded almost like a dog barking. Grandma hurried into the living room, closing the door behind her.

Mommy's crying made Klara's stomach hurt. She dropped her spoon. It clattered to the floor, splashing milk and bread. She needed to get away from that awful sound. She slid off her chair and ran to the lean-to door. She opened it and went out, shutting the door behind her like Mommy had taught her.

The lean-to floor was as cold as a snowdrift. Klara looked out the window and saw the moon like a yellow pancake in the sky. It made frost shine on the hooks that Daddy had screwed into the wall for hanging up clothes. Daddy's overalls hung on one hook. Klara's snowsuit hung on another one, then Mommy's brown coat.

Klara heard Mommy scream.

It sounded terrible. Klara wrapped the bottom of Mommy's coat around her ears, but she still heard the screaming. Then it stopped and she heard something else. Horse bells?

The outside door opened and the wind blew in. Daddy hurried in, smelling like snow and horses. His eyes looked wild. Doc Muirhead pushed around Daddy, yanked the lean-to door open, and rushed into the kitchen.

Mommy screamed again and Klara clamped her hands over her ears.

Daddy picked her up. As he carried her into the kitchen, Grandma came out of the living room. She went to the stove and dipped water from the reservoir into a basin. Doc Muirhead washed his long white hands, his eyes on the living-room door. Behind it Mommy was screaming and crying. Doc Muirhead turned to Daddy. "Go unhitch the horses. Take the little girl with you."

Daddy pulled Klara's snowsuit onto her, his hands shaking.

He put her socks on her feet, then her overshoes. He lit the lantern. She grabbed the dolly and they went out.

She and Daddy went to the barn and dug themselves into the straw pile beside the cows. Daddy hugged his arms around Klara. "God, if you're there," he prayed, "if you can hear me, please stop Tina's suffering. Please let her live. And if it's your will, please give us a healthy baby boy." Sometimes Daddy prayed in English, sometimes in German. Klara understood him both ways.

When he stopped praying, she said, "Pray for a girl, Daddy."

Daddy didn't say anything.

"I said pray for a girl."

He hugged her tighter. "I'd sooner have a boy myself. But you pray for a girl if you want."

Chapter 25

When Frank came home from taking Doc Muirhead home, he found Tina sitting in her living-room bed eating breakfast: scrambled eggs and toast on a blue plate. She looked good considering what she'd been through. She even had some pink in her cheeks.

Her mother sat on the couch, rocking the baby in her arms. "What a little sweetheart you are," she crooned. "I think you got your Great-Grandpa Thiessen's nose." She held the infant up for Frank and Tina to see. "Don't you think he has my dad's nose? Look how long and straight it is."

Tina smiled at Frank. "Ask his daddy."

Frank slipped a finger under the baby's chin and turned the tiny face toward the window. "Yup, that's the Thiessen nose all right." Maybe it was and maybe it wasn't. But if it made Rachel happy, fine. Today was a day for everyone to be happy.

Rachel held the infant out to Frank. "Do you want to hold him?"

He gathered Herbert into his arms, the practised father, and noticed again how long and wiry the baby was. Long was understandable; all the Warkentins were tall. But so thin? Was that normal? Doc Muirhead said it was nothing to worry about. He said Herbert's body just needed time to catch up with his length.

Firm little footsteps sounded on the stairs. A moment later Klara trudged into the living room clutching the rag doll, Lois.

Frank raised his eyebrows at her. "What do you think of your brother?"

Klara wrinkled her nose. "His face is sure red."

"Oh, that'll fade in time," Frank said. He laid the baby on the bed and measured him with his hand. "See how long he is.

He must be twenty inches or more. He's going to be tall, maybe even taller than his Grandpa Warkentin." Frank grinned. "He'll out-Warkentin the Warkentins." He winked at Rachel. "And with that Thiessen nose, he'll be a winner for sure."

* * *

Tina woke to slivers of light creeping in around the window blinds. She yawned and stretched in her living-room bed, still sore from giving birth two days ago, but feeling as contented as a queen bee in a hive. Love and caring surrounded her. Her mom managed the household—sweeping, dusting, looking after Klara, washing baby Herbert's diapers, cooking. Judging by the aroma from the kitchen, there'd be pancakes and bacon for breakfast this morning. Frank would be pleased when he came in from milking the cows.

Herbert whimpered in his bassinet, and Tina turned to stroke his cheek. What a little miracle the baby was. She slipped out of bed and rolled up a window blind so she could take a better look at him. Her lips curving into a smile, she returned to her son.

Tina's smile faded as she gazed into Herbert's face. His cheeks had a yellowish tinge. So did his wonderful nose. "Mom!" she called.

Her mother hurried in from the kitchen.

Tina lifted Herbert out of his bassinet. "Does the baby look yellow to you?"

Her mom took him in her arms, tilting his face toward the light. "I think he has jaundice," she said slowly.

Fear clutched at Tina's heart.

"Adeline's youngest son had it, too." Tina's mom seemed to be searching her mind for memories. "But Simon's jaundice didn't start so young, and he never got this yellow."

"What shall we do?" Tina's heart pounded like wings in her chest.

Her mom laid a hand on Herbert's forehead. "He feels too hot to me." She handed the baby to Tina, then hurried into the kitchen. Moments later she was back in the living-room doorway, putting on her coat. "I'll go tell Frank. I think he'd better get Doc Muirhead."

Chapter 26

Tina's stomach curdled with irritation as Adeline Epp loped into the living room. This was no time for a neighbourly visit. Frank would be back with Doc Muirhead any minute.

Adeline loomed over the baby lying in Tina's arms. She always reminded Tina of a vinegar bottle: small head and narrow shoulders sloping down to a wide body. "Huy yuy yuy," Adeline squawked. "I never saw such bad John Dust, not in all my forty years." She touched the soft spot on top of Herbert's head. "Do you remember the Dave Kellers? Their baby Lester died from John Dust."

Tina shuddered and turned Herbert's face away from Adeline. "There must have been something else wrong with Lester. Babies don't die of jaundice." Well, maybe some babies did, but it was cruel of Adeline to suggest it.

Tina's mom came from the kitchen carrying the coffee tray. "Herbert sure doesn't have much spunk. When I was changing his diaper an hour ago, I accidentally dropped the basin and he didn't even jump."

Adeline plunked herself down on the couch. "That's how it goes with bad John Dust."

Tina bit her lip, choking back tears. She wouldn't cry in front of Adeline, wouldn't expose her feelings to the woman's harsh pity.

Klara trudged in from the kitchen and headed straight for Adeline, holding the rag doll, Lois, in front of her like a figurehead. "Grandma and I made a dolly for Herbert. But he doesn't even like it."

Adeline stroked the doll's beige flannel chest. "She's a pretty dolly, but she needs a dress, *nicht?*"

"I was going to make her a nice red dress," Tina's mom said. "But then Herbert . . ." Her voice trailed away.

Adeline helped herself to coffee and a couple of date squares. "My Simon, he had John Dust." Herbert began to wail and she raised her voice. "But Simon's John Dust wasn't too bad and it disappeared soon. So we didn't get too worried."

Herbert's crying tore at Tina's heart. "You'll be okay," she crooned, trying to reassure herself. "Daddy and Doc Muirhead will be here soon."

Adeline shovelled sugar into her coffee. "You should take him to Doc Cohen instead."

Tina sighed. "It's a long way to Outlook."

"The train ride would be hard on such a young baby," her mom said.

Adeline sloshed cream into her coffee. "Doc Cohen was good when Simon had ammonia. Better than Manurehead. And when my shoulder went to nothing, Cohen made it right in five minutes."

Tina jostled Herbert in her arms, trying to calm his crying. "Doc Muirhead isn't perfect, but people say he's good with babies." Herbert was getting hard to hold onto. He kept arching his back, tilting his little yellow face toward the ceiling.

Adeline tasted her coffee and added more sugar. "I doubt if Manurehead is even a real doctor. Some people say he just named himself a doctor when he out-wandered from England."

"Adeline, please," Tina's mom said.

Tina prayed that Frank and the doctor would be here soon. Herbert was flopping in her arms like a fish. Was he in pain? Maybe he was just filling his diaper. She reached for a clean one, then dropped her hand as the outside door opened. Thank God.

She heard Frank's rumbling voice in the lean-to, then the doctor's smoother one. Tina's mom hurried out to the kitchen. Tina heard her dip water from the stove reservoir. Soapy hands squeaked, rubbing together. She rose and met the doctor in the kitchen doorway with Herbert in her arms.

* * *

"I'm sorry," Doc Muirhead said after he'd examined Herbert. The doctor's grey eyes looked wintry. "There's nothing I can do." He wrapped the baby in his blanket and held him out to Tina.

She turned away, clenching her fists. "There must be something."

Doc Muirhead shook his head and handed the infant to Frank. "Herbert's blood isn't right. Some babies are just born like that. You remember the Dave Kellers? Their baby Lester was—"

"Please," Tina wailed, clapping her hands over her ears. "I don't want to hear another word about Lester."

Adeline confronted Doc Muirhead, grabbing him by the shirtfront. "What kind of a doctor are you? Why are you giving up so soon? Herbert could grow into a tall strong boy if you'd just do something."

"I told you," Doc Muirhead said, pulling away from Adeline. "There's nothing I can do."

"You're not even a real doctor," Adeline squawked. "You should be ashamed to name yourself a doctor. I bet Cohen could do something already."

Doc Muirhead stood up straighter. "Doctor Cohen would just tell you the same thing."

Frank put his arm around Tina. "We'll take him to Cohen anyway. First thing in the morning. We'll catch the morning train."

But by morning Herbert's crying had dwindled to a thin hoarse mewling. As Tina dressed him for the trip to Outlook, his little voice whimpered away into silence. His breath rattled in his throat. "Frank," Tina shrieked, her voice bouncing off the kitchen walls.

Tina's mom grabbed Klara by the shoulder and steered her toward the stairs. "Go to your room. This isn't something for a child to see."

"Frank!" Tina screamed.

Her mother hurried toward the lean-to. "I'll get him. He's hitching up the horses."

"No, stay here." She held the baby out to her mother. "Can't you do something?"

Her mom peered into Herbert's face. "Oh, *du Lieber Gott.*"

Chapter 27

Tina lay in her living-room bed letting a fog of desolation drift over her. She heard Frank chopping firewood outside. Every day since Herbert's death, he'd been out chopping in the cold and snow.

How long was it since they'd lost the baby? Two days? Three? Everything seemed to blur together.

She heard the door open. Then the floor creaked.

"I made tea." Her mom's chirpy voice. "It's peppermint tea, your favourite."

"I don't want tea." Tina turned her face to the wall, scowling at the blue petunias on the wallpaper.

A spoon clinked against a cup, then the edge of the bed sank. Her mom's warm hand rested on Tina's shoulder. "You really should drink some tea. You'd feel better."

"I'll never feel better."

Her mom sat silent awhile. Finally she said, "Do you remember when your sister Greetje died?"

Tina nodded. She'd heard the story of Greetje a thousand times, but she understood her mom's fierce need to tell it. Now more than ever, having lost a baby herself, she understood.

"Greetje looked just like your Grandpa Thiessen, remember? Long nose, high cheekbones, eyes green as grapes."

Tina's heart groped toward her mom like a ship toward its harbour.

"We had no flowers for Greetje's funeral." Tina's mom poured a mug of tea, handed it to Tina, and filled one for herself. "It was a hard winter in Russia that year."

Tina half sat up, pressing the mug against her aching breasts. "I thought a neighbour lady brought you geraniums."

"Yes, Elvira Klassen brought red geraniums from her living room. The Klassens had a good window for flowers. I could see Elvira's geraniums from my kitchen. We Mennonites lived close together in Russia—"

"—not in the wilderness like here." Tina finished the sentence. All her life she'd heard those same words, over and over. They were a kind of slogan for her mom, who never stopped being lonesome for the Old Country.

"So Elvira brought the geraniums," her mom continued, "and I pinned them into Greetje's hair. I put her green dress on her and laid her in the box your dad had made. We loaded it onto the sleigh and took Greetje to her funeral. But the ground was frozen like cement that winter, and a lot of our men had typhoid. They couldn't dig her grave.

"So we brought Greetje home after her funeral. Your dad put her in the icehouse, where it was freezing cold. She had to wait till springtime to get buried."

Tina glanced out the window at the machine shed, where her son lay frozen in a box on Frank's workbench. Poor Herbert. At least he wouldn't need to wait as long as Greetje to be buried. This was Canada, where some things worked better than in Russia despite what her mom thought. The municipality had a steam shovel for digging graves.

Tina's mom shifted on the bed, making the springs creak. "Your dad didn't want anyone going into the icehouse."

Frank didn't want anyone going into the machine shed either. He'd locked the door and hidden the key.

Tina's mom sipped her tea. "But Greetje's face was always on my mind. One day while your dad was away, I put on my coat and sneaked out to the icehouse."

Tina knew why Frank had locked the door of the machine shed. He didn't want her and her mom visiting Herbert, upsetting themselves even worse.

Her mom continued. "When I opened the door of the icehouse, a ray of sunlight was struggling through the window. I lifted the lid of Greetje's box. She looked like an angel in the weak light from that window." Tina's mom fell silent and for several moments Tina heard nothing but the rhythmic cracking of Frank's axe. Would he never quit chopping?

"After that first visit," her mom said, "I went to the icehouse every chance I got. One afternoon when I was combing Greetje's hair, I thought I saw her eyelids flicker. I dared to hope she wasn't dead after all. My heart started pounding. Maybe her funeral had been a mistake. I clapped my hand to her chest, feeling for her heart."

Tina slumped back against the pillows. "But her heart wasn't beating."

"No, God had taken Greetje to heaven, just like Preacher Dirksen had said at her funeral. That's where Herbert is, too. In heaven, safe with Jesus."

Tina turned her face to the wall. Heaven was a wonderful place, far better than earth according to what the Mennonites believed. Greetje and Herbert were happy there. But what about their poor left-behind families?

If only some miracle would bring Herbert back. She let her mind drift away, picturing herself and the baby in a hospital. Maybe it was Uncle Yash's hospital in Vancouver. Green walls, smell of antiseptic. Herbert lay in her arms, cold as clay. Uncle Yash and the other doctors took the baby and locked him in a machine. The doctors pushed buttons. Lights flashed. Something beeped. Then Uncle Yash opened the machine and lifted Herbert out. The baby was pink and thrashing, crying the astonished cry of a newborn.

Tina groped across the bed for her son. Part of her believed her waking dream, but most of her realized it couldn't be true. Her searching fingers touched only the cold blue petunias on the wallpaper.

Chapter 28

Tina sat at the kitchen table drinking coffee with Frank, hoping the caffeine would make her feel livelier. She felt like a limp dish-towel. She'd been exhausted ever since Herbert's death. How long ago was that? Four days? Five?

Frank reached across the table and curved his hand around hers, pressing her fingers against her warm coffee mug. "We need to talk about the funeral." His voice was tender.

Of course. She tried to summon logical thoughts. "Maybe we could have a service right here at home. Then I wouldn't need to go out."

Frank glanced into the living room. "Our place wouldn't be big enough, even if I carry the bed upstairs. A lot of Scandinavians will want to come. Brits, too."

Tina nodded. Frank was right of course. She'd only been considering the Mennonites.

Frank buttered a slice of the raisin bread the Fehrs had brought along with their condolences. "We could have the funeral at the Friesens' house, except their kids have the mumps."

"Do they? That's too bad." Tina's small reserve of energy was dwindling.

Frank jabbed a fork into the jar of pickled herring that his bachelor friends Thor and Sigurd had brought with their sympathy cards. He laid three chunks of herring on his slice of raisin bread and balanced another slice on top.

Tina's stomach churned at the sight of Frank biting into his sandwich. Her husband seemed able to eat anything in any combination. In four and a half years of marriage, she'd never gotten accustomed to that.

She sipped her coffee. It settled her stomach a bit. "Has anybody ever held a funeral at the school?"

"I guess so, but there's no kitchen there. Your mom and Adeline thought it would be too hard to serve a funeral lunch without a kitchen." Frank paused. "So they decided—"

"They decided? They already decided?" Indignation jolted some energy into Tina. "So why are we even talking about the funeral? Let me guess: Adeline persuaded you and Mom to have it at the Epps' house."

Frank swallowed a mouthful of raisin bread and herring. "That's the most logical, isn't it? The Epps have the biggest living room anywhere around here. Adeline's got tons of dishes and—"

"Why didn't anybody even ask me?"

Frank patted her arm. "You weren't well. You might not remember this, but you were having hallucinations, seeing things that weren't there. Hospital rooms, doctors, black machines, vultures flying around the ceiling. Your parents and I could hardly talk to you."

Tina remembered some of those dreams or visions or whatever they were, though they seemed otherworldly now. "I'm not seeing things anymore," she said. "And I don't want the service at the Epps'."

"Aw, Tina, try to—"

"Adeline will turn it into a circus." Her voice broke. "Why can't we use one of the town churches?"

"Adeline thought they might want to charge."

"How much would they charge anyway? Couldn't you ask?"

Frank stared down at the floor. "I'm sorry. It's too late. I already put up the announcements."

"You what?"

Frank sat up straighter. "I wrote the announcements and put them up. All over town, and at Lindbergs' store and post office."

"How could you?"

"Come on, Tina. It had to be done. Adeline said—well, she's just so efficient. We won't have to worry about a thing." His eyes begged for understanding.

Somewhere deep inside, Tina wanted to understand her husband. He'd made the arrangements with everybody's best interests at heart. She realized that, but he should have consulted her. "Why doesn't anybody care what I think?" She bolted away from the table. "I might as well be wallpaper for all the attention anybody pays me." She stumbled toward the living room.

"I said I'm sorry." Frank threw his hands up in a helpless gesture, though his voice sounded defiant. "What was I supposed to do?"

Tina turned in the living-room doorway, looking back at her husband.

He hunched into his chair like a boy in a man's body, his eyelids drooping. Maybe he was praying. More likely he was shutting her out, protecting himself from her harshness. She stood still a moment, then went to him and laid her hands on his shoulders. "I'm sorry." She choked out the words. Frank was suffering as much as she was, maybe more because he wouldn't let himself rage against God, or sob aloud, or escape into denial. He was trying to be strong for her sake—be the man of the family. She should appreciate that.

"You did the best you could, I guess," she said, massaging his shoulders. His muscles felt as tight as knotted clotheslines under his flannel shirt.

Chapter 29

At the lunch following baby Herbert's funeral, Tina sat halfway down the women's table in the Epps' living room, choking back tears. She refused to cry. She wouldn't make a spectacle of herself, especially not in Adeline's house. If she kept counting the daisies on the wallpaper, she might get through this meal without breaking down. Thirty-two, thirty-three, thirty-four—were daisies ever that shade of mauve? Evidently with wallpaper all things were possible.

Her mom nudged Tina's arm, handing her a plate of buns. "You should try to eat something. You'd feel better."

Tina stared at the plate in her hand, then let it sink to the table. Eat? How could she eat when she had a lump like a baseball in her throat? Everybody in the room was watching her, though they pretended not to be. Roland Fast caught his wife Dorrie's eye and raised his eyebrows. Tina could just imagine what the Fasts were thinking: *Poor Tina. She isn't taking it well. Look at those hollows under her eyes. And her face. As pale as cottage cheese.*

Tina wondered how Frank could act so normal. He was presiding over the men's table as calmly as a Sunday School superintendent . . . eating sliced sausage on a bun . . . passing the dill pickles . . . even laughing at a joke Dave Friesen had apparently made. Frank was so strong. At least he knew how to act strong; it was almost the same. Tina wished she could borrow some of Frank's strength for a couple of hours, just till this funeral lunch was over.

Thor sat on one side of Frank, Sigurd on the other. Frank's bachelor buddies were loyal; Tina had to give them that. Sigurd was acting something out, flinging his arm so vigorously that

Tina thought the sausage would slide off his bun. He must be explaining, again, how the municipality's steam shovel worked.

Thor twitched his bushy eyebrows, making digging motions with his hands.

Tina let out a whimper in spite of herself. How could Frank have let Thor and Sigurd dig Herbert's grave so far from home? Her little boy should have been buried with the Mennonites in the Schellenbergs' pasture, not in the Lutheran cemetery twelve miles away. She half-rose, tempted to shout that out now, here—with other Mennonites to support her. It would be a relief to say what she thought for a change.

No, she decided, sinking back onto her chair. She'd better not. Frank would be mortified. Maybe she could ask Preacher Schellenberg to speak to him. He and Frank could dig Herbert another grave at the Schellenbergs'. The coffin would be easy to move if they did it before the ground froze hard. Surely Thor and Sigurd would understand. As Tina glanced around the room, looking for the preacher, she heard a crow-like voice from the Mennonite end of the women's table. "I never lost a baby," Adeline squawked.

How could the woman talk babies now, here, right after Herbert's funeral?

Adeline cleared her throat, leaning across the table toward Dorrie. "First Justina was born the year after Isaac and I married ourselves. Then Wally, then Manfred. Then thirteen years later, Simon. My little Simon." Adeline put her arm around her scrawny three-year-old. "I think God made him out of the leftovers."

Simon munched a jelly bean cookie, gazing up at his mother with luminous blue eyes.

Dorrie frowned across the table at Adeline. "You shouldn't talk about Simon like that. You'll make him feel bad."

Good for Dorrie. She wasn't afraid to speak her mind. Marrying Roland had given her more confidence, not less.

Dorrie gathered little Roland Junior into her arms and lifted him to his feet, letting his head bounce against her shoulder. "See, Rolly, there's your cousin Simon. What a nice boy he is."

Tina swallowed hard, stifling a sob. Dorrie didn't even know how to hold her baby, but Roland Junior was gurgling with delight, bright-eyed as a gopher, while Tina's son lay under six feet of cold earth in the Lutheran cemetery. She lurched to her feet, her heart convulsing with grief. "Excuse me," she muttered, pushing her chair back from the table.

Her mom caught her arm. "Tina, what are you doing? Are you all right?"

"I just need some fresh air." She turned and fled to where the coats hung in the Epps' sunny hallway.

"Poor Tina." Adeline's squawky voice followed her. "She's not strong. I told Frank and Rachel we should have waited longer for the funeral."

Tina put on her coat, stumbled out the door, and staggered into the Epps' snowy garden. As she plunged past a row of shrivelled corn stalks, she heard Frank's voice from the porch. "Tina, come back here."

She quickened her pace, heading for the Epps' pasture, arms pumping, eyes straight ahead. She needed to get away from her husband, from everybody. If only she could get away from herself. What a relief that would be.

Frank caught up to her near the pasture gate, his jacket flapping around his hips. "You shouldn't let Adeline upset you," he said, putting his arm around her. "Everybody knows what she's like."

Tina tried to wrench herself out of her husband's embrace. "Why bother about me? I'm just Herbert's mother."

Frank's eyes were smoky brown with concern. "Tina, please don't go all sarcastic on me. Everybody sympathizes with you. You know that."

She did. But she couldn't endure being around all those sympathetic souls in the Epps' living room. There were too many of them. They suffocated her. Tina tried to pry Frank's fingers off her arm.

He tightened his grip. "Everybody wants you to stay, but I'll gladly take you home if you've had enough. Just come in and keep warm a few minutes while I hitch up the horses."

"Don't bother. Go back and enjoy yourself with your friends."

Frank sighed. "I'm not enjoying myself. This isn't a time to enjoy. It's a time to get through."

Tina's eyes brimmed with tears. "I'd get through it better if we'd buried Herbert with the Mennonites. You should have asked me where I wanted his grave."

Frank shook his head. "I told you. Your parents and I couldn't talk to you. You weren't making sense."

"Well, I'm making sense now and I think we should dig Herbert another grave at the Schellenbergs'. Then he'd be with his relatives. Your aunts are buried there. So is my grandpa."

Frank stared down at his boots. "I already paid for him to be with the Lutherans."

"But he's got no family in the Lutheran cemetery. He's all alone there."

"Herbert's soul is in heaven. Isn't that what the preacher said? That's just his body in the coffin. So why get so excited about where it's planted?"

Tina gulped. "Maybe it doesn't matter so much for Herbert's sake, but what about us? We can't even visit his grave without driving all the way to town."

"If we move him now, people will think we're crazy. I can just hear the gossip: That Gypsy—unstable as molasses."

"I never hear people talk like that."

"They wouldn't say it in front of you, would they."

Tina blew out a breath, feeling like a balloon losing air. She was too exhausted to argue, too exhausted to think of

anything but crawling into bed and pulling the quilt over her
She slumped out of her husband's grasp.

* * *

Frank stood shaking his head, watching Tina trudge along the
pasture fence toward home. He wished she wouldn't shut other
people out like she did. It couldn't be healthy. She should have
at least tried to visit with the other women at the funeral lunch
She might feel better if she shared her grief more.

He'd felt better himself after baring his heart to Thor and
Sigurd. The Norwegian bachelors were true friends, the best
friends he had. They accepted him just like he was. He couldn't
very well have refused when they offered to dig Herbert's grave
Anyway he wasn't sure he wanted his son buried with the Mennonites. They'd never accepted him, not really.

Frank turned and plodded back toward the Epps' house
He'd better get his horses, go home, and be with his woman.
Cry with her, make cocoa, lie down beside her—whatever she
needed.

Chapter 30

Tina stood at the stove trying to force herself to cook porridge. She needed to fetch the yellow saucepan from the pantry. Then she needed to pour water into it, get the oatmeal, get the salt. Everything seemed so difficult now that her mother was gone. Her mom had been Tina's anchor through Herbert's birth, short life, and death. Now she'd returned to her own family, and Tina felt like a rowboat drifting in a dark sea.

Frank emerged from the pantry carrying a plate of buns and cheese. "Next time you're expecting, we'll have you in the hospital in Moose Jaw or Saskatoon." His voice sounded brisk and businesslike. "I don't care how much it costs." He set the plate on the table. Tina shuddered at the harsh thud of cold earthenware against the oilcloth.

Klara wandered into the kitchen and sank onto her chair, looking as forlorn as Tina felt. The red bow at the back of the little girl's dress had come undone. Frank retied it—crooked— then poured milk for Klara, and coffee for Tina and himself.

Tina slumped into her chair, ignoring the coffee. "I don't want any more babies."

Frank's eyes widened. "What do you mean? Doctor Muirhead says you can have more."

"Doc Manurehead," Tina muttered. "What does he know?"

"Well, he seems to understand the problem Herbert had. Muirhead says our next baby might be born with the same condition, but city doctors could handle it better. They have more staff, more equipment."

"How can you talk about more babies when Herbert's hardly in the ground?"

Frank reached across the table and took her hand. "Tina, we can't keep living in the past. Sooner or later we need to move forward with our lives. Isn't that what Preacher Schellenberg said? He said we should accept God's will and—"

"God's will!" Tina jerked away from her husband. "You don't even believe in God."

"Tina, please." Frank glanced at Klara. "Remember who's listening."

Klara scrunched down in her chair, her eyes swimming with tears.

Tina put her arm around her daughter. "I'm sorry. I'm not fit company for anyone today."

Frank pushed the plate of buns and cheese toward Tina. "You'd feel better if you'd eat something."

"Eat something." A runaway train of anger rattled up from Tina's stomach. She picked up the plate and banged it down on the table, hearing the earthenware crack. "I don't want to eat something," she shrieked. "And I don't want to move forward with my life. Why can't anybody understand that?" She reeled out of her chair and fled to the living room, slamming the door behind her.

Tina flung herself down on her living-room bed, crying in big honking gulps. Finally she couldn't cry anymore. A mournful silence fell on the room. Tina felt herself get smaller and smaller. At last she disappeared into sleep. Blessed sleep.

She woke with a jolt, her eyes darting to the clock on the wall. It was nearly one-thirty in the afternoon. Klara and Frank must be hungry.

Tina dragged herself out of bed, trying to summon enough energy to make soup. She shuffled down to the cellar and grabbed a couple jars of canned beef off a shelf. She returned to the kitchen and dumped the meat into the soup pot. Added some water and set it on the stove. Stared at it. Cabbage. It needed cabbage. And tomatoes. She returned to the cellar. Got more jars. Emptied them into the pot, found a wooden spoon, and sloshed them around. What else? She'd made cabbage borscht a thousand times before. Why couldn't she remember?

Oh, yes, it needed dried dill. She headed for the cellar, felt sobs rise in her throat, and retreated to the living room.

She dozed awhile, then woke to the sound of Frank's heavy tread in the kitchen. She heard Klara's firm little footsteps. A ladle banged against the soup pot. Chairs scraped up to the table, then spoons rattled against bowls.

"Mommy likes soup," Klara chirped, her voice hopeful. "I'll take her some."

"Maybe later, Princess," Frank said. "I think Mommy's sleeping now."

The silence that followed was broken only by the clinking of spoons. "I wish Grandma was here," Klara finally said.

"So do I," Tina whispered. "So do I."

The next day she hardly got out of bed except to eat a few spoonfuls of borscht. It tasted like dishwater. It needed dill, salt, pepper, parsley, a bay leaf, maybe some carrots. But Tina didn't have the gumption to find those things, add them, stir, taste. What was the point? What was the point of anything? She dumped her bowl of soup into the slop pail and returned to her bed in the living room. Sinking back against the pillows, she pictured Herbert in the sailor suit she would have made for him if he'd lived.

After a few minutes she dozed off. She woke to the sound of Frank's rumbling laughter in the kitchen. Klara giggled. Their feet thumped against the floor. They must be playing hopscotch, one of their favourite games. Tina pictured the chalk lines Frank must have drawn on the linoleum, the buttons he and Klara used for markers. When was the last time she herself had played or laughed? She couldn't remember but she knew one thing for sure: she'd been happier in Vancouver than she was here. She should have stayed there instead of marrying

Frank. She could have saved herself a lot of heartache. Frank would probably have been happier without her. He could have married his little Goldilocks, Dorrie Harms.

Tina closed her eyes and let her mind drift across the miles to her office in Vancouver. Seagulls screamed outside her window. She pictured herself typing a report for Uncle Yash, her fingers dancing across the keys. In her waking dream, Tina finished the report with a flourish, released the lever, and pulled the last page out of the typewriter.

She hurried down the stairs and out to the veranda, where Victor Graf awaited her, his blue-grey eyes full of love. Tina poured orange spice tea for Victor and watched him sip it, his freckles like nutmeg sprinkled across his ruddy cheeks.

She rolled over in bed. She should have married Victor when she'd had the chance. If Vic was her husband, she might still believe God cared about her. Now she was clinging to faith by her fingertips. One gust of wind and she'd reel off into some howling void of—what? She didn't know; she'd never not believed before.

Her heart felt like a blind sparrow crashing from one rib to the other. She had no godly Victor to lead her through life. Only her Gypsy infidel of a husband. Frank would never be the spiritual guide she needed or the Christian father Klara needed. Dear God, what had she done with her life?

Chapter 31

It seemed to Frank that an essential part of Tina was no longer there. Her body lay on the bed in the living room, but her spirit was somewhere else. "Shall I ask Preacher Schellenberg to come and see you?" he asked one morning as he brought her breakfast on a tray. Bread, slices of sausage, dried apples, glass of milk.

Tina ran her fingers through her limp hair. "I'm not sure I believe what Preacher Schellenberg says anymore. If God loves us so much, how come he let Herbert die?"

"I don't know." Frank set the tray on the bedside table and took Tina's hand. "Maybe the preacher could explain it to you."

She pulled her hand away. "I need more than words. I tried reading Psalm 23 — 'The Lord is my shepherd' — but it didn't mean a thing to me."

Frank got the Bible from the bookcase. "Do you want me to read you a parable or a miracle or something?" He flipped through the flimsy pages, half afraid of where this conversation might lead.

Tina reached over and flipped the Bible shut in his hands. "Don't bother reading it to me. I think it's mostly empty promises."

Frank stared at his wife. She didn't mean what she'd said. She couldn't. Her faith had been a guide rope for their lives together. He hadn't often clung to that rope or even touched it, but just knowing it existed had made him feel steadier.

"It makes me feel kind of shaky," he said, "hearing you say you don't believe."

Tina's dark thoughts must have temporarily derailed her faith. Talking about them might help her. "What's on your mind these days?" he asked, returning the Bible to the bookcase. "Half the time when I come in here, you don't even notice me. You just sit here staring out the window like a zombie."

"Well, pardon me. If you can't stand the sight of me, I'll spare you the agony." She flopped down on the pillows, turning her face to the wall.

"That's not what I said, Sweetheart. Please."

"Go away. Can't you see I need to be alone?"

Frank sighed and retreated to the kitchen. At noon he tried again. He brought Tina a bowl of borscht and offered to get Doc Muirhead or take her to Doc Cohen in Outlook. But she didn't want borscht. She didn't want a doctor. She didn't want her mom either, or her dad, or anybody, including her husband.

Frank returned to the kitchen and dumped the borscht back into the soup pot on the stove. He was trying to be patient with his wife. He'd been more than patient, but Tina didn't seem to care whether he was here or not. In fact, she'd rather he wasn't here.

So why stick around? There was no rule saying he had to spend every minute of his life on this farm. He'd go to town tomorrow, see his friends, laugh, joke, breathe. Tina could take care of Klara for a few hours. She wasn't too sick to do that.

Chapter 32

Before baby Herbert's death, Tina hadn't paid much attention to the soap operas on the radio—*Ma Perkins, The Right to Happiness, The Guiding Light.* Now she tuned them in regularly. Listening to other people's problems seemed to take her mind off her own. One afternoon as she lay in her living-room bed sniffling over a bride deserted at the altar, she heard someone pounding on the outside door. "Tina!" That was Adeline Epp's squawky voice. "Open up."

What did the woman want? Tina was in no mood to talk to her.

"I know you're in there," Adeline called.

Tina sighed and shut off the radio. She grabbed her housecoat, threw it on, and padded to the door. Almost before she had it open, Adeline thrust a soup kettle at her. "I made you some chicken noodle soup."

"You shouldn't have bothered," Tina muttered, trying to smooth her stringy hair. How long since she'd washed it? A week? More like two.

Adeline elbowed past her, loped into the kitchen, and set the soup kettle on the stove. "As soon as I heard about you and Frank, I prayed and it seemed like God said, 'Addie, something's wrong at the Warkentins'. You gotta go to Tina.'"

"As soon as you heard what?" What were the neighbours saying?

"That you can't keep your man at home." Adeline navigated her bulk into the living room.

Tina followed her. "I'm not trying to keep Frank home."

She gulped. What a stupid thing to say to a gossip like Adeline. The words would be like gasoline on a fire. Adeline plopped herself down on the couch, and Tina sank onto the bed, trying to think how to dampen the flames. "I mean, I haven't been well lately, so I'm glad Frank runs our errands in town."

What a flimsy explanation. Of course Frank went to Dayspring to buy groceries, go to the bank, recharge the radio battery. But Tina knew his main reason for going: his wife was on strike and he needed cheerier company.

Adeline peered at Tina like she was a grasshopper in a bowl of soup. "My son Wally says Frank eats at the Chinese café almost every day."

"How does Wally know what happens at the Chinese café? I thought he was in high school. Or is he a government spy now?" Tina wondered if Adeline detected the sarcasm in her voice. Probably not.

"Of course Wally's in high school, but he walks downtown every noontime. He likes to see what the grown-ups are doing."

Just like his mother. "Did Wally mention what Frank eats at the Chinese café?"

"Sometimes the roast beef dinner, sometimes the pork chop dinner with mashed potatoes and peas. He usually eats with the Norwegian bachelors."

Tina clicked her tongue in mock disapproval. "Isn't that awful." Actually it was tame compared with what Frank could be doing, like getting drunk or chasing women.

"It is awful," Adeline said. "Our Mennonite men don't waste money on café dinners. Sometimes they drink coffee with the Norskies, grab a piece of pie. But they've got better dinners at home and cleaner places to eat, as long as nothing's wrong with the missus."

Tina's scalp prickled with irritation. Adeline made it sound like cooking and housecleaning were all a wife was good for. What about the companionship she offered, the encouragement, humour, love-making? Tina winced. Frank wasn't getting any of those from her anymore.

She heard footsteps on the stairs. Klara. The little girl wandered into the living room, her eyes sludgy with sleep, her nightgown grimy.

Tina sighed. What a terrible mother she was. She only had one chick and she couldn't even take care of her.

Adeline gave Klara a pitying smile. "Come and sit with me?"

The child went to her like a dime to a magnet.

"Tina, whaddaya think you got?" Adeline asked, setting Klara on her lap. "Is it flu?"

Tina shook her head. Why try to explain? Adeline wouldn't understand.

"I don't feel so good neither." Adeline found the hairbrush under the bed and started working the tangles out of Klara's curls. "But I never let feelings stand in the way of doing God's work. I said to myself, 'I'll make chicken soup for Tina, even if noodles are a lot of work. She can't feed her man right now.'"

Tina faked a coughing fit.

Adeline nodded. "It's flu. I thought so."

Tina said nothing but her mind was shrieking, *Not flu, Adeline, but a thirsty heart.* Her heart was parching with grief, but she couldn't get spiritual water from Adeline. The woman was like a poisoned well. She claimed Jesus poured springs of living water into her heart. Maybe he did, but Adeline poisoned them with her rudeness as fast as he poured them in.

Adeline set the hairbrush on the coffee table. "Do you want me to take Klara home awhile? Just till you find your feet? With Frank gone at the Chinaman's every day—"

"No!" Tina bolted off the bed. She seized Klara by the shoulders with a suddenness that made the little girl whimper. "You can't take Klara away. She's the only baby I've got left."

"My children, they all lived, even Simon," Adeline said. "I know it's hard for you, not giving your husband a son. You're not getting any younger neither. You need rest. Do you want

me to clean your place up—sweep around a little, do the dust
ing, wash clothes?"

Tina sank back on the bed. "You're worse than Job's com
forters," she wailed. "Please just go away and leave me to my
mess."

After Adeline had left, Tina made a pot of tea and sat a
the kitchen table, staring out the east window. She was twenty
nine years old. Only twenty-nine. She had a long time left in
this world. Was she going to spend all that time sulking in the
shadows, nursing her grief, making other people miserable:
Klara was miserable. So was Frank, though he probably
wouldn't admit it. She loved them. She owed it to them to star
acting like a proper wife and mother again.

Tina sat up straighter. She'd start now. Why wait? She'c
heat some water and wash Klara's hair and her own. Then they'c
both take a bath and put on clean clothes before Frank got back
from town.

By the time he arrived, Tina had made raisin scones
opened a jar of applesauce, and heated the chicken noodle
soup. She was setting the table when Frank came in with the
groceries.

"Hey!" he said with a grin. "Look who's risen from the
dead." He kissed her and Tina wondered if he'd noticed the
sugar-pink lipstick she was wearing. Her parents wouldn'
approve of it. Neither would most other Mennonites. But dic
God really care whether Tina Warkentin wore lipstick or not?
He hadn't cared enough to let baby Herbert live. So why woulc
he care what colour her lips were?

She gave Frank her brightest smile. "I hope you'll stay
home tomorrow. I thought we'd make ice cream." Frank lovec
homemade ice cream, especially with coffee in it.

He shook his head. "We'll make ice cream another day
okay? I've gotta get to town tomorrow. Sigurd wants me to meet
his cousin Axel."

Tina felt like her husband had splashed cold water in her face.

"You understand, don't you? I've been spending a lot of time with Sigurd lately. He's looking forward to his cousin coming from Montana. He'll be disappointed if I don't show up."

She sighed. "You're right, of course." She couldn't expect Frank to drop all his plans the moment she decided to restart her life. It would take time to get their marriage back to where it had been before Herbert's death, or better. But thank God she and Frank had time, lots of it.

Chapter 33

Frank felt like a schoolboy sitting in the café across from Sigurd and his Montana cousin. The cousin, Axel, had a fat-cat face, the kind some people get from being rich. He wore a camel coat, a white shirt, and a purple tie with a diamond pin in it. At least it looked like a diamond.

Axel's grey eyes seemed to drill into everything he saw — the red lanterns hanging from the ceiling, the army-recruiting poster above the jukebox, the coffee mugs on the table. Frank's face.

Sigurd shifted his toothpick to the west side of his mouth. "Axel here, he's one important guy."

"Is that so?" Frank didn't doubt it.

"He's a recruiter for the Anaconda mining company."

Axel smalled his eyes at Frank. "We've already got some Canadians working in our copper operations in Butte, but there's more jobs available." He stirred his coffee, then gave his spoon a businesslike tap on his mug. "For the right guys."

Frank reared his chair back on its hind legs. "What makes you think I'd be interested in a mining job? I've got responsibilities here — a farm, wife, little girl."

Axel leaned forward. "We pay thirty-eight dollars a week. Imagine what you could buy for your family with that."

"Money isn't everything," Frank said, shifting his face into neutral. Thirty-eight dollars a week! Amazing. He'd be lucky to average that much in a month, farming.

Axel waved a manicured hand toward the army-recruiting poster. "You'd be helping the war effort. The Allies are desperate for copper these days."

Sigurd inserted his toothpick between two of his back molars and worked it around. "So what do you figure, Frank?"

he asked, removing the toothpick. "It's a nice opportunity. I'd take it myself if I didn't have this bum leg."

Frank drummed his fingers on the table, considering the prospect. It would be great to see Montana again—mountains, waterfalls, bars with bullet holes in them. He owed it to himself. He'd hardly left the farm since he'd taken it over from his folks. He'd done okay for a half-Gypsy prodigal—sticking with the same line of work, rubbing shoulders with the same small-minded people, standing by his woman.

Chapter 34

Frank allowed his horses to dawdle on the way home, letting them paw aside patches of snow and eat the frozen weeds underneath. He wished he could delay telling Tina about his new job, at least till he was sure she was really feeling better. But Sigurd's cousin Axel was no time-waster. He'd already bought Frank a train ticket to Butte, Montana. That meant the station agent knew, and of course Sigurd knew. Soon everybody in Dayspring would know. Frank couldn't risk letting Tina hear the news secondhand.

He broke it to her while she was making supper.

"You don't love me anymore," she said in a jerky voice. "I think you just want to get away from me." She yanked the frying pan off its hook, her elbow knocking against the dish of sauerkraut that sat on the counter. It crashed to the floor.

Frank scowled at the broken glass and kraut on the floor, then got the broom and started sweeping them up. "We could use the money," he said, trying to speak in a calm, logical tone. "I'd like to buy my sister's land. She and Alvin are never going to farm; they're settled in Winnipeg. If we bought Fania's quarter-section, we could—"

"You don't love me." Tina's voice came out high, like a child's.

"Of course I love you." He propped the broom against the table and reached for her.

She pushed him away. "If you loved me you'd stay here."

Frank's scalp tingled with—what? Guilt, anger, a longing for freedom. Since he'd lost his son, he had to admit he'd been hankering for new horizons, fresh winds. But he couldn't tell Tina that. She wouldn't understand. He retrieved the broom and started sweeping again. "I'd be helping the war effort, working in the mine. I feel guilty, letting all those soldiers risk their lives for me and my family."

"We're raising food for the soldiers. That's important, isn't it?"

"Yeah, sure, but . . ." How could he explain? Since Herbert's death, he seemed to have lost his concentration. He dithered from one task to another without finishing anything, then had to double back and figure out where he'd left off. He felt like a machine whose controls had gone off-kilter. He needed to reset himself somehow. A change of location might help. It had worked when he was single.

Tina picked up the butcher knife and began slicing sausages in the frying pan. "You're mad at me because I've been sleeping in the living room."

"It's not that. It's just—I need to get away," he blurted. "I'll only be gone a few months. Manfred can do the chores."

"Adeline's Manfred?" Tina waved the butcher knife at him and for a crazy moment Frank was afraid she might run it through him.

He backed away from his wife. "The kid's sixteen. He can handle the chores. If he can't, he can always—"

"Ask his dad or his blessed mother. Adeline would love that. She'd be here every day, checking up on things. I'd be a stranger in my own home."

Frank cleared his throat. "Actually I hadn't figured on you staying here." Tina didn't like this farm anyway. She only lived here for his sake. With him in Montana, she'd be free to leave.

Tina stared at him like she was counting his eyelashes. "What do you mean?"

"I figured you and Klara could live with your parents."

"With my parents?"

"Isn't your brother leaving for army training camp? You and Klara can sleep in his room."

Tina banged the frying pan down on the stove. "You've go this all planned, haven't you." Anger flared in her eyes. "I be you even discussed it with my folks already."

"Of course not. I wanted to talk to you first."

Tina collapsed into a chair, her anger dissolving in tears "Frank, what's happening to us?"

"Come on, Tina. You know I'm right. A few months with your folks will do you good. Your mom is better at cheering you up than I am. Besides, you'll be close to town. Isn't that wha you always wanted?"

Tina lurched out of her chair and stumbled into his arms "Not without you, Frank." She buried her face in his shoulder her tears soaking into his shirt. "Please don't go. I need you Klara needs you."

Chapter 35

Bunkhouse 2, Mackenzie Mine, Butte, Montana,
Nov. 21, 1944
Dear Tina,

I got here okay. The trip would have gone
better if the train hadn't got stalled in Great Falls.

I worked three shifts so far. Klara, you should
see my helmet. It's got an electric light so I can see
where I'm going in the mine. There's a cord
attached to a battery on my belt. The other guys and
I go down the mine shaft in a cage like an elevator.
Underground, it's like a spider's web made of
tunnels and train tracks. We blast the copper ore
out of the rock, then the trains carry it out.

I'm writing this in the bunkhouse. The beds
aren't great. They're just cots really. The mattresses
are just stuffed with straw but I sleep pretty well.
Must be the mountain air.

I miss you, but it's great having something new
to do and the money's good. See cheque enclosed.

   Love, Frank

Box G, Dayspring, Sask., Nov. 30, 1944
Dear Frank,

Thanks for your letter and cheque. I'm glad
you enjoy your job though I don't like the idea of
you blasting. What do you use, dynamite? Watch
out that you don't get hurt. Are they feeding you
enough?

I'm glad you didn't join the army anyway. My

brother says training camp is quite the eye-opener.
Dad is mad at him for enlisting. He says the army's
no place for a Mennonite, etc., etc. But Gary's
stubborn. He says he won't quit now. He'll finish
what he started. I hope he doesn't get hurt or killed.

Klara and I sleep in Gary's room since he left.
Klara is lonesome for you. Sometimes she cries
herself to sleep.

Klara and I both miss you but we try to keep
busy. We draw pictures. We help Mom and Dad.
(I'm learning to chop wood. Dad's teaching me.)
Mom and Klara and I are cutting up old clothes and
making things for ourselves. I made a new dolly for
Klara but she likes ragged old Lois better.

We got lots of snow this week. Klara and I took
shovels to the cemetery and cleared off Herbert's
grave. I still don't like the idea of him being buried
in the Lutheran cemetery, but at least he's close to
Mom and Dad's place. I walk to his grave almost
every day. I took Herbert some red geraniums from
Mom's plants. That was silly, I guess. They froze
right away.

Klara drew a picture of her and me shovelling.
I'll send it along.

Love, Tina

Bunkhouse 2, Mackenzie Mine, Butte, Montana,
Dec. 10, 1944
Dear Tina,

Klara, thanks for the picture. I'm glad you're
taking care of Herbert's grave. Next summer when
the ground is settled, we'll put up a stone for him. I
wonder what we should write on it.

Tina, I don't do any blasting myself so don't

worry. My job is what they call mucking. I run a machine that cleans up rock and mud and stuff from the blasting.

They feed us okay but some of the food isn't too tasty. I miss your cooking, especially borscht and cabbage rolls. We don't get stuff like that here. I guess it's easier to just slap a hunk of meat and a baked potato on a plate. We get salad too, and sometimes a veg like corn.

We're having quite the cold snap here. I sure freeze in this bunkhouse. You can probably see that from my shivery writing. There's a coal stove in the middle of the floor, but it doesn't heat the edges too well when the wind blows.

I'm sending another cheque. I hope it gets there in time for your Christmas shopping.

Love, Frank

P.S. While you've got the sewing machine out, maybe you could run me up a couple of flannel shirts. I could try to buy some but you know the sleeves are always too short.

Box G, Dayspring, Sask., Dec. 19, 1944
Dear Frank,

About Herbert's gravestone, maybe we could just write the name and the dates. I can't think of a Bible verse to use without sounding bitter or hypocritical.

Thanks for the cheque. I'll use part of it to buy Mom a new colander. Hers is chipped, and the handle came loose when I strained the noodles last night.

Leif Lindberg's mother died of tuberculosis in the sanatorium in Qu'Appelle. They brought her body to Dayspring for the funeral. It was in the Lutheran church. Dad and I went. Mom stayed home with Klara.

I met Thor and Sigurd in town yesterday. They said hello and thanks for your letter. They'll write soon. Thor's still pumping gas. Sigurd took over his father's dray business because his dad's not feeling good. Sigurd delivers both water and freight now. He bought a bigger wagon.

I'm sending one shirt with this letter. I hope it gets there in time for Christmas. I'm making another one. It's brown plaid to go with your eyes.

Will you get Christmas dinner at the cookhouse? We're sending you some cookies. Klara put coconut beards on all the gingerbread daddies. I don't know why. Maybe she forgot what you look like. Do you have any idea when you'll be home?

Love, Tina

P.S. I got a nice Christmas card and letter from your sister. She says the weather's very cold in Winnipeg this winter. She probably wrote to you, too.

Bunkhouse 2, Mackenzie Mine, Butte, Dec. 25, 1944

Dear Tina,

Yes, I got a card and letter from Fania and Alvin. I'd sure like to buy her land off her. It's so handy right next to ours. If I keep my nose to the mucking machine here, maybe I can save enough money.

Being that it's Christmas, I went out looking for a church. I ended up at a little Episcopalian one that smelled like varnish and old hymn books. I

didn't get much out of the service. The Episco-
palians stand up and sit down a lot, and they read
their prayers from a book. Maybe it seems better
once you're used to it.

Thanks for the shirt. It fits fine. And thanks for
the cookies. I'm rationing them out to myself and
my buddies Clemence and Mehil. They're Gypsies
from Nebraska. It's interesting to hear how they
were brought up. Pretty free and easy compared to
Mennonites.

The relief cook made Christmas dinner for us
poor schnooks that couldn't go home. He sure doesn't
cook like you and your mom. See cheque encl.

Love, Frank

Box G, Dayspring, Sask., Jan. 5, 1945
Dear Frank,

How are you enjoying the New Year? Life is
kind of boring here now that the frenzy of cooking
and visiting is over. I've been copying some of
Mom's recipes to take home with me. She's got lots
of them pasted into Dad's old farming magazines. In
between the recipes I find little nuggets of wisdom
like:

— Manure is a useful source of plant nutrients.
— Cutworms can cause serious damage to
    seedling crops.

Dad is getting on my nerves with his farming
lectures. He must have told me at least ten times:
"When you're farming out east of town like Frank
does, you've got to start harvesting earlier than
around Dayspring. There's more sloughs out east,
which means more ducks. Ducks like oats and
barley but they'll take wheat, too."

And so he rambles on and on. I don't know
if I can hold out till spring. Maybe you'll be home
before then. I hope you can come for Easter. Klara
is sure growing up. She's quite the young lady in the
patent-leather shoes Mom bought her for Christmas.

Love as ever, Your Tina

Bunkhouse 2, Mackenzie Mine, Butte, Jan. 7, 1945
Dear Tina,

I got a part-time job! Last Saturday night I went
downtown to tour a few saloons. In one of them—
The Hungry Dog or some such—I met this rancher
Joe Topps. He's got a horse-riding school just outside of town. It's got a winterized barn and everything. Joe seemed kind of fassinatted facinated
(can't spell it) about me being a Gypsy since they're
so apparently good with horses.

Anyway the next day Joe takes me out to his
barn, watches me work with a couple of his geldings,
and offers me a job. It's part-time. I only work
Sundays so it doesn't interfere with my shifts in
the mine.

Joe teaches riding a bit different from what I'd
do. He lent me a book on it. Pretty interesting. I've
got it here in bed with me. Wish it was you instead.
A guy can get lonesome sleeping with a book.

Clemence and Mehil got jobs at the riding
school, too. They're better horsemen than me,
according to them. Clemence has two sisters
coming up from Nebraska. He's trying to get jobs
for them in the cookhouse. It'll be interesting to see
what they're like. Do you realize I've never met a
Gypsy woman besides my mother?

Love from your riding teacher, Frank

Box G, Dayspring, Sask., Jan. 18, 1945
Dear Frank,

That's interesting about your part-time job, but
I wish you wouldn't tour saloons. Remember, you're
a family man.

Also I wish you wouldn't work Sundays.
Why don't you go to church? If you don't like the
Episcopalian, there must be others. How much does
this Joe Topps pay? Is it worth ignoring the Lord's
Day for?

Thanks for the cheque but I'd rather have you
home than any amount of money. Why won't you
tell me when you're coming? You'll want to be here
in time for seeding, won't you? Manfred says he and
his dad are sorry, but they can't handle our seeding.
They'll be too busy on their own land.

Klara sure misses you. Mom bought her a
Bible story colouring book and she tries to colour
inside the lines. Sometimes she adds her own draw-
ings, so cute. I'm sending you her picture of Daniel
in the lions' den. Notice the angel she added to
"help keep Daniel safe."

Love from your lonesome Tina

Chapter 36

Bunkhouse 2, Mackenzie Mine, Butte, Montana,
Feb. 4, 1945
Dear Tina,

I see by the papers that the price of copper
went up. Too bad my wages don't go up with it, but
I guess I can't complain. See cheque encl.

The weather has been warm lately. A bunch of
us went trail-riding in the mountains.

Last Saturday night we went to a movie called
National Velvet. It's about this girl who wins a horse
in a raffle. She trains him, enters him into the
Grand National Sweepstakes, and rides him dressed
up like a boy. Not too believable but interesting
anyway. I liked the horse.

I hope you and Klara are doing fine. Say hello
to your folks for me.

Love, Frank

Tina slumped across the red-quilted bed in her brother
Gary's room. What kind of a letter was that? Frank hadn't mentioned anything she'd written in her last letter. He hadn't said
how much Joe Topps paid, or promised to stay out of saloons,
or even hinted at when he'd be home.

Frank hadn't sent her a card for her birthday either. He'd
always remembered her birthday before, even when she still
lived in Vancouver.

Tina stared out Gary's white-framed window, watching the
willows bend in the wind. Frank wouldn't let another woman
turn his head, would he? Who did he mean by "a bunch of us?"

If they were all men, he would have said "me and the guys," wouldn't he? Probably women were involved, maybe Clemence's sisters. What did they look like? Probably willowy young beauties with fluttery eyelashes and flat stomachs.

Surely Frank wouldn't let himself be tempted. He had principles even if he didn't believe in God. On the other hand, what basis did people have for behaving themselves if they didn't believe? Actually Frank did seem to believe, sometimes. He was like the wind in those willows, usually blowing from the west but sometimes shifting to the east.

She heard pans clatter in the kitchen, then her mother's voice. Klara giggled. They must be making the peppermint cookies they'd been talking about. Tina rolled off the bed. She'd go and help them. It would be better than lying here stewing about Frank.

In mid-February Frank wrote, "Clemence's sisters are doing real good in the cookhouse. They made us a venison soup with lots of garlic and pepper. It sure is tasty."

What else were the Gypsy sisters doing for Frank? Tina wondered, tossing his letter onto the nightstand beside Gary's bed. Trying to ignore her own question, she picked up the newspaper she'd bought in town. With a sigh she sank onto the bed and scanned the headlines: *Allies push toward German Siegfried Line. Coffee rations due to rise. Toronto blacksmith declared war hero.* Then an advertisement at the bottom of the page caught her eye: *Help boost the spirits of our guys and gals overseas. A letter from home can mean so much.*

Tina had seen that ad a hundred times before. This time a light dawned in her mind. Why couldn't she write to her old boyfriend Victor Graf? He was one of the "guys overseas." There'd be no harm in writing, as long as she remembered she was married. She had Victor's address. It was in one of the Baptist newsletters that Aunt Irmie had sent her. Vic must be lonesome over there in England. A letter from her might help cheer him up. Frank would never need to know. There'd be no point in giving her husband the wrong impression.

She rummaged in the nightstand for a writing pad, pen and bottle of ink. Then she filled the pen, propped herself against the pillows, and began to write:

General Delivery, Dayspring, Sask., Canada,
February 20, 1945
Dear Victor,

I see by the Baptist church paper that you're a hospital corpsman now. Good for you. I'm glad you found a way to help the war effort without participating in armed combat. The Mennonites would be proud of you if you were a Mennonite.

You'll be surprised to hear from me after all these years, but I've decided to start writing letters to the "guys and gals overseas." We get lots of ads in our newspapers about that. I'll go to the town office tomorrow and ask for some addresses, and I found yours in the Baptist paper.

My husband, Frank, took a job at a copper mine in Butte, Montana. I'll be glad when he gets home. In the meantime I'm living with my folks near Dayspring with our daughter, Klara (four years old on her next birthday). We try to keep busy. We sew, draw pictures, cook, gather eggs, feed the pigs—anything for excitement, ha, ha. But time still hangs heavy on my hands. It doesn't seem fair, me without enough to do while you and Frank and so many others help the war effort. If writing letters would help make a difference, I'm happy to do it.

If you write back, please address it to me in care of General Delivery, Dayspring, Sask. Mom and Dad might get the wrong idea if they see a letter from you in their mailbox.

A friend, Tina (Janz) Warkentin

Canadian Military Hospital, Sussex, England,
Feb. 28, 1945
Dear Tina,

I just got back from praying with Nigel, one of our patients. He's not going to make it, poor fellow. The whole side of his face is blown off and—well, I'll spare you the details. But I think he accepted Jesus as his Saviour before he lost consciousness. I pray that he understands and that I'll get another chance to talk to him about it.

Your letter was a wonderful surprise, though I wouldn't want to correspond with you if it would threaten your relationship with your husband in any way. On the other hand, you've made it clear that your feelings for me are those of a sister only. An older sister, I might add.

So please write if you feel you can do so in good conscience. But be careful of my heart.

Your corpsman/corpseman, Victor Graf

P.S. I wish I could see you one more time. Sometimes that fond hope is all that keeps me from despair. I get so tired of all the senseless slaughter. Then I think of your lovely face. Sorry. Just my pathetic fantasy, but there's so little to keep a man going here. Enough. I'd tear this letter up and start over if paper wasn't so scarce. That's a lame excuse, *nicht?*

Tina read and reread Victor's letter, frowning over it every time. Was he still in love with her? If he was, she shouldn't keep writing to him. It wouldn't be fair to him or her husband. On the other hand, writing to Vic might be okay if she kept reminding him they were only friends. Her letters to Victor didn't need to be much different from those she wrote to any other "guy or gal overseas." She'd treat all her correspondents alike, keeping her letters cheerful and breezy, full of hope and news from the home front.

Chapter 37

Klara's red jacket fluttered in the breeze as the child pranced across the cinder-surfaced train platform. Tina followed more slowly, her boots crunching out the words of Frank's telegram: *April 7, 1945. Got thrown off horse. Arm injured. Quit jobs. Arrive train Friday. Love, Frank.*

She twisted the frayed leather handles of her purse—a nervous habit she should break. How bad was Frank's injury? Was he in pain? Was he coming home just because he'd hurt his arm, or because he missed her and Klara? How had her husband changed in the months he'd been away?

Klara was running circles around the cream cans that stood in a gleaming row near the station house. Tina allowed herself a fond smile. The little girl was pretty: creamy-brown skin, dark eyes, dimple in her chin. Her arms and legs were growing long like Frank's. He'd be surprised to see how tall she was.

He should be here soon. It was three-thirty according to the station-house clock. Tina peered down the track that ran south out of town. Sunlight glittered on the rails, making her eyes water. Where were her sunglasses? She rummaged in her purse, feeling more frantic than she should over a pair of sunglasses. She pushed aside her extra set of combs, then her compact and lipstick, but she didn't see her glasses. She dug deeper in the purse, then froze at the wail of a train whistle.

"Mommy!" Klara ran to her, boots spurting cinders. "It's coming! The train is coming!"

Tina stood like a statue, watching the locomotive chug out of the valley. As it approached the crossing near the Lutheran cemetery, Klara started jumping up and down. "Daddy's coming. Daddy's coming." The train clattered over the crossing and rattled past the Knutsons' stubble field, then the sports ground at the edge of town. With a lurch and a whoosh of steam, i pulled into the station and shuddered to a stop.

Tina scanned the passenger coaches, her eyes skimming over heads and shoulders. Heads and shoulders that weren' Frank's. Where was he? Oh, there in the doorway of the las coach behind a woman in a hat with fake cherries bobbing Frank looked thinner than he had when he'd left. His cheek bones were sharper. More teeth showed in his grin.

He stepped onto the platform clutching his suitcase in his left hand, his right arm hanging at his side. "Daddy!" Klara shrieked. She ran to him and threw her arms around his legs.

With one swift motion, Frank set his suitcase down and scooped Klara up in his left arm. "How's my princess?" He kissed her. "How's Daddy's big girl?"

Tina hurried to join them.

"Darling!" Frank called, setting Klara on the platform. He pulled Tina into a one-armed hug. "It's been too long." His lips found hers. "Way too long."

Chapter 38

"Just smell that land, Tina." Frank threw his head back and sniffed the breeze like a young colt. It was Saturday morning, the morning after he'd returned from Montana. They were out walking across the stubble field, Klara darting ahead with the dog. The horizon surrounded them like a distant wedding ring.

Frank squeezed Tina's hand. "There's nothing like the smell of nice loamy land in the springtime. It makes me almost glad I hurt my arm."

"Would you have come home if you hadn't?" Tina tried to keep her voice light, teasing.

"Of course." He nuzzled her ear, a fleeting butterfly kiss. "I love you. You know that."

"Yes, I guess so, but—" She gulped. "Frank, why didn't you write more often?"

"I'm sorry." His voice stiffened. "I said I'm sorry. I was busy. I hardly had a free moment. But you were on my mind, you and Klara. All the time."

Tina sighed. No matter what Frank said, she couldn't help wondering what he'd been doing in Butte besides working. Had there been another woman? She hesitated to ask, afraid of the answer—or lack of it.

He planted his feet wide apart in the stubble and swung an imaginary bat in his left hand. "I feel like a home-run hitter stepping up to the plate. I can hardly wait to start seeding. I'll get out on this quarter tomorrow. My machinery's all ready, thanks to Manfred and his dad."

"What about your arm?"

He massaged his elbow. "I think it's some better."

"Didn't the doctor in Butte tell you to rest it?"

"I rested it on the train. Anyway, driving a tractor is easie
than running a mucking machine."

"Why don't you wait till Monday at least? We should go t
church tomorrow." Tina had gotten back into the habit o
church, living with her parents.

"The weather's perfect for seeding." Frank pressed his boo
into the stubble and examined his footprint. "See how moist th
soil is? If I wait much longer, it'll dry out."

Tina frowned. "You never seeded on Sunday before. Doesn
it seem kind of disrespectful?"

How could she explain? She wasn't even sure she believed
in God anymore. Not the kind of God she'd grown up believing
in anyway. But she couldn't shake the feeling that God, or some
body a lot like him, was always just around the corner, keeping
score.

The sun slid out from under a cloud and Tina blinked ir
the sudden glare. She tied her scarf over her head, pulling i
forward to shade her eyes. "Klara finally got brave enough to g
to Sunday School. I'd like her to keep going."

"Your parents could take her. I'm sure they'd be glad tc
pick her up."

"What'll we say when they ask us to come to church?"

Frank gave her a sly wink. "I'll tell them my ass fell into ;
pit."

"That's no way to talk." Tina glanced at Klara, who wa
throwing a stick for the dog. "You're not in the mine anymore.

"That's not mining talk; it's in the Bible. Didn't Jesus say
that if your ass or ox falls into a pit, you're allowed to pull it ou
on Sunday?"

Part of Tina felt like laughing, part like screaming. She'c
forgotten Frank's way of teasing, keeping her off balance. With
him she never knew what to expect. Victor Graf had neve
made her feel this way. Victor was a more predictable person
more restful. Tina blushed, picturing the letters Vic had written

her while Frank was away. They were hidden in her sweater drawer, tied with yellow ribbon. She'd better burn those letters.

By five-thirty the next morning, Tina was up making pancakes and frying sausages for Frank. After breakfast she milked the cows so he could get an early start in the field.

But after only a couple of hours of driving the tractor, he slouched back into the kitchen, where Tina was listening to the *Back to the Bible* broadcast, feeling guilty about not being in church. She switched off the radio. "What's the matter?"

Frank rummaged through the medicine chest that hung on the wall. "My arm's gone all numb and tingly. Where'd you put the liniment anyway? I wish you wouldn't keep hiding things."

Tina went to the medicine chest, grabbed a brown bottle off the bottom shelf, and handed it to him. "It would've bit you if it was a snake."

"You hid it behind your Lydia Pinkham pills. How would you expect me to find it?"

"Here, let's see your arm." Tina led him to a kitchen chair and helped him roll up his sleeve. "It looks awfully swollen."

"I guess driving the tractor aggravates it worse than I figured."

"Maybe you should take the seeding a little slower."

A look like thunder darkened his face. "How can I? A guy's gotta seed when it's seeding time." He poured some liniment into his left hand and rubbed it on his right arm. "You wanna bandage it for me? It feels like it needs support."

Tina got an elastic bandage from the medicine chest.

"Pull it tight," Frank directed as she wound it around his arm and wrist.

When she'd pinned it, he clumped over to the phone and called some of the neighbours, asking if they knew anybody he could hire to help with the seeding.

"No luck," Frank said after he'd talked to Pop Wolford. "They're all short-handed themselves." He grabbed his brown fedora, plunked it on his head, and went out. Tina watched him slouch across the road to the south quarter and start left-handedly picking stones off it. He tossed them onto the rock pile near the fence, looking as sad as an eagle with clipped wings.

After an hour she made some lemonade and took it out to him. "You should stop and rest," she said, handing him the sweating glass. "These stones are hardly big enough to bother with."

Frank grunted and tossed a pincushion-sized chunk of granite onto the rock pile.

Tina sighed and called Klara from the house. The three of them made a game of it. Finding stones, laughing as they kicked them out of the earth and tossed them onto the rock pile—competing to see who could make the loudest clatter. It was a pointless exercise in Tina's opinion, but that didn't matter. What mattered was that they were together doing what Frank seemed to need to do: keep busy.

The next morning Tina re-bandaged his arm and he went out to try seeding again. This time he was back after only three quarters of an hour. "I tried to ignore the pain but it's getting worse. I think it's spreading into my hand."

Tina unwound the bandage. "Looks like it's swollen worse than yesterday." She touched his arm. "It feels hot. Soaking it in cold water might help."

"It might."

"I'll get a fresh pail from the well."

"Thanks." The lines around Frank's eyes softened. "Tina, I just want to tell you." He cleared his throat. "It means a lot to me, having a little woman to take care of me."

Had he had a little woman taking care of him in Butte? Tina didn't feel like asking. She couldn't face the explosion of anger that might result. Anyway, if there had been another woman, Frank was hundreds of miles from the trespasser now. He was all Tina's again—she hoped. "I'm not a little woman," she said and headed for the lean-to.

He followed, laughing and pulling at her apron strings. "If you're not a little woman, what are you?"

"I'm your nurse," she snapped, retying her apron. "So you better do what I say."

He gave her a left-handed salute. "Yes, ma'am."

Tina took a water pail off the shelf. "If the swelling in your arm's not down by morning, we'll go see Doc Muirhead."

Chapter 39

Tina sat in Doc Muirhead's waiting room paging through the latest issue of *Life* magazine. It was full of *Victory in Europe* celebrations: parades, flags, fireworks, people dancing in the streets. The Germans had surrendered, thank God. But Canada and the other Allies were still fighting Japan in the Pacific. Would this crazy war never end?

The waiting room was empty, silent except for muffled voices behind the door of the doctor's office. Doc Muirhead's voice sounded smooth and steady; Frank's angry, explosive.

A few moments later her husband barged out into the waiting room. "Muirhead can't do anything for me. All he can say is, 'Rest your arm and it should improve in a couple of months.'"

"A couple of months!" Tina dropped the magazine. "How will we get our seeding done?"

"You'll have to do it."

Tina jumped to her feet. "I can't drive the tractor. You know that. I've never driven anything but horses."

"You'll have to learn," Frank said, jamming his fedora onto his head. "What else can we do?" He followed her out of the waiting room. "All the men are busy around here. Agatha Gunther is good on a tractor, I hear, but she's gotta help her brother."

"I'm no Agatha Gunther," Tina said as she and Frank hurried to the livery barn, where they'd left their horses and wagon. "That woman is as strong as a man."

Frank managed a half-smile. "Maybe I should ask Adeline Epp."

"You're joking, right?"

He shrugged his left shoulder. "Adeline would do it just to prove she could."

"I'll bet. I can just hear her bragging."

Could she herself learn to handle the tractor? Tina pondered the question as she drove the horses home. She had learned to split wood; her dad had taught her, though she'd been terrified of cutting her feet. But the tractor was a monster, an exhaust-spewing monster. It could kill a person. On the other hand, Agatha Gunther had tamed it. And Adeline Epp could if she tried. Maybe Tina Warkentin could, too.

The next morning she put on a gardening shirt, a pair of Frank's overalls with the legs pinned up, boots, sunglasses, and work gloves. She tied her straw hat on her head and walked out to where Frank was checking the oil in the tractor. She gave him a smart salute, clicking her heels together. "Little woman reporting for duty."

He looked up, dipstick in hand.

She twirled to show him her outfit.

Frank grinned. "You look good. Now let's see how smart you are." He replaced the dipstick and stepped over to the long, low implement behind the tractor. "This here is a one-way disk seeder," he said. "Most people just call it a one-way. The seed wheat is in this box, see? It trickles out these little tubes. Then the disks cover it with earth."

"Sort of like planting a garden."

"Much the same, only the machines do the work. All you need to do is guide them."

Tina frowned. "Couldn't we hitch the horses to the one-way instead?" The horses were familiar at least.

Frank shook his head. "The tractor is stronger than twenty horses, and it's not temperamental like horses can be."

"It might get temperamental if I try to drive it."

"Naw, you'll do fine. Come on." He went to the back of the tractor. "The first thing to do is get on. Climb up there. That's it. Okay, now sit down."

Tina perched on the metal seat, wrinkling her nose at the

smell of gasoline and engine grease. "How do you make it go?" she asked, not that she really wanted to know.

Frank stepped up behind her. "First you push in the clutch—that's the floor-pedal to your left." He peered over her shoulder. "Push it down. Good. Then you turn on the ignition—that's this switch here. Good. Now ease the throttle forward." He placed her left hand on it.

She scowled at him. "I can't remember all this."

"Sure you can. It'll get to be second nature after awhile."

"It's not the kind of second nature I want."

"Maybe not, but we can't always do what we want, can we?"

She sighed. "No, I guess not." Marriage was a partnership, as Preacher Schellenberg kept saying. She and Frank were supposed to help each other, shore up each other's weaknesses.

Frank pointed at another button. "Pull that out—give it some choke."

"Choke—just what I need. I'm already choking with fear."

He nudged her with his hip. "You're not. You're enjoying this."

"I am not."

"You are so. You can hardly wait to get rolling and feel all that power—you, the boss of twenty horses."

Chapter 40

Once Tina got started, she was surprised at how quickly she learned to manoeuvre the tractor around the field. The pattern Frank had taught her was easy. Start at the outside of the field, work around the edge, then make smaller and smaller rounds till you reach the middle. Finally make one straight track out.

Tina also discovered that she liked leaving Klara with Frank—she liked letting her husband cook and wash the dishes. She enjoyed getting dusty and sweaty, and not caring because it was part of the job, a badge of honour. Most of all, Tina liked being so tired at night that she slept like a stone. No worrying about the state of her soul or Klara's or Frank's.

If only the sunlight wasn't so hot and bright. It strained her eyes and burned her skin till she felt like fried steak, even when she wore a hat and plastered herself with cold cream. She tried oils and lotions. Nothing worked very well. Frank borrowed a big umbrella and rigged it up to give her shade on the tractor. It helped, though she couldn't use it when the wind was too strong. In desperation she made a mask out of a pillowcase, but Frank didn't want her wearing it. "It's dangerous. You can't see enough through those holes."

Tina tried to ignore the discomfort and kept seeding, day after dogged day. Never again would she take lightly all the field-work Frank had done in his life. On the other hand, tractor-driving was easier for him, at least when his arm was okay. Frank's skin was dark enough to tan, not burn, and the sun didn't seem to bother his eyes like it did hers.

"How did it go today?" Frank asked one evening as he and Tina and Klara sat down for supper.

"Better," Tina said. "I like cloudy weather."

Frank opened the jar of meatballs he'd brought up from the cellar. "Clouds are fine as long as they don't dump rain on us." He speared a meatball with a fork and put it on Klara's plate. "We can't seed if the field is too wet."

Tina helped herself to a couple of meatballs, hoping for rain though she realized that was selfish and short-sighted of her. "I caught a stone between a couple of one-way disks today," she remarked, making conversation.

Frank slid a baked potato onto Klara's plate. "Did you get it out okay?"

Tina smiled, feeling a new confidence in herself. "I took a wrench and pounded it out."

"Yeah, that's what I generally do. Or I pry it out with the crowbar."

From her husband's carefully casual tone, Tina knew he enjoyed talking shop with her like this. She enjoyed it, too.

What other adventures could she recount? Oh yes, the duck. "I saw a mallard duck's nest near the fence," she said, spreading butter on her baked potato. "I steered around it. I didn't want to run over the mother and her babies."

Klara grinned through her milk moustache.

"Yeah," Frank said, passing Tina the pickles. "I usually steer around the duck nests. I figure birds have as much right to live as we do."

* * *

As the days grew longer, the sun bothered Tina more. Her skin blistered and she developed eyestrain headaches. Finally she and Frank decided she should work only in the early mornings while the sun was low in the sky, and in the evenings as it went down.

"Why couldn't I work at night?" she asked one afternoon while she and Frank were resting in their bedroom.

He reached over and started massaging her throbbing temples. "You couldn't see the furrows well enough. Anyway it would be dangerous for you to *putz* around in the field after dark."

"You should be a doctor," she murmured. "There's healing in your hands."

"It's the Gypsy in me." He swung his legs out of bed. "I'll wring out a towel in cold tea. It might take some of the burn out of your eyes."

"Are you sure we can't find someone to help us?" she called as he started down the stairs.

He reappeared in the doorway of the bedroom. "Who? Nobody's answered my ad in the newspaper. And we can't ask the Epps or your dad. They're already busier than a one-armed paper-hanger with the chickenpox."

Chapter 41

Tina trudged across the field toward the house, hungry from driving the tractor since before dawn. Her stomach growled for the second breakfast Frank had promised to cook. Her face was sore and hot under her mask of dust. Her eyes had that too awake feeling that signalled a headache coming on. She'd need to take aspirins after second breakfast. Aspirins gave her heartburn but what else could she do? She needed to be able to sleep this afternoon. By seven o'clock this evening, she'd be out on the tractor again. Tomorrow would be the same unless it rained. So would the next day and the next. Could she keep going till the seeding was done — another month or more? God only knew.

As she approached the road, she noticed a winged shadow skimming across the earth. She looked up and saw a bird circling overhead. It was a fair size, with a fan-like tail and rounded wings tipped up at the ends. Probably a hawk. Too bad it wasn't bigger, big enough to blot out the sun. She watched it plummet from the sky into the clover along the roadside. A gopher exploded out of the clover and streaked away. The bird dived after it, streamlining its brown-speckled wings against its body. The gopher popped into a hole and the hawk's talons snapped at empty air. The bird screamed and flapped away, its shadow darting across the clover and the figure of the man who stood in it.

A man standing in the clover? Why? Who? Tina removed her sunglasses, wiped her eyes with her handkerchief, and looked again.

There was a man standing in the clover all right, but it wasn't Frank. This was a shorter, wider man with a knapsack on his back. If she hadn't known better, she might have thought it was her old boyfriend Victor Graf. But of course Victor was overseas.

She walked toward the man, and saw his hair flame fire-red like Victor's. His nose beaked like Victor's.

He smiled at her, his teeth as wide apart as ever. "Tatia-meana, how are you doing?"

The familiar nickname gave Tina a jolt. Her hands flew to her face. "Victor, what are you doing here? You're supposed to be in England." Why was her heart kicking like a horse? It had no right to do that; she was a married woman. She crossed her arms over her chest. "I'm almost fainting with shock," she said when she found her voice. "How did you get here?"

"They discharged me from the army early because of my stomach problem. I stopped to visit my cousins in Regina, and figured I'd drop in here while I was in the area."

"In the area?" Tina felt like she was floating outside her body, like her voice belonged to someone else. "Dayspring's not exactly close to Regina."

"No, but your letters were so nice, I thought I'd take a little detour—"

"My husband is back from Butte," she blurted, glancing toward the house.

"Yeah, I know. I met this guy Leif Lindberg on the train platform. He said Frank was back. "

"I suppose Leif dropped you off here."

"Yeah, it was good of him."

Tina's head throbbed. "Frank and I are trying to make a fresh start in our marriage." She massaged her temples.

Victor's blue-grey eyes darkened. "I don't want to come between you and Frank. I just hoped to spend a few hours with you."

"What for?" Surely Victor hadn't come all this way for a few hours' visit.

He ran his finger over the scar that snaked across his forehead. Where had that come from? Sniper fire? Bomb blast? "I need to see you as a wife and mother." Victor's voice was so quiet, Tina almost lost it in the buzzing of bees in the clover. "I want to meet your husband. See what kind of little girl you got. Then maybe I can finally forget you." He swallowed and his Adam's apple bobbed. "I prayed a lot before I decided to drop in here."

"And what did God say?"

"I don't think he said no." Victor paused. "Tatiameana, please try to understand. Not seeing you married is like not seeing my grandma in her coffin. I still have a hard time believing she's dead."

Tina's lips twitched into a half-smile. "Are you saying I remind you of your grandma?"

"Of course not. I'm just saying I need you to do this one little thing for me." He gulped. "Your dream came true. Mine didn't."

Tina stared down at her dust-caked boots. Her dream had come true. She'd married the man she wanted. Of course their lives hadn't been all roses. But she loved Frank and their marriage was getting stronger. Surely she could be generous enough to share a few hours of her family life with Victor.

She smiled. "You might as well come up to the house. We don't have anything fancy to eat though. Too busy seeding."

"Leif said you were driving the tractor." Victor's eyes scanned her dusty shirt and overalls.

"Yes, Frank hurt his arm. He got thrown off a horse."

She and Victor walked to the house in silence, Tina trying to ignore the pounding in her temples. "Frank?" she called, opening the screen door. "Darling, we've got company." She led the visitor into the kitchen, where Frank stood at the stove left-handedly cracking an egg into a frying pan. "Darling," she said, "this is Victor Graf, a friend of Uncle Yash's."

Victor extended his right hand, then withdrew it. "Sorry. I hear you bunged up your arm."

Frank grinned. "It only hurts when I cook." He wiped his fingers, then thrust out his left hand. "Welcome here, Victor. Would you like two eggs or three?"

"Oh, just one." Victor removed his knapsack and dropped it in a corner.

Klara wandered down from upstairs, her eyes widening when she saw the stranger.

Victor snapped his fingers at her. "One egg's enough for us little guys, *nicht?*"

She giggled and ducked behind Tina.

During second breakfast Victor mentioned that he'd grown up on a farm near Kelowna, BC. "We didn't grow wheat though, mostly cherries and peaches."

Frank helped himself to a couple of fried eggs. "Can you drive a tractor?"

"Of course."

Tina's heart stumbled over a beat. Was Frank thinking of hiring Victor to finish the seeding? If he did, she could stay out of the sun like a lady. She pictured herself wearing a frilly pink apron, cooking for Frank and Victor.

It was a nice picture but it might be tricky. If Victor stayed here, the two of them would need to keep their former connection a secret. Letting Frank know would only cause trouble.

After second breakfast, Klara took charge of the visitor, leading him out to see her sandbox.

Frank stayed behind, helping Tina gather up the dirty dishes. "What do you know about this Victor Graf?" he asked, scraping egg yolk off a plate.

Tina shrugged. "He's just a guy who worked at Uncle Yash's hospital." It made her sick to mislead her husband like this, but what else could she do? If she told Frank that Victor had once been her sweetheart, he'd get mad and send him away.

"Why did he drop in here?" Frank asked.

"I guess Uncle Yash suggested it."

"I guess so." Frank emptied the leftover coffee into the slop pail. "What kind of work did Victor do at the hospital?"

"I think mainly carpentry and repairs. He was in the maintenance department."

"Did he work at anything else before he joined the army?"

Tina took the dishpan off its hook. "I believe he ran a carpentry shop in Chilliwack. Then Uncle Yash's hospital offered him his old job back so he took it."

"He must be a good worker if the hospital wanted him back."

"I suppose so."

Frank took the dishpan from her. "Leave the dishes, Sweetheart. I'll wash them later." He hung the pan on the hook. "You go take a nap and I'll show Victor around. I like the look of him. He's got an honest face."

"What do you mean?"

Frank laughed. "Anybody with teeth that far apart—any lies are gonna fall out before he gets a chance to tell 'em."

Tina laughed but a cold feeling crept in around her heart. What if Victor told Frank she'd once been his girl? "Please don't be too honest, Vic," she whispered, watching her husband head out the door. Part of her hoped Frank would hire Victor so she could stay out of the cruel sun. Part of her thought the idea was preposterous. Maybe she wouldn't feel so confused if her head weren't aching. She swallowed three aspirins with a glass of milk. She should take a nap but she was too nervous. She fetched her sewing basket from the living room. As she sat down at the kitchen table to thread her darning needle, she heard the men come into the lean-to.

"It's strange you showing up here all of a sudden." Frank's rumbling voice. "Almost like it was meant to be."

Tina leaned forward, straining to hear.

Frank cleared his throat. "You couldn't stay and help us seed, could you?"

She held her breath, waiting for Victor's reply.

Vic said nothing.

Frank led the visitor into the kitchen. "But you probably want to get home to the wife." He seated himself at the table, motioning for Victor to do the same.

"I'm not married." Victor glanced at Tina as he sat down. "I'm as free as a meadowlark."

She retreated to the pantry to get some cookies. She didn't want to influence the men. If Victor stayed she wanted it to be his and Frank's decision, not hers. Of course she wasn't in love with Victor anymore, but it would still be awkward having him around.

Tina took the tin of raisin cookies down off the pantry shelf. Then she remembered that Victor didn't like raisins. She found a jar of molasses cookies. As she carried it into the kitchen, she saw Victor waving his arm through the air in a grand gesture. "A few weeks in the country is just what I need after all that mud and blood overseas."

Tina's heart clenched. She really should try to persuade him to leave.

She set the molasses cookies on the table. On the other hand, things might work out fine if Victor kept his mouth shut. Of course nothing could come of his love for her; she'd be sure to make that clear. If he stayed here in order to be near her, it was a dead end for him. But if he stayed because he'd enjoy a few weeks in the country—and wanted to earn some money helping her and Frank—things might turn out just fine.

Chapter 42

Tina stood in the lean-to putting the cream separator together
Through the screen door, she heard Frank and Victor approach
ing from the barn. Their voices sounded hearty, friendly. Good
The men had gotten along fine since Victor's arrival, though
she shuddered to think what would happen if Frank discovered
she and Vic had once been sweethearts.

The screen door opened and Frank clumped in carrying a
pail of milk in his left hand, his sore arm hanging at his side
Victor followed with two more pails.

"It looks like a great day for seeding," Frank said, setting
his pail on the table beside the separator. "I figure we'll finish
the west quarter today."

Victor's eyes widened. "It's Sunday. I thought we'd be
going to church."

"The wife and I don't attend church steady," Frank said
helping Tina set the milk tank into the separator. "But we figure
the Lord helps them that help themselves. Right now, the best
way we can help ourselves is get the seeding done."

Victor put his pails on the floor. "You don't think you need
to ask God's blessing on that?"

Frank gave a short sneeze-like laugh. "We asked God to
bless our son and he died."

The sudden mention of baby Herbert made Tina's heart
ache. Had Frank really prayed for him? She'd never known her
husband to pray.

Victor fetched the cream and milk containers from the
kitchen, and set them under the separator's spouts. "Your son
didn't die because you prayed."

Frank grunted. "I guess not, but praying didn't help neither, did it?"

"God doesn't always answer our prayers like we—"

"No more preaching, okay." Frank's voice sounded tight. He lifted a pail of milk with his good arm. Using his chest to tilt it, he started filling the separator tank. The pail wobbled, spattering milk on the floor. Frank muttered a curse and slammed the pail down on the table.

Victor sickled an eyebrow at Tina, probably wondering how seriously to take Frank's anger.

She kept her expression neutral. Let the men work things out between themselves. If she interfered, it might only cause trouble.

Frank stomped into the kitchen and returned a moment later with the scrub-bucket and a floor-cloth. "You're entitled to your beliefs, Vic." He squatted and began washing the spilled milk off the floor. "But I'll thank you not to ram them down my throat."

"I'm sorry if I was too pushy." Victor stepped aside so Frank could wash around the separator. "But while we're talking religion, I might as well tell you. I won't do any work on Sundays except what's absolutely necessary, like feeding the cows and milking."

Frank's lips curled into a sneer. "You're sure narrow-minded for an army man."

A muscle in Victor's jaw twitched. "After the hell I went through overseas, the Lord's Day is more important to me than ever." He hitched up the straps of his overalls. "If you want to fire me, that's fine. But I'd hate to leave you and Tatiameana—" He broke off, his face flushing under his freckles.

Tina sucked in her breath. What would Frank think of Victor calling her by a nickname he'd never heard?

Her husband mumbled something she didn't catch, then said, "Never mind. I guess Tina and I can muddle through by ourselves for one day."

She blew out her breath, her head light with relief.

Victor poured a pailful of milk into the separator, then grasped the handle and started turning it. "I'll walk to church then, if you'll point me in the right direction."

"There's no Baptist church nearby," Tina said, though Victor already knew that from her letters. "But the Mennonites hold services in each other's homes. They're meeting at the Friesens today. You go a quarter-mile west to the turnoff, then half a mile—"

She stopped as a horrible thought struck her. What would her mom and dad think of Victor suddenly showing up at church? They'd probably recognize him from the pictures she'd sent years ago. If her parents told someone Vic had been her boyfriend, the news would spread like the flu.

She watched the floor-cloth flop in Frank's good hand as he washed the baseboard behind the separator. Poor darling. He was part of a love triangle and didn't even know it.

No. She stood up straighter. This wasn't a love triangle. She didn't love Victor, though she had to admit she enjoyed knowing Victor loved her. Frank would be devastated if he knew. Tina forced a smile. "Why don't we all go to church together? It's such a beautiful day."

Frank threw the floor-cloth into the scrub-bucket. "Don't it seem kinda small-minded of God, giving the farmers a nice day and then telling them not to seed?"

What could she say? Seeding on Sundays hadn't seemed too bad before Victor had arrived. But with him here, it seemed sinful again. She felt like a rubber band stretched between her husband's principles and Victor's. Victor's were right; she realized that. But she couldn't afford to side with him against Frank. She needed to keep things peaceful around here, at least till the seeding got done.

Frank carried the scrub-bucket back to the kitchen. Tina followed. "Darling, if you don't feel like going to the Friesens',

Klara and I could walk with Victor. It would give us a chance to wear our spring dresses."

More important, it would give her a chance to tell her parents to keep their mouths shut about her and Victor.

* * *

Tina hurried to her parents' car, which her dad was parking in the grass near the Friesens' garden.

He rolled down his window. "Good morning, Tina. It's great to see you at church."

"Is Klara here?" her mom asked, leaning past him.

Tina jerked her head toward the house. "She's playing with the Friesen kids." She hesitated. "Listen, I've got to talk to you. I'll sit in the car for a minute, okay?"

Her mom moved over to make room.

Tina circled to the passenger side and got in. "Mom, Dad," she said, shutting the car door, "Victor Graf is here." She reached around her dad and rolled up his window.

Tina's father stared at her. "Victor? Here? What does he want?"

"He happened to drop in, so Frank hired him to finish our seeding."

Her father's stare hardened. "Victor happened to drop in? How did he know where you live?"

"I guess Uncle Yash told him," Tina said, watching one of the Friesens' cats stalk a robin in the grass. She hated lying to her parents. On the other hand, she couldn't tell them Victor had come because of the letters she'd written him. Her folks wouldn't understand.

Her mom frowned. "Doesn't Frank mind having your old boyfriend around the place?"

"Victor and I didn't tell Frank we used to go together."

"Didn't tell him?" Her mom's voice squeaked. "It's got to be a sin not to tell your husband something like that."

Tina sighed. Her mother was probably right. It was a sin, but what else could she do?

Her dad sucked a breath between his teeth. "It seems wrong to me. Have you prayed about it? We should pray right now."

Tina opened the car door. "Dad, there isn't time. We'll be late for the service." She got out of the car, then stuck her head back through the open door. "Look, I didn't ask Victor to come here, but he showed up at a good time. Frank enjoys having another man around the place, and the seeding is getting done without me getting burned to a frazzle. Please don't tell anyone about Vic and me. It would only cause unnecessary trouble."

Chapter 43

Frank woke to the wind flapping the blinds against the bedroom windows. The soft thump, clack, thump was irritating yet soothing at the same time.

From the chicken yard came the squawky crow of a rooster ready for another day of strutting, preening, and lovemaking. Lucky rooster. He felt like making love. Frank didn't. He hadn't for a month now.

Tina yawned, sat up in her sleeveless blue nightgown, and took a jar off her nightstand.

Frank turned away, trying not to watch his wife smooth cold cream over her shapely shoulders.

She reached across the bed and dabbed a bit of cold cream on his ear.

He grunted and wiped it off.

"What's the matter?" Tina's voice sounded girlish, teasing.

"Nothing."

"You seem cold toward me lately. Don't you find me pretty anymore?"

Of course she was pretty. She was gorgeous. But he wasn't in the mood for lovemaking. "It's seeding time," he growled. "No time for futzin'."

Tina creamed her lovely throat. "You had lots of time when I was the one driving the tractor."

"Sorry. I'm jumpy lately."

"Why?" She unbuttoned her nightgown, slipped it off her shoulders, and began creaming the tops of her full round breasts.

What could he say? He couldn't tell Tina he was jealous because their hired man took her and Klara to church every

Sunday. That was okay anyway. He knew he should take hi. family to church himself, but with Victor here, he didn't need to worry about it.

On the other hand, something was wrong. He didn't like the way Victor and Tina talked. The way they laughed at each other's jokes like they knew things he didn't. Of course they did they'd both lived in Vancouver. But there was something else Tina had a new softness in her voice, a new light in her eyes Was that because of Victor?

Frank rolled out of bed, opened a dresser drawer, and fum bled for a pair of socks. "We should be finished seeding in a week or so. Then Victor will go back to Vancouver, and we'l have the house to ourselves again." He turned and gave his wife a half-hearted wink.

Chapter 44

A warm breeze riffled through the locoweed on the north side of the machine shed, where Frank and Victor were cleaning the one-way. Frank's heart felt as light as the leaves on those weeds. The seeding was done, thank God, and Victor would be leaving for Vancouver soon.

Victor gave him a gap-toothed grin. "I feel good here. You and I get along good, *nicht?*"

"Sure, you're a great hired man. Steady, smart, cheerful. But I'm afraid I don't need you anymore. We're finished seeding."

Victor's grin faded.

Frank rummaged in his toolbox for an oil can. "I'm sorry." The sooner he got rid of the guy, the better. Victor and Tina had too much in common—church, memories of Vancouver, non-Gypsy mothers.

Frank began squirting a little oil into each seed cup to keep them from rusting. Victor took an oily cloth from the toolbox and started cleaning the disks. "I could stay and help you with the summer-fallowing."

"Nah, it's okay. I'll manage. My arm is a lot better. Those exercises you showed me really help. "

"It's funny," Victor said. "In Vancouver my nose ran in the springtime. My eyes itched till I could scratch them out. Allergies. It was the same in England, but not here."

"Maybe your allergies fixed themselves," Frank said. The dry air of the prairies might have something to do with it, but he wouldn't bother mentioning that. No point giving Victor any excuse for staying.

He and Vic soon finished with the one-way, and went into the house for coffee. Tina and Klara weren't there. They must

be out cleaning the chicken coop like Tina had said they might
But she had made coffee, and left buns and plum jam on the
table. "Time to settle up," Frank said, pouring the coffee. "How
much do you figure I still owe you?"

Victor slumped into a chair, his face as glum as ditchwater

Frank trundled down to the cellar and got his safe. Back at
the kitchen table, he unlocked the safe and counted out a handful of bills. "Do you figure that's right?"

"Yeah, sure." Victor stuffed the money into his pocket.

"I hope you understand," Frank said, locking the safe. "It
doesn't make sense for me to keep you on anymore. There isn't
enough work for both of us."

"What if your arm gets bad again? You might not find
another hired man."

Frank took a bun and split it in two. "I'll take my chances
There's more men coming home from overseas now." He spread
jam on the bun. "If I was you, I'd hightail it to Vancouver and
find a job before the returning soldiers take them all."

Victor gulped. His Adam's apple bobbed. "Some of your
granaries look kind of saggy. I could fix them for you."

Frank shook his head. "You're a city fella. Why would you
want to stay in this backwater?" If Tina was the attraction, the
guy was pathetic. Pathetic and dangerous.

Victor hunched over his coffee mug, wrapping his freckled
fingers around it. "I just started teaching Sunday School. I don't
want to leave those kids now."

"Somebody else can teach them." Frank pushed the plate
of buns toward Victor.

Vic pushed it back. "What about my stomach treatments?
I hate to think of stopping those. That doctor in Moose Jaw
really helps me."

Frank sighed. "I'm sorry. Believe me, it's better for everybody if you go."

Victor's eyelids drooped like a sick chicken's. "All right,

Frank, if that's what you want. You're the boss." He rose and
trudged to the stairway.

Listening to Vic climb the stairs, Frank wondered if he was
doing the right thing. What if there was really nothing between
Vic and Tina, and little possibility of anything? Maybe he was
sending Victor away for no good reason. There was no shortage
of work around the farm. He could certainly find enough for a
hired man to do over the summer.

On the other hand, maybe his gut feeling was reason
enough. From the rummaging sounds Frank heard upstairs, he
gathered that Vic was packing his stuff. Good. The guy would
be better off in Vancouver anyway. He was young, smart, citi-
fied. He shouldn't waste any more time around Dayspring.

Chapter 45

Tina stood in the spare room staring at the bed Victor had slept in. Its orange quilt looked forlorn without his slippers peeking out from underneath. The closet yawned like an empty cave without his shirts, trousers, belts, and boots. The suit he'd worn to church was gone. So was the blue-grey tie that almost matched his eyes.

Victor had packed and left without saying goodbye. Why? Tina had asked her husband, but he'd just grunted and said, "We don't need a hired man anymore. We're finished seeding." Was that the real reason, or had Frank and Victor fought?

A small hand tugged at her skirt. Klara peered up at Tina through her dark bangs. "When is Victor coming back?"

Tina put her arm around her daughter. "He's not coming, Sweetie. Daddy says he's going to stay with the Schellenbergs for a few days. Then he'll move back to Vancouver."

Klara sighed. "I'm lonesome for him."

Tina was lonesome for Victor, too, more lonesome than a married woman should be. She patted Klara's shoulder. "I see Victor left you the Noah's ark he made," she said in her brisk 'mommy's-in-charge' voice. She reached up to the closet shelf and brought out the bag containing the ark and its clutter of wooden animals. "Here, you can take this downstairs if you like."

"I wanna play with it here," Klara said.

"All right, but I'm going down." It was dangerous to stay here with Victor's woodsy scent still on the bedding, stirring up memories.

She'd make a pot of tea, Tina decided as she trudged down the steps. Tea always made her feel cheerier.

The fire needed more wood. She went to the lean-to to

etch some, and was surprised to see her neighbour Adeline's four-year-old standing outside her screen door, silent as an owl. What was the little boy doing here without his mother?

"Good morning, Simon," Tina said, not really expecting an answer. He hadn't learned to talk yet, though he was two months older than Klara.

Tina opened the door for the child. "Where's your mom?"

Simon's moist little lips moved like he was reading to himself.

"Yoo-hoo," Adeline called from the north pasture. "I'll be here in a minute. I just need to clean up this patch of stinkweed first." She hiked her skirt between her legs and yanked out a handful of weeds.

Tina rolled her eyes. The woman was bizarre. Who else would weed a pasture, especially on someone else's land?

She laid a hand on Simon's skinny back, steering him into the kitchen. "Can you say hello? Try."

He hitched up his overalls, which bulged around his bum because of the diaper Tina knew he wore underneath.

"Klara," she called up the stairs, "Simon's here."

She heard running feet. Then Klara appeared at the top of the steps, a grin lighting her face. She was clutching the Noah's ark in one hand, the animals in the other.

Tina hurried upstairs and helped her carry them down. As the children settled on the bottom step with the ark and animals, Tina added more wood to the fire. She was putting the kettle on when the screen door creaked open.

Adeline loped into the kitchen. "How are the Warkentins today?" She thrust a pail-full of *pyroshki* at Tina—huge turnovers of flaky pastry oozing rhubarb filling.

"Adeline, these look great," Tina said, taking the pail from her.

Her visitor plopped herself down at the kitchen table. "My son Wally is leaving for summer school at the university in Saskatoon."

"That's sudden, isn't it?" Tina said, setting some rhubar[b] turnovers on a plate.

Adeline lifted the edge of her hairnet and pushed sever[al] escaped curls under it. "This summer school class came up re[al] sudden. Wally has to go. If not, the returning soldiers will tak[e] all the places."

"What's he planning to study?"

"The insides of farm animals." Adeline beamed. "M[y] Wally is smart. He's going to learn himself up real high. Mayb[e] he'll be a vettermarion."

Tina turned away to hide her amusement. "A what?"

"A vettermarion. A doctor for cattle and horses and stuff."

"Oh." She wouldn't bother correcting Adeline. Wall[y] apparently hadn't.

Adeline grabbed a magazine off the bookshelf and fanne[d] her face with it. "Whew, it's hot in your kitchen."

Tina opened a window. "Doesn't Isaac need Wally thi[s] summer? I don't think he and Manfred can handle the sum[-]mer-fallowing alone, can they?"

"Of course not." Adeline rolled down her stockings alon[g] with the rings of elastic that held them in place. "That's why w[e] thought we'd hire Victor if he's willing."

"Victor Graf?"

"Victor who else? He's not working for Frank anymore, i[s] he?"

"No," Tina said carefully, pouring boiling water over th[e] tea leaves in the pot. "But I don't think he plans to stay aroun[d] Dayspring, does he? Isn't he going back to Vancouver?" It woul[d] be better if he did. Better for her heart and her marriage.

Adeline shook her head. "No, I don't think Victor's leaving[.] Preacher Schellenberg said he decided to stay. Maybe he has [a] sweetheart around Dayspring?"

The woman's guess had hit too close to home. Tina retreate[d] to the pantry to refill the sugar bowl. "Where would Victor fin[d] a sweetheart around here?" she called. "In the field? Behind a granary?" She returned with the bowl and set it on the table.

Adeline reached for a turnover. "Maybe in church? Maybe he's sweet on Lydia or Agatha."

"Could be." Tina hadn't thought of that. She suppressed a twinge of jealousy. "Your *pyroshki* are always so good," she remarked, changing the subject. "But I'm surprised you find time to bake them since you're still washing diapers."

Adeline grimaced, glancing from Klara's trim bum to Simon's bulky one.

Aha! Tina had hit a sore spot that time. But mixed with her sense of triumph was an unaccustomed feeling of gratitude toward her neighbour. Thanks to Adeline, Victor might soon be working only half a mile from her. It wouldn't be Tina's doing either. Not her fault, just circumstances.

Chapter 46

"Whoa, Heppner," Victor called, pulling on the grey gelding' reins.

The horse stopped with a wheezing snort, and Victor leaned on the plough handles, watching Frank stride across the Epps' potato field toward him. Thank God he and Frank were on speaking terms again. His former boss had avoided him for a few days, but their frosty relationship had thawed once Victor had started working for Adeline and Isaac.

"Do you know where Isaac is?" Frank asked, stepping over a row of dark-green potato plants. "I need to get my post-hole auger back."

"I think he's in the machine shed," Victor said. "What do you want with your auger?"

"I've gotta fix my pasture fence. Zelma broke out again."

Victor grinned. "Yeah, you better keep that ornery cow o yours out of Isaac's wheat." He jerked a nod at the Epps' west quarter. "It's growing good, *nicht*?"

"Not as good as mine."

Victor puffed out his chest. "Yeah, but look who seeded yours."

Frank laughed. "Look who taught you how."

The doors of the machine shed opened with a rumble that echoed across the potato field. Frank squinted toward the shed, shading his eyes against the sun. "There's Isaac now. See you later, Vic."

Victor watched him hurry across the field to the shed. Then he turned and pushed the plough back into the earth. "Giddyap, Heppner." Guiding the plough along behind the horse, he congratulated himself on the good job he'd done with the Warkentins' seeding. But what a shame he'd made a mess of things when it came to Tina. He should have told Frank she'd once been his girlfriend. It would have been the honourable thing to do, no matter what she said.

Of course his long-ago romance with Tina didn't matter much anymore. After their tense reunion on the driveway, he'd never mentioned it to her. More important, he wasn't in love with her anymore. He still found it hard to believe that God had brought another wonderful woman into his life.

Victor turned the horse around and started ploughing the other side of the potato row. It had been selfish of him to come to Dayspring. He realized that now. He should have left Tina strictly alone; she was another man's wife. On the other hand, God seemed to be overruling his mistake and working things out for the best. Look how Frank was changing. At the beginning he wouldn't listen when Victor tried to share his faith in Christ. Now he sometimes did. And what about Klara and the other children in the Sunday School class? Their hearts were so tender, so open to the gospel. What a joy to share it with them.

"Coffee time!" Adeline called, her voice squawking across the field. Victor looked up and saw her bustle past the clotheslines with the coffee tray. "Yoo-hoo, Isaac," she called outside the door of the machine shed.

Isaac and Frank emerged with the post-hole auger.

Victor tied Heppner to a fence post, hurried across the field, and joined the others in the cool grass beside the shed.

Adeline trampled out a nest in the grass and set her tray in it. "While Frank was in Montana," she announced, seating herself between Isaac and Victor, "Tina had no man except her dad. Then she had two men, Frank and Vic."

Adeline paused to pour the coffee. "Now Tina has only one man and I've got three." She counted them off on her fingers. "Isaac, Manfred, and Victor. Four if you wanna count Simon."

Victor leaned back on his elbows. "I'm glad you're keeping score, Addie." The woman was a scorekeeper all right. But she didn't know everything, did she? She and Isaac would sure be surprised if they knew he visited their auburn-haired daughter every time he went to Moose Jaw.

Adeline passed Frank a mug of coffee.

Frank blew on it and took a sip. "Tina and I thought we might go to the auction sale this afternoon. I'd like to buy another guitar, and she wants to take the Hudson for a spin."

From the way Isaac's jaw dropped, Victor wondered if he knew that Frank had bought Pop Wolford's car. Isaac was hard to read sometimes. *Shtelle Isaak,* the Mennonites called him Quiet Isaac. "How does she ride?" Victor asked, envy edging into his voice as he pictured the Hudson Terraplane with her shiny waterfall grille and wide blue fenders.

The corner of Frank's mouth twitched into a smile. "She rides not bad. I'd say pretty good."

"I'll bet." Victor would love to take the Hudson for a spin himself. He could almost feel her steering wheel in his hands. Maybe he'd invite himself along to the auction if Isaac could spare him for a few hours. He might find some Bible storybooks for his Sunday School class.

Chapter 47

As spring blossomed into summer, Frank often invited Victor over after the day's work was done at the Epps'. Victor was happy to go. Frank was more talkative than the Epp men, and more fun.

"I'm thinking about building a veranda," Frank announced one evening as the two of them sat on the Warkentins' porch playing checkers. "Would you want to help me? I could pay you by the hour."

"I guess I could." Victor jumped one of Frank's checkers and slid it off the board. "I'd have time once the Epps' summer-fallowing is done."

Frank gestured toward the northeast corner of the house. "I thought I'd run the veranda from that corner over to the lean-to."

Victor eyed the stretch of wall Frank indicated. "Yeah, that would work. Or you could wrap it right around the lean-to, *nicht?*"

Frank's eyebrows rode up and down. "I never thought of that. I wouldn't need the porch then, would I?"

"Nope. You could take it right out."

Frank rose and began pacing out dimensions. "I'd like to make this veranda big enough so Tina can put a table on it, a couple of chairs, even her painting easel—everything in the shade. My wife likes shade."

"I guess the sun bothers her eyes."

"Yeah," Frank said, "and you saw how her skin burns. If we had a veranda, she wouldn't be stuck in the house so much. She could paint outside, darn socks, shell peas, chop rhubarb, write letters, read. Whatever she wants."

"You could plant trees around it." Victor pictured the spruce-sheltered veranda in Vancouver, where he and Tina had spent so many happy hours.

Frank shook his head. "I'm not crazy about trees. They make a house feel too crowded." He found a stick and began sketching a plan in the bare earth near the porch.

A few minutes later Tina emerged from the house with mugs of cocoa on a tray. "That's a wonderful idea," she said when Frank had told her about the veranda. "Maybe we could plant trees around it. Maybe spruce trees? I love the sound of the wind blowing through spruce branches."

"Spruce trees!" Frank exploded. "Do you have any idea how much water spruce trees would take? Not to mention the roots growing down into the cellar. Besides, they'd block the view summer and winter."

"What view?" she murmured, handing Victor a mug of cocoa. "There's nothing to see around here except fields and pastures." She jerked a mug at Frank, sloshing cocoa onto his fingers.

Frank winced and wiped them on his trousers. "The sunset is nice tonight. Or doesn't it meet with your ladyship's approval?" His voice dripped sarcasm.

Tina sighed. "Sure the sunset looks pretty. But we'd see sunsets from our house near town, too. It's the same sun, the same sky."

Frank snorted. "Tina, I told you. I'm not moving an inch closer to Dayspring." He turned to Victor. "This wife of mine is never satisfied. I work like a serf trying to make something out of this farm. I try to give her shade with a veranda and all she can do is nag me about moving. Moving, moving, moving. Me and my farm ain't good enough for her. I'm just a Gypsy chore boy—"

"You're as good as anybody else," Victor broke in. "God loves everybody the same." His heart ached for Frank. It must be terrible, going through life feeling like you had two strikes against you. On the other hand, that was no excuse for being mean to his wife. Were those tears in Tina's eyes? Victor raised his eyebrows at her, trying to telegraph his sympathy without being too obvious about it.

Frank dragged his boot over his sketch in the earth, erasing the lines. "Do you really figure God loves everybody the same? The Mennonites around here sure don't. You must notice how they clam up every time I come around."

"It might be your imagination," Victor said. He was almost sure it was.

"Hah!" Frank's laugh was as sharp as a Russian thistle. "It sure ain't. They've been slighting me ever since I was a kid. Or outright tormenting me."

Tina laid her hand on his shoulder. "Frank, please."

"You're too sensitive," Victor said. "You're like a crayfish, crawling around with your feelers out, looking for somebody to offend you. Maybe that's why people go quiet around you, if they do."

Frank shook his head. "You never walked in my boots. You don't know what it's like."

Victor sighed. Frank was almost impossible when he got into one of his poor-me moods. There was no point staying here and getting sucked deeper and deeper into a circular argument. Victor drained his mug of cocoa. "Speaking of walking, I'd better get back to the Epps'."

As Victor headed across the north pasture, watching the sunset fade from gold-red to blue-violet, he wondered what it would take to give Frank more confidence. The guy had a lot to be confident about, but he didn't seem to realize it. On the other hand, Tina should try harder to appreciate her husband instead of complaining so much. Frank's opinion of himself might improve if she boosted his ego more.

Tina was sure different from Victor's new sweetheart, Justina. That girl was no complainer. He sighed, wishing she

was here instead of a hundred miles away in Moose Jaw. He'
love to stroll through the pasture with her, holding her sma
rosy hand, watching the breeze lift her auburn hair.

Chapter 48

Frank sat near the front window of Mah's Café, stretching his legs under the enamel table. It was good to be finished harvesting, good to be drinking coffee with his Scandinavian buddies on this dill-pickle-crisp morning. Now that the weather was cooler, the café seemed even cozier with its red lanterns hanging from the ceiling, the jukebox in the corner, the cloudy window framing the clear blue sky.

Frank's buddy Lars took a sip of his coffee. "I think you got a pretty fair crop, Frank."

"Not bad."

Sigurd plucked a toothpick from the red holder on the table. "My cousin Axel says there's not many mining jobs in Montana this fall. There's lotsa men back from the war, lookin' for employment."

"Yup." Thor sank his fork into his slice of lemon meringue pie.

That pie looked good. Frank glanced at the counter, where Ming Sun Mah sat reading his newspaper. "Hey, Ming."

Ming peered over his glasses, slim and sprightly in his green shirt and brown trousers.

"You got any more lemon meringue?"

As Ming headed for the kitchen, Frank wondered if it bothered him, being the only Chinese guy in this little fishbowl community. It must be something like being the only half-Gypsy. Everybody watched what you did, never forgetting you were different, no matter how friendly they acted.

Ming brought the pie and set it in front of Frank. As he returned to his newspaper, pushing his glasses up on his nose,

Lars leaned across the table toward Frank. "How's that red headed friend of yours?"

"Victor? Not bad. He's still working for the Epps, fixing granaries."

Lars pulled a blue polka-dotted handkerchief from his pocket and blew his nose. "Is he a pretty good carpenter? The wife wants some cupboards built."

Frank chewed a forkful of pie, pretending to consider the question. He'd learned to adjust himself to the conversational pace of the Scandinavians. They were more meditative than the Mennonites, less likely to blurt out the first thing that came into their minds. "Yeah, Vic's not a bad carpenter," Frank said after a suitable pause.

Another meditative silence followed. A fly buzzed in mindless circles, pinging against the window. Ming turned a page of his newspaper.

A moment later the door opened and the postmaster, Ross McNab, came in flapping a big brown envelope in his hand. He headed for Frank's table and handed it to him.

Frank glanced at the envelope, then flipped it over. No address, no writing at all. "What's this?"

Ross jerked his chin at it. "I put a letter in there for you, Frank. It's old news now, I guess." He looked around the table, including the other men in the conversation. "I lost a few letters last winter when I moved stuff to fix the floor. They slipped under the counter and some of them got ripped. I sorted the scraps the best I could by the handwriting."

"Thanks, Ross," Frank said. The postmaster left and Frank opened the envelope. He shook several ragged scraps of paper onto the table, immediately recognizing the rounded blue writing. He pushed his pie aside and flattened one of the scraps: Klara sure misses you. We'll both be happy wh. The sentence ended with a torn letter e. He read another scrap: the weather in Butte lately? realize you don't get much time to enjoy it. Here it's been snowi

Frank grinned at his buddies. "Letter from the wife."

Lars blew his nose again. "She musta wrote that while you were in Montana, gettin' rich."

"Musta." Frank read a few more scraps, looking for a date, then froze as he read: *Victor, remembering those foggy evenings in Vancouver, when we—*

What? Had Tina written to Victor? When? Why? She'd hardly known Vic before he'd come to Dayspring, had she? The café swirled around Frank, a blur of lanterns, jukebox, and cloudy window framing the blue sky.

Sigurd grabbed his arm. "Frank, what's the matter? You don't look good."

"N-nothing's the matter." Frank blinked, then blinked again, trying to stop the swirling. When it slowed he forced a smile. "I've just had some surprising news, that's all." He lurched out of his chair, pawing the scraps of letter back into the envelope.

Out in the street, he hurled himself into the Hudson and roared out of town, his tires spurting gravel. He jolted the car past the Hundebys' farm, hardly slowing for the potholes, then passed the Berndts' place with its neat black and white buildings. A half-mile past the Stoeszes', he turned into a farmers' pull-off and cut the engine. He dumped the contents of the brown envelope onto the seat beside him and began sorting the scraps.

The letters weren't easy to separate since each scrap had so few words on it, and Tina had written on both sides of the paper. Frank couldn't piece together her whole letter to Victor, but he read enough to make him groan. When he read *remember when we picked rose hips at the beach and you kissed me,* he whimpered and slumped over the steering wheel.

Frank sat there like a lump of clay for he didn't know how long. A magpie screamed. The wind whistled through the clover. Wild geese honked overhead, flying to wherever geese went for the winter.

He sighed, gathered the scraps of the Victor letter, and stuffed them into the envelope. Then he drove home like a man in a nightmare.

"Tina!" he called, stomping in through the lean-to. "Come here and explain this to me." He shook the Victor letter onto the kitchen table and began putting the scraps together like a jigsaw puzzle.

"I'm painting shelves," Tina called from the pantry. "Can't it wait till later?"

"No, it can't."

She emerged from the pantry, Klara tagging after her. Tina approached the table, peering at the partly put-together scraps. Her face flushed under its speckles of white paint. She nudged Klara. "Go out and play with the kitties. Daddy and I need to talk."

"I don't wanna play with the kitties."

Tina gave her a little push. "Go upstairs then. Play with your dolly."

As Klara lagged up the steps, Tina squared her shoulders like a general preparing for battle.

"You're quite the correspondent," Frank said, his voice shaking despite the sarcasm he tried to inject into it.

Tina snatched a couple of scraps off the table. "What are you doing with this letter?" Her eyes blazed with anger, blue as a gas flame. "It's not yours."

Frank pried the scraps from her hand and threw them on the table. "Of course it's not mine. Ross got it mixed up with a letter you wrote me. What were you doing writing to Victor Graf? I thought you hardly knew him before he came here."

Tina hitched up her paint-smudged trousers. "I told you. I wrote to several 'guys and gals overseas' while you were in Montana. I was trying to help the war effort."

Frank stabbed his finger at the scraps on the table. "This is no ordinary letter to a soldier. Why didn't you tell me Victor was your boyfriend?"

"He's not."

"But he was, once. How do I know you're not still—"

Her eyes flashed. "That was before I met you. You don't think you're the only boyfriend I ever had, do you?"

"No—but—but Tina, you lied to me. How could you betray me, your own husband?" He felt like he was seven years old again, screaming with fear as Mama ran away with the soldier.

Tina set her hands on her hips. "You had girlfriends besides me. You used to take Dorrie Harms to church, and to the Chinese café, and community picnics, and who knows where else? And I think you were sweet on Marya—Mara—Meeka—whatever her name is—that stringy-haired cook at the lumber camp."

"Maybe so, but I didn't write love letters to those women after I got married."

Tina gulped. "Those weren't love letters I wrote to Victor. It was just that he and I were acquainted in Vancouver, so it was only natural to write about things that happened in the city."

"Like kissing on the beach."

Her eyes darted like a gopher looking for its hole. "Frank, please try to understand. That happened before I met you."

"But why remind Victor of it after you married me?"

"Vic was lonesome. So was I. I didn't even know if you were coming home from Montana. I thought you'd found another woman. You hardly ever wrote to me."

Frank rolled his eyes. "I was working two jobs, trying to make money for my family. Pardon me for being too exhausted to pick up a pen and paper." He felt hot all over, then cold. "I'm your husband, for Pete's sake. You should have known I'd come home."

"What am I, a mind-reader? A Gypsy with a crystal ball?"

From the way Tina sucked her breath through her teeth, Frank knew she was sorry she'd said those words.

He snorted. "I'm the Gypsy, remember? I couldn't hold a kerosene lamp to a clean-blooded German like Victor. I'm surprised you haven't divorced me and married him."

"Please don't start with that Gypsy stuff again. Nobody thinks any less of you because of your mother." She reached for Frank's hand.

He jerked it away. "You do. Otherwise why did you make a fool of me when Vic showed up here? Letting me think he was an angel sent by God to help us poor farmers—"

"I thought Vic was only going to stay to help with the seeding. What was I supposed to do when he didn't leave? Make an announcement in church? Put up a poster in Mah's Café— HIRED MAN TURNS OUT TO BE LOCAL WIFE'S FORMER BOYFRIEND?"

"That's enough. Any more of your sarcasm and I'll vomit." Frank stuffed the scraps of letter into the envelope.

Tina grabbed his arm. "What are you doing?"

"Going to the Epps'." He folded the envelope in half. "I'm going to have it out with that red-headed angel of yours. Imagine, he pretended to be my friend."

"Victor wasn't pretending. He is your friend."

Frank yanked his arm out of his wife's grasp. "It makes me sick, remembering how he preached at me. 'Give your heart to Jesus. Get yourself saved. Make sure you're going to heaven.'" Frank burped. "That religion of Victor's is pretty feeble if it couldn't even make him tell the simple truth."

Tina collapsed onto a kitchen chair. "It's not feeble. There's power in it. I'm not a good Christian myself but that doesn't mean faith in Jesus isn't—"

"Your precious Vicky isn't much of an advertisement for it." Frank grabbed his jacket off the hook, put it on, and jammed the envelope into the pocket. "Imagine, he even teaches Sunday School. Who knows what he fills those innocent kids' minds with? My poor daughter—"

Tina pressed her hands against her temples. "Please don't blame Victor. This whole thing is my fault. I begged him not to tell you about us."

"Why?"

"I didn't want to cause unnecessary trouble."

Frank wheeled toward the door. "I'll show you trouble." He stomped out through the lean-to and slammed the door behind him.

Chapter 49

"Klara," Tina called up the stairs. "Come down here right away please."

"Why?"

"We're going to the Epps'." Tina dashed up the steps, grabbed Klara's hand, and hurried her down.

"Mommy, don't go so fast. I wanna get my dolly."

"You don't need your dolly. Here, let's put your jacket on." Tina snatched it off its hook and shoved her daughter's arms into it. "We've gotta run and catch Daddy."

She rushed the little girl outside. As they hurried along the north pasture fence after Frank, Tina's heart pounded so hard, her eardrums hurt. She'd deceived her husband; she couldn't deny that. She'd had good reasons, or what seemed like good reasons at the time, but the situation had backfired on her. Her marriage would never be the same again.

Tina steered Klara around a badger hole. *Dear God*, she prayed, *please help Frank calm down. And please don't let him hurt Victor.* As she and Klara passed the Epps' pond-like dugout, she stopped praying. She'd almost forgotten: she wasn't on speaking terms with the Lord anymore.

Maybe he'd take pity on her anyway.

By the time she and Klara reached the Epps' yard, gasping for breath, Frank was on their porch, banging on the door. "Adeline." His voice rumbled across the yard. "I've gotta see Victor. It's an emergency."

"Frank," Tina called, hurrying Klara around the shrivelled vegetable garden, "we need to talk." She needed to explain herself, but how?

She dashed to the porch and up the steps. But before she

reached Frank, Adeline opened the door, bulky in a brown housedress with a denim apron over it. "Victor's not here," Adeline squawked. "He caught a ride to town with the Lindbergs."

A current of relief flickered through Tina's veins. It would take Frank nearly an hour to catch up with Victor. His anger might cool in that time.

Frank turned and hurled himself down the porch steps, almost knocking Tina over.

"Wait," Adeline called. "Victor said he's not staying in town. He's taking the train to Moose Jaw."

Tina's heart jumped. If Victor got to the city before Frank found him, he'd be safe. Safer anyway, harder for her husband to find.

Frank frowned over his shoulder. "What does he want in Moose Jaw? Doctoring again?"

Adeline wiped her hands on her apron. "I think he went for stomach treatments, but there might be something else, too. He said he'd be gone a week, maybe more."

"Thanks." Frank turned and bounded across Adeline's garden, heading toward the pasture.

"Not over my rhubarb," she wailed. "Come back here. Maybe I can help."

"No time," Frank barked over his shoulder.

Tina and Klara hurried after him, careful to avoid Adeline's rhubarb. By the time they reached their own yard, Frank was in the car, revving up the engine. He scowled at Tina and rolled down the window. "Get Manfred Epp to help you with the chores."

"Please don't . . . go." Tina felt like her lungs would burst from running. "I need to—talk to you." She grasped the driver's door handle. "I love you."

Frank locked the door and set his elbow over the lock.

"Daddy!" Klara called.

Frank leaned out the window. "Be a good girl, Princess."

He kissed one of her round brown cheeks, then the other. "Tell the truth. Always tell the truth. Lies are poison." He gave Tina a long look, his eyes like a wounded animal's. Before she could think what to say, he stepped on the gas and roared away.

Chapter 50

The days after Frank left were anguish for Tina. Why didn't he come home, or at least write to her? Where was he? Still in Moose Jaw, or had he gone somewhere else?

She'd betrayed Frank, at least according to him, but she needed him. Her heart never stopped aching unless she was asleep. Even then the nightmares came. Sometimes she dreamed she was still living at her uncle and aunt's in Vancouver. She dreamed Frank was writing to her, letter after letter. Each letter was colder and more impersonal than the last. In her dream, Frank was never proposing to her, just letting her grow old and grey on her relatives' veranda, alone. Waves of nausea sometimes woke Tina from this dream, and she hurried out to the backhouse to vomit.

Every afternoon she and Klara rode the mare, Reyna, to Lindbergs' post office and store to look for a letter from Frank. But after a week, the bounce and sway of horseback-riding upset Tina's stomach too much, so she asked Manfred Epp to bring her mail and groceries when he came to do the chores.

Tina began to wonder if she could be pregnant. No, not if there was any justice in the world. A pregnancy now would be too much on top of everything else.

If only she knew where Frank was. His friends might know, but how could she get in touch with them? She couldn't phone. The wind had blown the phone line down again. If she got herself to Dayspring, she might discover something. But how could she do that? The wagon was in the shed but Reyna couldn't pull it by herself, and Tina knew she couldn't force the bit between Maynard's stubborn teeth. She didn't trust herself to take the truck; she'd never driven it on the road before.

After ten days without a word from Frank, Tina swallowed her pride, left Klara with Leif Lindberg's wife, and caught a ride to town with Leif.

Leif dropped her off in front of the Co-op store with its broken brown shutters. She stood on the sidewalk scanning the main street, looking for someone who might know her husband's whereabouts. Someone she could ask without feeling like a fool. Maybe Sigurd Olsen. "Do you know where Sigurd is?" she asked Ross McNab when he ambled out of the Co-op with a box of groceries.

"Try the Chinese café," Ross said, shifting his grip on the box. A milk bottle clinked. "Sigurd was out with the dray wagon this morning, but I think he's finished hauling water now. Prob'ly having coffee."

Tina hurried to the café. As she creaked the door open, all conversation stopped. Had the customers been gossiping about her and Frank? She could just imagine what they'd been saying: *Poor Tina. Frank probably left her. Otherwise he'd be back by now. She's probably pregnant. See how flushed her cheeks are. See how her eyelids droop.*

Tina squared her shoulders and strode into the café, trying not to look like an object of pity. She scanned the tables and booths, and caught sight of Sigurd's blond head. As she sauntered toward him, trying to appear relaxed, a muscle in the corner of her eye jumped. "Sigurd, how's it going?"

"Not bad." He half-rose, shifting his toothpick to the west side of his mouth. "How're you doing, Tina?"

"Fine." Her eye muscle jumped again. "I wonder, could you come outside and help me for a minute?"

Out in the vacant lot, Sigurd stood staring down at his boots.

"You probably know," she began, "that Frank left home on important business."

"Yup." Sigurd gnawed on his toothpick.

"He wanted to see Victor Graf. Did he?"

"Nope," Sigurd said. "Missed him."

"How come? Frank must have been in town by train time."

"Yeah, but Vic had already left for Moose Jaw. He caught a ride with the Sorensons. They hadda take their kids to the dentist."

Tina's eye muscle relaxed. At least there hadn't been a noisy, bloody confrontation in the streets of Dayspring. "Do you know where Frank is now?"

Sigurd shrugged. "He drove to Moose Jaw as far as I know."

"Is he still there?"

"Sorry, I didn't hear from him."

She sighed. "Okay, thanks. Thanks anyway."

Sigurd waved his toothpick at her. "You bet."

As he clumped back into the café, Tina hurried across the street to the telephone office. She asked the operator to connect her with her father-in-law in Calgary, then stepped into an empty booth. "Hello, Dad," she said when Frank's father came on the line. "Frank left Dayspring to take care of important business in Moose Jaw. Did he happen to phone you?"

"No, but he dropped in," Herb shouted. He always shouted during long-distance phone conversations because they cost so much.

"Dropped in? In Calgary?"

"Yeah, here in Calgary." Herb's voice rumbled like Frank's, but it was twice as loud. "Frank's business didn't go so good in Moose Jaw, so he came here for a visit."

Tina pursed her lips, mulling over the situation. If Frank didn't plan on coming home, why would he visit his dad and stepmother? They'd tell him to go home unless he'd managed to turn them against her.

"Is everything all right?" Herb shouted. "Klara okay?"

"We're as well as can be expected." Tina summoned all her courage. "Could I please speak to Frank?"

"He's not here."

Her shoulders sagged. "Where is he?"

"Went to the lumber camp," Herb bellowed. "He said he needed to see somebody."

Nausea swirled through Tina's stomach. What did Frank want at the lumber camp? A job? If he got one, he'd probably be away all winter. Tears gathered in her eyes. "Listen, Dad, do you have a phone number for the camp?"

"No, sorry."

"A mailing address?" Tina asked, rummaging through her purse for her pen and a piece of paper.

"Wait. I'll find my glasses."

Tina peered out through the door of the booth. The clock above the switchboard said twenty minutes after three. She didn't have much time. She was supposed to meet Leif at three-thirty.

When her father-in-law came back on the line, she scribbled down the address and said a hasty goodbye. Outside, she hurried along the main street looking for Leif. Maybe he was on the train platform getting the mail bags. No, nobody there, nobody except a short broad man with a knapsack on his back. A man with flaming red hair. Tina's breath caught. Victor! She hurried across the platform to him, relieved to see that his eyes weren't blackened as she'd thought they might be. Every tooth was accounted for in his gap-toothed grin. "You're back," she blurted.

"Yup, back in God's country. Do you know where the Epps are? They're supposed to pick me up."

"No, sorry. Did you happen to see Frank in Moose Jaw?"

Victor raised his eyebrows. "Frank? Should I have seen him?"

"I thought you might have. He was looking for you." Tina glanced around to check that nobody was listening. "I need to talk to you."

"What about?"

"A personal matter," Tina said. "I can't discuss it here."

Concern clouded Victor's freckled face. "I could come over this evening after the Epps' chores are done."

"Okay, I'll see you then."

Tina left the platform and hurried along the main street, watching for Leif and wondering what Victor would think when he discovered that Frank wasn't home yet. The Epps were sure to tell him, first thing. Maybe Vic would consider it improper to visit her when her husband wasn't there. But where else could the two of them talk? Not at the Epps' for sure.

Chapter 51

Klara twisted her small hand out of Tina's. "I don't wanna go to sleep. It's not night yet."

"It's almost night," Tina said, pointing out the kitchen window. "See, the sun's going down." She wanted to get Klara to bed before Victor arrived. The evening would be complicated enough as it was.

Klara squinted at the dishes Tina had set on the table. "Why did you put the pretty cups on? Is Daddy coming home tonight?"

"No, he isn't." Tina's voice sounded sharper than she intended. She softened it. "I don't know when your daddy's coming home. He didn't say."

"I hope he comes soon. I wanna show him my necklace."

The rosehip necklace hung around Klara's neck, gleaming orange-red in the light from the window. "It was nice of Mrs Lindberg to help you make such a pretty necklace," Tina said. "I bet it'll look nice with your blue nightgown. Shall we go upstairs and see?"

Klara fingered the necklace, her forehead furrowed with concentration, then sighed and followed Tina to the staircase.

As Tina followed her daughter up the stairs, her mind drifted to the rosehip necklace Victor had made for her at the beach in Vancouver. He'd strung the rosehips with careful hands, like a surgeon's, his needle piercing each one through the heart. He'd tied the ends of the thread, hung the necklace around her neck, and kissed her—a long tender kiss. Then they'd strolled along the beach with their arms around each other, happy as sand fleas.

Tina shook her head to dislodge the memory and followed Klara into her room. She helped her daughter change into the blue nightgown and held the mirror so Klara could see how nice the necklace looked with it. "All right, Sweetie," she said. "Say your prayer and I'll tuck you into bed."

Klara knelt beside the bed, her dark curls silky against the sheets. "Now I lay me down to sleep. I pray the Lord my soul to keep." The child's shoulder blades quivered and Tina felt a wave of remorse. She simply had to stop daydreaming about Victor. It wasn't fair to Klara or Frank. On the other hand, how fair had Frank been to her? He should have tried harder to understand why she'd written to Vic. She and Frank might have worked things out if he'd stayed here instead of raging away like a mad bull. Why didn't he at least write and say where he was, for Klara's sake if not her own?

The little girl had stopped praying.

Tina leaned over her. "Did you forget the words? 'If I should die before—'"

"No, no." Klara shook her shoulders. "I said that part already. I want to ask God something else."

This daughter of hers was no creature of mindless ritual. "All right but hurry, okay. I've got things to do."

Klara hauled in her breath. "Please bring Daddy home." She gulped. "And please help Mommy and Daddy not to fight. A-MEN!"

"Amen to that," Tina murmured as Klara scrambled into bed.

When Tina answered Victor's knock at the door, his breath was misting out white in the chilly air. "Are you sure you didn't see Frank in Moose Jaw?" she asked, leading him into the kitchen.

"No, I didn't. The last I saw Frank was at the Epps' wiener roast."

Tina pulled out a chair for Victor, her spirits lifting a little. Vic evidently had no idea how angry Frank was at him. She sat down, served the tea and cookies, and told Vic the story, careful not to mention her fears about Frank not returning home. Of course her husband would come home. Sooner or later.

On the other hand, what might Frank do when he saw Victor? When she told Vic about her concern for his safety, she was surprised that he didn't seem too worried. "Frank and I will talk things over," he said, brushing cookie crumbs off his fingers. "We'll understand each other, *nicht?*"

Tina's heart lurched. How could Victor treat the situation so lightly? Was he that good an actor, that he could pretend to Frank that he wasn't in love with her? Of course nothing could come of Victor's love. She'd made that clear from the day he'd arrived at Dayspring. On the other hand, she'd come to depend on Vic's love. Just knowing it existed made her feel more attractive and confident.

Victor was still talking but she wasn't listening. She blinked. "Sorry. You were saying?"

"I said I hope Frank gets home before I leave for Vancouver."

Tina jerked her head up. "You're going to Vancouver? For a visit?"

"No, to stay." Victor gave her a gap-toothed grin. "Your Uncle Yash got me a job at Vancouver General Hospital."

Tina felt like the ceiling was caving in on her. "But—but— I thought you liked it here. You're part of the community now. What will the church do without you?" The shrillness in her voice made her cringe.

"The church got along fine before I came. It'll get along after I leave."

Tina tried for a mellower tone of voice. "What are you going to do at Vancouver General? There aren't many jobs left, with all the military personnel coming home."

Victor's eyes shone. "Your uncle talked the hospital into hiring me to supervise all the orderlies, because of my experience and service in the army. Isn't that great?"

"Sure, Vic, great." Tina managed a weak smile.

"Who knows? I might even 'learn myself up higher,' as Adeline would say. "I could become a doctor someday. I'm not old yet. I'm only twenty-seven."

"No, you're not old." Tina forced another smile. "I'm thirty and I don't feel old." But she did. And what Victor said next made her feel even older.

Chapter 52

Tina couldn't sleep that night. When she lay on her right side the moonlight irritated her, seeping in around the window blinds. When she lay on her left side, her arm seemed to be in the way. She couldn't find a comfortable position for it.

She tossed from one side to the other, her mind chewing over what Victor had told her. She should be happy for him, happy he'd found a girl who loved him as he deserved to be loved. She herself had never given Victor her whole heart. He'd been a friend, possibly the best friend she'd ever had. But she'd cheapened that friendship by using his love to prop up her own ego. That wasn't fair to Victor or to Frank. She was a terrible person who deserved to lose them both.

But she loved Frank. Tina reached under the pillows and pulled out his green pajamas. She buried her face in the soft flannel, recalling the last time they'd made love in this bed. After the act, lying in the darkness beside Frank, she'd wondered if she'd moved him to the core of his being, as he had her. She'd doubted it and felt empty inside, like she'd lost a piece of herself and Frank had that piece.

She hated to admit it to herself, but she'd often felt empty lying next to her husband. She'd never been sure of his love. From the beginning he'd kept her off balance, taking forever to propose, dithering over Dorrie Harms. It was her insecurity about Frank that had led her to reassure herself with Victor's love. But that love had turned out to be an illusion. He loved Justina Epp, not her. And Frank was disgusted with her deception and might never come home.

Tina rolled over for the fiftieth time, the bed-sheet dragging at her shoulders. Did God care about a dishonest, selfish woman on a wilderness farm with only her daughter, the brute animals, and Manfred Epp for company? A pregnant woman? Imagine how the tongues would wag once she started to show. Dayspring gossips could be cruel. *Whose baby is it? It might not be Frank's. Otherwise he'd be here, wouldn't he? It could be Victor's baby. Maybe that's why he went to Vancouver.*

A wave of nausea rolled up from Tina's stomach. She hung her head over the edge of the bed. She should get the chamber pot or walk out to the backhouse. On the other hand, what did it matter if she threw up on the rug? It would match the mess she'd made of her life.

Chapter 53

By the first week of October, Frank still wasn't home, so Tina put on an old pair of his overalls and went out to dig the last of the potatoes. The simple rhythm of the job soothed her troubled spirit. First came the moment of anticipation as she thrust the potato fork into the earth beside one of the dried-up plants. Then the moment of revelation as she flipped the fork over and saw the potatoes poking through the soil like little bald heads. At last the moment of fruition when she picked them up and threw them into the gunny sack.

Life should be more like this, Tina thought. Straightforward, with less anxiety about the future.

She leaned on the potato fork to look out at the road. Watching for Frank's car had become a ritual, almost meaningless after three weeks with no sign of the blue Hudson.

She stared at the dusty road running ribbon-like between the weedy ditches. It was empty. With a sigh, she turned and thrust the potato fork back into the earth. As she flipped the fork over, the corner of her eye caught a flash of blue. She whirled around and saw a blue vehicle passing the school, heading in her direction. Her heart quivered. Was that Frank's car? It looked like the Hudson: wide fenders, waterfall grille.

She dropped the potato fork and headed for the driveway. Straining her eyes for a first glimpse of her husband, she hurried across the shrivelled vegetable garden, where Klara was making a nest of dry corn stalks. Would Frank be frowning or smiling when she saw him? Her heart raced with anxiety and anticipation. The Hudson turned into the driveway and Klara erupted from her nest of cornstalks. "Daddy!" She sprinted toward the car, her dark curls flying. "Daddy! It's Daddy's car!"

The little girl skidded to a stop.

Tina swayed on her feet, her heartbeat stuttering. Who was that driving Frank's car? Not Frank. No, it was a younger man. Ruddy face, hair the colour of sawdust. Manfred Epp. Why? Where was her husband?

Manfred pulled the Hudson up beside Klara, braked, and cut the engine. "Hey there, Princess." He slid out of the driver's seat, reaching out to rumple the child's hair.

Klara ducked away and ran to Tina, who stood in the garden like a pillar of salt. Was this somebody's idea of a joke? Maybe God's.

Manfred climbed out of the car and stumped toward her, dangling the car keys from his hand. "Frank—um. He said—um—you might as well use the Hudson. You can still drive it awhile before the roads get snowed in."

Frank said? That meant Manfred must have seen Frank, talked to him. Tina reached for the keys, trying for a neutral expression. "Thanks, Manfred. Did Frank happen to mention how his business is going?"

Manfred kicked at a clod of earth. "I didn't see Frank."

"Didn't see him? So how'd you get his car?"

"Sigurd give it to me. He said Frank said to bring it to you."

A chimney fire of anger roared up from Tina's stomach. That husband of hers, what a coward. He'd talked to Sigurd but he hadn't found a way to talk to her, his own wife.

Manfred cleared his throat. "Do you need me to do the chores tonight?"

For a wild moment Tina thought of saying, *No, Manfred, hang the cows. Hang the chickens. Hang the horses. Hang the potatoes. Hang everything. Klara and I don't need Frank or the farm. We'll run away to Vancouver, where Uncle Yash and Aunt Irmie will help us start a wonderful new life. You'll see.* Instead she murmured, "Yes, if you would, please."

Chapter 54

At two-thirty that afternoon, Tina pulled the Hudson up in front of the Chinese café, her heart lifting with pride. She'd driven all the way to Dayspring, twelve miles. It was the farthest she'd ever driven a motor vehicle. She turned to Klara, who sat beside her clutching her rag doll, Lois. "I'm going into the café for a few minutes, okay?" She kissed the top of her daughter's head. "You stay here and take care of your dolly."

Tina walked into Mah's Café with a firm step, glad she'd worn her blue suit and rayon stockings. Nice clothes always gave her confidence. She scanned the tables and booths, looking for Sigurd. He must know her husband's whereabouts.

"Tina," Frank's buddy Lars called from a booth near the back, "how are you doing?"

"Not bad." Tina stepped toward him, her high-heeled shoes clicking on the linoleum floor. "Klara and I are going to the Lutheran Church bazaar, but I need to see Sigurd first. Do you know where he is?"

"Could be out with the dray wagon." Lars glanced at Thor, who sat across from him. "Have you got any idea where Sigurd is?"

Thor scratched one of his woolly eyebrows. "He mighta quit early and went home." He paused. "Now that he's got help."

"Help?" Tina stared at Thor. "Who's helping Sigurd?" As far as she knew, he ran the dray business by himself. His horses and wagon were a familiar sight around town, delivering freight and water.

Thor jerked his head toward the door. "Tina, you better come outside a minute."

Out on the sidewalk, Thor blurted, "Sigurd's got Frank workin' for him."

"Frank?" Tina's stomach dropped to her ankles. Frank was right here in Dayspring? Why hadn't somebody told her he was back from BC? Why hadn't he told her himself instead of letting her hear it second-hand? He was making a fool of her.

Thor dragged his boot along a crack in the sidewalk. "Yup. Frank didn't find a job in BC, so he come back here and Sigurd hired him."

"Is—that so," Tina stammered. "Th—thanks, Thor. Thanks a lot."

Why hadn't Frank come home, where he belonged? she asked herself, watching Thor clod back into the café. Was her husband still mad at her? Where had he been living since he'd been back?

Enough questions without answers. She hurried to the Hudson, got in, and roared the car along the main street.

"Mommy!" Klara yelped over the squeal of the tires. "Why are you driving so fast?"

"Hang on, Kiddo. We're going to find that daddy of yours. And when we do, he's going to have some explaining to do."

Chapter 55

Frank steered the dray wagon into the alleyway behind Petersons' Farm Supply, enjoying the steady clopping of the horses' hooves. The water tank seemed like a pot-bellied friend, riding along behind him. This new job was working out fine, even if some people he delivered water to were less pleasant than others. Roland Fast for one.

The Fasts' house loomed ahead of him now, the tallest one in town. The afternoon sun glinted on its ridiculous stained-glass windows: gold, green, blue, pink. What a showoff, that Roland. How was he going to belittle Frank this time? He always found a way.

Oh well, might as well get the ordeal over with. Frank urged the horses forward. As he approached the Fasts' fence with its silly flower-shaped medallions, he heard a car pull up behind him. He steered the wagon to the edge of the alleyway to let it pass.

It didn't pass. Instead, it crept up beside him, its engine purring like a cat. Frank peered over his shoulder and jumped like he'd been scalded. What was Tina doing here? In the Hudson? She must have driven all the way to town. How had she managed that? She'd never driven more than two or three miles before.

Their little daughter, Klara, leaned out through the passenger window, looking like a doll with her curls tumbling over the collar of her green coat. "Daddy!"

Her sweet voice pierced Frank's heart. He'd missed his baby, missed her sparkling laughter, her chocolate eyes gazing at him like he was the world's most wonderful dad. He longed to tell her he loved her, that he would always love her even though he didn't live at home anymore. But he couldn't yell that out here, now, with his wife and maybe the Fasts listening.

Tina waved at him, smiling like nothing was wrong.

A sauerkraut soup of anger seethed in Frank's stomach. Tina had made a fool of him, writing love letters to another man. He should have realized sooner that she'd end up hurting him like his mama had. Tina hadn't deserted him physically like his mama, but she'd abandoned him in her heart, in her spirit.

Tina stopped the car and got out. "Listen, Frank," she said, leaning across the Hudson's blue roof. "I'm sorry I wrote to Victor." She hesitated. "He doesn't mean a thing to me, not anymore."

"Why are you bothering me?" Frank growled. "Can't you see I'm working?" He didn't want to talk to her; the pain was still too fresh. He clucked to the horses. "Vang, Slidre, let's go."

"Daddy!" Klara called, her flute-like voice clear and high. "Don't go."

"Giddyap!" Frank shook the horses' reins. It hurt him to leave his daughter, but he couldn't risk a fight with Tina behind the Fasts' house. He could just hear Roland: *What a pity you Warkentins can't get along together. Dorrie and I are still crazy about each other. We feel like we're still on our honeymoon.*

Frank flapped the horses' reins against their broad brown rumps. "Move."

He had to get away from Tina. He reached under the seat, found the whip, and flicked it across the horses' rumps.

They snorted and clumped forward.

Tina got back into the Hudson and motored along beside the wagon.

Frank urged the team past the Fasts' woodshed with its silly rooftop garden. "Come on, you bangtails. Move."

As the horses passed the vacant lot beyond the Fasts', Tina leaned across Klara and called through the passenger window,

"Frank, if you won't talk to me, at least give your daughter a hug. She's been terribly lonesome for you."

"Daddy," Klara piped up, "I wanna ride on the wagon."

He sat still a moment, considering. "I guess that would be okay." It would give him a chance to talk to the child.

He reined the horses in and his daughter scrambled out of the car. Tina led her to him and lifted her into his arms. He kissed Klara's cheek, breathing her familiar scent. Soap and coriander. Her soft hair tickled his face. "Tell Mommy you and I will finish the water route," he said, setting her on the seat beside him. "Then we'll meet her at the park."

Klara wrinkled her nose. "You tell her, Daddy. Mommy's right here—"

"Okay," Tina broke in, "I'll see you at the park." As she stepped back to the car, a sudden roar shattered the quiet of the alleyway. Frank wheeled around and saw a motorcycle barrelling into the alley, its tires spraying gravel. The rider crouched low over the handlebars, a leathery-looking fellow with a scowl on his face.

"Tina, look out!" Frank yelled.

She flattened herself against the Hudson.

The motorcycle vroomed between the car and the wagon, clipping one of the wagon wheels. The water tank groaned, rocking from side to side. Vang whinnied and reared onto his hind legs.

"Easy, Vang, down." Frank hauled back on the reins.

The motorcycle swerved into the vacant lot, bounced over clumps of weeds, and backfired. The sound was like a gun-shot. Vang leapt forward, breaking into a gallop, pulling Slidre along with him. Tina shrieked as the wagon lurched sideways, then bounded ahead. Klara clutched Frank's jacket, sobbing and screaming.

"Get down," Frank yelled. "Sit on the wagon bed." Klara was too small and light to stay on the seat.

Klara scrambled down and he wedged her between his shins. "That's right," he yelled. "Hang onto my legs."

Frank caught a flash of movement to his right. A portly figure was dashing up beside the wagon, blond hair flying. Roland Fast. For once Frank was glad to see the snob. Maybe Roland could help stop these crazy horses.

Frank pulled on the reins. "Calm yourselves," he called. "You're okay. It was just a bit of noise."

Roland was gaining on the wagon, hauling air in loud gulps.

Frank lurched to his feet, braced himself against the wagon frame, and strained at the horses' reins. "Whoa." If he could just slow them, there was a chance Roland could grab Vang's harness.

Frank might as well have been yelling at the wind. The team plunged ahead, leaving Roland in the dust. With a jolt the wagon hurtled onto the street and hit a pothole. The water tank shifted and slipped its moorings. As it rolled off, the wagon bed tilted and Frank skidded across the seat, feeling Klara dragging along with him. "Whoa," he roared.

The horses sped forward and the wagon settled back onto its wheels, thank God. Klara was still clinging to Frank's legs, though she was screeching like a bobcat.

As the team stampeded toward the skating rink, Frank remembered a trick his dad had taught him. He pulled first on the horses' right reins, then on their left. Maybe the seesaw motion would distract them from their desperate race. Or maybe not.

Chapter 56

Tina froze against the car, horrified to see the horses and wagon disappear behind the skating rink. Her daughter's voice echoed into the distance. Then Tina heard a crash like boxes falling.

Moments later relief almost choked her when Frank's wagon emerged from a cloud of dust south of the rink. It was still in one piece and he was still on it. But the horses were speeding up, plunging into the Knutsons' whiskery stubble field.

"Get in the car," Roland yelled, running toward her.

She'd barely slid into the passenger seat before Roland hurled himself in on the driver's side. He powered up the Hudson and roared it along the alleyway toward the street.

"Dear God," Tina prayed above the squealing of the tires. "Oh God, oh God, please stop those horses. Please don't let Klara and Frank get killed." The car careened around the water tank that lay in the street, and she clutched the dashboard, stifling a scream. Roland leaned forward like a race-car driver and vroomed onto the road that ran past the field. Tina scanned the stubble and spotted a yellow-grey blur bouncing across the field. Through the dust she saw Frank pulling on the horses' reins.

But nobody sat beside him. Where was Klara? Tina's heart almost stopped. Had her daughter been thrown off the wagon? Was she lying in the field somewhere, injured, crying for her mommy? Or worse, not crying? "Please, no."

Roland tramped on the gas and the car shot ahead. Moments later, it was passing the wagon, then the team. Tina craned her neck, watching them disappear in a whirl of dust.

Just short of the hill that led down to Knutson Lake, Roland rammed his foot on the brake, grinding the Hudson to a halt. He threw the driver's door open and leapt out.

Tina jumped out on the passenger side.

Roland ran into the stubble field. Tina hesitated an instant, then followed him.

She could hear hoof-beats. Then the horses came pounding through a fog of dust, the wagon rattling along behind them. Frank was still on the seat, thank God, but still no Klara.

Roland dashed through the stubble, waving his arms at the approaching team. "Whoa, Vang. Whoa, Slidre."

Tina followed, praying that the horses would stop before they plunged down the hill to Knutson Lake. The wagon was no match for that terrain. Frank might get thrown off and hurt, or even drowned in the lake.

Vang and Slidre were so close now, she could see the whites of their eyes. Foam sprayed from their mouths. Lather streaked their necks. They were finally slowing, evidently tiring.

"Whoa," Roland roared, wind-milling his arms.

"Whoa," Tina called. "For the love of God, whoa."

Vang whinnied and veered away from her and Roland. The wagon wheels squealed, ploughing sideways into the soft earth. Slidre stumbled. Frank dragged on the reins, and the horses' pace slackened to a trot. Dust settled around them like feathers from a quilt. Then a child's wail floated across the stubble.

"Thank the Lord," Tina murmured, seeing Klara scramble up from the wagon bed.

"Mommy!" the child screamed, her face streaked with dust and tears.

Tina dashed after the moving wagon, reaching for her daughter.

"Easy, Vang, Slidre." Frank's rumbling voice. "Steady, boys. That's right."

Roland ran up alongside Vang and grabbed his belly band. The team lurched to a halt, their sides heaving.

Sobbing with relief, Tina caught up to the wagon and gathered Klara into her arms.

Frank stepped off the wagon, handed the reins to Roland and threw his arms around his wife and daughter. "Klara, you're a brave—little kid," he gasped. "Mommy's—brave, too."

Tina smiled through her tears and Frank elbowed her in the ribs. "Or maybe Mommy's just foolhardy." He glanced at Roland. "How's our rescuer?"

"Just winded, I think."

Frank gave him a sheepish grin. "You saved our lives, guess. How can I thank you?"

"Go home with your wife and daughter. That's all the thanks I need."

A dark-red flush of anger crept up Frank's neck into his face

Tina bit her lip, tasting dust and tears. Roland was trying to help her, but he was going about it the wrong way. Frank didn't like him; everyone knew that. Whatever Roland said, Frank would feel like doing something else.

Vang whinnied and took a step forward.

"Whoa, Boy." Roland pulled back on the reins. As he crooned to the horse, stroking his steaming side, Tina heard a vehicle roaring along the road. She squinted against the late afternoon sun and saw Frank's employer, Sigurd Olsen, parking his truck behind the Hudson.

Sigurd got out of the truck. "Dorrie phoned," he called. "She said you had a runaway. Is everybody okay?"

"We're alive anyway," Frank answered, "thanks to Roland."

"I'm glad to hear it." Sigurd clumped across the field toward them, chewing on a toothpick.

"I think the wagon's still in one piece," Frank said as his boss approached.

Sigurd kicked the wheels and peered at the axles, then inspected the hitch. "Yup." He switched the toothpick to the other side of his mouth. "It's not too bad. A little fixing here and there."

"The horses look okay, too," Tina volunteered. Not that she was an expert.

Sigurd patted Slidre's heaving flank. "Yeah, I think they just need rubbing down and blanketing. Frank, do you wanna help me get them to the barn?"

No, please no, Tina's heart begged. She and Klara hadn't seen Frank for weeks. The three of them needed to talk, hug, get reconnected as a family. She couldn't let Sigurd take her husband away so soon.

She raised her eyebrows at Roland. "Do you think you could help Sigurd with the horses?"

"Sure, I don't mind. Frank, you go home with your girls."

Would her husband do that? Tina wondered, watching Roland and Sigurd leave with the team and wagon. Had the near-accident made Frank realize how much he loved her? She gave him a timid smile, feeling like a girl on a first date.

He avoided her eyes, brushing dust off Klara's coat. "How do you feel, Princess?"

"I'm tired, Daddy."

Frank squeezed her hand. "Me, too. I'd better get to Sigurd's house and catch some sleep."

Sigurd's house? No. Tina gathered all her courage. "Frank, your bed is waiting for you at home."

The corner of his mouth twitched. "I've got a bed at Sigurd's. Room and board go with the job."

A volcano of anger erupted from Tina's stomach, pushing words out before she could weigh them. "You're a married man. You should sleep at home."

He backed away from Tina, dropping Klara's hand.

Tina wanted to follow and throw herself at Frank, cry, plead. But those tactics didn't work with her husband. They never had. What did work? She'd been married to the guy for five years and she still didn't know.

The sun was setting, blood-red on the horizon. Klara trembled with cold or shock, maybe both. Tina carried her to the Hudson and tucked her into the back seat with a blanket around her.

"Come on," she called to Frank. "Let's go. Klara needs he
dad."

He stood in the stubble field like a botched sculpture, hi
arms awkward at his sides. There was something lonesome
about Frank. There always had been. Had she ever touched the
core of that loneliness and eased the pain deep inside him? She
doubted that she had. Not enough anyway. Maybe she wasn'
the right woman for Frank. A different woman might have given
him more of what he needed, with a lot less effort. But she loved
him and clung to the belief that he still loved her.

Tina took the car key from the ignition and plodded across
the stubble toward him, dangling the ring of keys from her out
stretched hand. "I guess you'd better drive. I doubt if I can turn
the car around so close to that hill." She probably could, but
her pride in doing so would be hollow without Frank beside
her. She jingled the keys. "Let's go home. Klara's cold."

He followed her to the Hudson without a word.

Chapter 57

Tina's eyes were sore and red at breakfast the next morning. She wiped them on the hem of her apron.

Frank scowled at her, his face more wrinkled than she remembered. "It's not my problem if you're crying for your sweetheart Victor." He stabbed at the sausage on his plate. Missed. It slithered off the plate, bounced onto the floor, and rolled under his chair. He cursed and Tina flinched like she'd been slapped. She'd never heard her husband use such strong language.

She reached under Frank's chair and picked up the sausage. "I'm not crying for Victor." She handed him the sausage, not bothering to wipe it off or rinse it. "I'm exhausted. You kept me awake all night, wandering around the house."

"I couldn't sleep. Why do you keep that stupid corduroy cushion on the couch? It's as lumpy as a sack of kittens."

"Don't blame me. Your stepmother left it there and you decided to sleep on it." If Frank didn't like the cushion, he could have asked her for a pillow. Or he could have slept in his own bed. With her.

Frank fetched the corduroy cushion from the living room and tossed it to her. "Put it in the rag bag. It gave me a headache. By the time I found a decent pillow, I was wide awake. Then I went looking for liniment for my sore neck. Of course you hid the liniment bottle again, so I gave up and made myself some hot milk and honey. I still couldn't sleep so I—"

"Okay, okay, I get the idea. I was up with Klara anyway. She was having nightmares."

The wrinkles in Frank's forehead softened. "Poor kid. Is she sleeping?"

"Yes, thank God." Tina sighed and pushed her plate away.

She'd thought she could eat a sausage, but now it was turning her stomach. She rose, got a jar of plums from the cellar, and set it on the table. As she opened it, Frank clutched a fried egg in his fist. He gave her a sidelong look and stuffed the egg into his mouth.

She stiffened in disgust. What was he trying to do, act like such a boor that she'd throw him out of the house? Well, she wouldn't give him the satisfaction of showing how he sickened her. She ignored the egg yolk dribbling down his chin, and spooned three plums into a bowl along with their juice.

Frank clutched another fried egg in his hand, shook his straggly hair into his eyes, and shoved the egg into his mouth.

He was acting like an animal, not a man. What had happened to the Frank she knew and loved? Could she jolt him back to himself?

"I heard some interesting news the other day," she remarked as if she and Frank had been having a pleasant chat over the breakfast table.

"Yeah?" he said, chewing the egg.

She raised a spoonful of plum halfway to her mouth. "Victor's getting married."

Frank choked on the egg, spewing gobs of it across the table. "Married?" he sputtered, reaching for his coffee.

Ha! Tina thought. *Got you.*

He gulped some coffee. "Your Victor?"

"No, our Victor," Tina said, trying to ignore the mess on the table. "Our friend Victor. He's coming back from Vancouver this summer to get married."

"Who's he marrying?" Frank asked. "Must be somebody from around here. Is it Lydia?"

"Guess again." Tina dared to smile. They were making progress, talking almost like normal people.

He rubbed his neck. "Could be Agatha, but I only saw her and Vic together a couple times. Unless they've been sneaking around behind the granaries."

"Frank, you'll never guess. It's Justina."

Frank's mouth dropped open like a bag. "Adeline's Justina? She's too young for him."

"She must be twenty-one, maybe twenty-two." Tina tore off a piece of brown bread to eat with the plums.

"Justina Epp? Are you sure? How would Victor get to know her? I don't think she's been back to Dayspring since she ran away from home."

"No, but you remember how Victor went to Moose Jaw for his stomach treatments? Well, one day when he left the doctor's office, he went to the army surplus store to buy some boots. Of course that's where Justina works so he met her."

"Did he know who she was?"

Tina finished her piece of bread and took another. "I guess he recognized her from the picture the Epps keep on their china cabinet. He asked her out for supper on the spot."

"That Victor's a fast mover."

Tina shrugged. "Apparently he and Justina liked each other right away. After their first supper together, he visited her every time he went to Moose Jaw."

"He didn't go that often."

"Often enough, it seems."

Frank pulled his chair close to the stove, opened the oven door, and set his feet on it. "So Adeline will have Victor for a son-in-law. She must be shouting hallelujah all day long. I'm surprised we don't hear her from here."

"Oh, Adeline doesn't know yet. Victor and Justina aren't telling anybody till he comes back in July."

Frank snorted. "So how come you and I are in on this big secret?"

"Why do you think?" Tina rose and laid a timid hand on Frank's shoulder. "Victor asked me to tell you so you'd finally believe there's nothing between him and me."

When Frank didn't shake her off, Tina began massaging his

neck. The smears of egg on his face needed wiping off but that could wait. Frank was like a lion requiring slow careful taming.

He drummed his fingers on the arm of his chair. "That Victor's no dummy. Maybe he's just marrying Justina to get close to you. He probably thinks the Epps will give him land once he's their son-in-law. Then he and Justina can live right across the north pasture from us. Won't that be cozy?"

Tina jerked her hands off Frank's neck. Forget the slow careful taming. "How can you say such a terrible thing? Something like that would never occur to Victor. It wouldn't be fair to the Epps or Justina or anybody."

"There you go, sticking up for your Vicky-pie again."

Anger blazed through Tina's insides. She seized her husband's head and turned it so he was looking past his shoulder.

"Owww, watch my sore neck!"

"Never mind your neck, Frank Warkentin. You listen to me. I've tried to be patient with you, but I've had enough. You're acting like a three-year-old. I don't want to hear another word about Victor and me. I've apologized more than once. The subject is closed." She paused. "And another thing. I want you to stay home this winter. I'm expecting a baby." She released his head and stepped back to watch his face.

He stared at her, his expression blank as dough.

Tears stung Tina's eyes. Didn't he care?

"Are you sure?" Frank finally said.

"Yes, I'm sure. I thought you might be pleased." When Frank said nothing, she stalked to the table and began scraping the breakfast dishes.

He swung his feet off the oven door. "I thought you didn't want any more babies. I thought your Aunt Irmie told you how to—"

"No method is foolproof." She banged the porridge pot down so hard that he jumped.

"Are you happy about the baby?"

"Of course I'm happy, you fool." She dipped warm water into the dishpan, biting her lip to keep from crying. "But I'd be happier if I had a husband I could count on."

He rose and threw a clumsy arm around her. "It's great news, Tina. I'm just surprised, that's all. And I'm exhausted."

"Go upstairs and take a nap," she said, tugging at the strands of hair that straggled over his collar. "And when you're done napping, I'll cut your hair. It's driving me crazy."

Chapter 58

Frank leaned back on the living-room couch, enjoying the creaking sounds the house made on cold winter nights like this. The isinglass windows of the heater glowed, reflecting the red of the fire. Tina's knitting needles clicked in a soft quick rhythm. She was knitting a sweater for the baby. The back part was almost finished. Tina said the whole sweater might be done by Thursday, when he got back from working in town.

Tina rested her knitting on her bulging stomach for a moment, then started a new row. "I wish you'd quit your job. Adeline says you're just doing it to get away from me."

Frank rolled his eyes. "Why do you listen to Adeline? She poisons your mind. I'm home three days a week, ain't I?"

Tina turned a page of her knitting book and frowned down at it. "A lot of men stay home all winter."

"Sure, that's fine for drudges like Adeline's men. Farming is all they know. But I've lived in different places, worked at different jobs. I need variety in my life."

Her needles began clicking again, though the frown stayed on her forehead. "How much variety do I get, stuck here in this wilderness? I wish we could go to church. Then at least I'd get to visit with other Mennonites."

"I told you, Tina. I'll drop you and Klara off at church any time you want." Even as Frank said the words, he wished they didn't sound so grouchy. It wouldn't hurt him to go to church with his wife once in a while. Maybe he would sometime, but not now. Too busy.

Tina pulled the footstool closer and put her feet up. "I feel like a widow in church without you."

"You went without me when Victor was here." The old

anger smouldered in Frank's gut. Tina still didn't understand how much she and Victor had hurt him.

"That was different," she said. "Victor didn't know anybody. I had to introduce him. When he started teaching Sunday School, I wanted to make sure Klara got there."

"Don't give me that." Frank bolted off the couch. "I know what you and Vicky-pie were up to."

Tina's eyes widened. "What do you mean?"

"I'm not going to spell it out for you. Let's just say I hope that baby of yours looks a lot like me." Frank turned and stomped out to the lean-to.

Tina hurried after him. "Frank, what? Surely you don't think . . . How can you even suggest such a thing? Maybe you're feeling guilty. Have you got some fancy woman in town?"

"That's ridiculous and you know it." He didn't chase other women; he had his principles. Frank grabbed his mackinaw, put it on, and went out.

Before he even reached the barn, he was sorry for what he'd said. What made him torture Tina like that? He didn't really think she and Victor had had an affair right under his *schnauz*. Why even suggest it? It seemed something almost dev-ilish got into him sometimes. Something that wanted to keep stirring up trouble between him and Tina.

Chapter 59

Tina stood near the rock pile in the west pasture, shaking a stovepipe into the weeds. Her nose wrinkled at the smell of the soot that trickled out. She'd never cleaned stovepipes with Frank before, but she'd insisted on helping this spring, at least as much as her pregnant belly would allow. Maybe she and Frank would get along better if they worked together more. Maybe he'd make love to her again.

No, that was too much to expect, she decided, watching her husband stomp toward the house for more stovepipes. She and Frank didn't even sleep in the same room anymore. He just muttered good night and slouched down the hall to the spare room. He claimed his sore neck made him too restless to sleep with, but she was almost sure that was just an excuse. He was still bitter about her "betraying" him with Victor.

Klara burst out of the house. "Daddy yelled at me," she shouted, running to Tina with her rag doll flopping in her arms

"Why?"

Klara's round brown cheeks were flushed with indignation. "I asked him to fix my dolly and he yelled, 'Get out of my way.'"

Tina set the stovepipe on the ground and put her arm around her daughter. "Daddy's busy, Sweetie. He didn't mean to hurt your feelings." Poor Klara. Frank's outburst had probably had little to do with the child. Tina was the one he was mad at, but his anger sometimes spilled over onto their daughter. It wasn't fair but that was how it worked.

Klara's doll, Lois, was a sorry sight. Her rag stuffing oozed through a rip in her neck. Her embroidered face drooped over her right shoulder. "Why don't you play with your new dolly?" Tina asked, pushing the stuffing back in. "She's nicer than Lois."

Klara thrust out her bottom lip. "No, she isn't. I love Lois."

Tina sighed, took her handkerchief from her pocket, and tied it around the rip in Lois's neck, propping the doll's face up as best she could. "That'll have to do for now. I'll patch her tonight, okay?"

Klara nodded and tucked the doll under her arm. "Come on, Lois, let's go play in the sandbox."

As Tina watched them leave, she decided that if the kitchen stovepipes were re-hung by five-thirty or so, she'd suggest to Klara that they make tuna casserole for supper. They both loved creamed tuna with crisp bread crumbs on top. Tuna casserole wasn't Frank's favourite, but at least it was a home-cooked meal. He didn't get many of those at Sigurd's house.

She'd be glad when he quit working for Sigurd. He'd need to quit soon to get ready for seeding. Maybe she and Frank would get along better once he was home full-time and back in the familiar rhythm of farm work.

Tina picked up an elbow-shaped length of stovepipe. As she tapped it with a stick to loosen the soot, she heard someone yoo-hoo from the north pasture. Adeline.

"Justina's coming home!" the woman squawked, loping along the fence toward Tina. Her burlap-beige dress flapped around her wide legs.

Tina dropped the stovepipe and went to help her neighbour with the gate. "That's good news, Adeline, but I'm sorry I can't offer you coffee today. We're cleaning our stovepipes."

"I don't have time for coffee anyway," Adeline said. "I just wanted to tell you Justina's coming home."

Tina brushed soot off her overalls. "Why now all of a sudden?"

Adeline shrugged. "I don't know. She said she's staying a whole month. She wants to fix up the guesthouse. Red-striped wallpaper, frilly white curtains."

"What for?"

"For some friends she's bringing home in July."

Sudden realization dawned on Tina, and she faked a coughing fit to hide her laughter. "Those friends must be pretty special," she said when she caught her breath. Apparently Justina still hadn't told her mother she was getting married in July.

Frank emerged from the house with an armload of stovepipes.

"Justina's coming home!" Adeline called, following him to the rock pile.

He leaned the pipes against it. "What brought that on?"

When Adeline told him, he grinned and clapped her on the back.

Watching them, Tina felt her stomach growl in disgust. If she'd told Frank the same thing, he would have snapped at her. He was treating Adeline better than his own wife, and he didn't even like Adeline. He often complained about how rude she was.

Frank's eyes glittered with mischief. "Those friends of Justina's are probably hoodlums. Probably a motorcycle gang looking for a new pasture to roar around in."

"No, no," Adeline said. "They're Christians."

"I told you they were hoodlums."

Tina scowled at Frank. "You shouldn't tease Adeline about something so important."

He gave the woman a playful slap on the rear. "Why shouldn't I tease her? She can take it."

Adeline batted her eyelashes at him like a twenty-year-old. But the next moment the woman's eyes grew round and solemn. "Frank, Tina, listen. Justina isn't the same person anymore. She changed."

"She must have," Tina said. "Otherwise she wouldn't be coming home." It was still difficult for Tina to equate the Epps' runaway daughter with the poised young woman Victor had described as his fiancée.

Adeline rolled her eyes toward heaven. "Thank the dear Lord. Justina told me and her dad she's sorry she ran away from home. And—" Adeline looked heavenward again. "She accepted Jesus as her personal Saviour at a revival meeting in Moose Jaw."

Personal Saviour. Tina sighed. She herself had almost given up on Jesus as her Saviour. He seemed so far away.

Frank picked up a stovepipe, raised it like a telescope, and peered at Adeline through it. "Maybe Justina's friends are preachers or missionaries." His voice echoed through the pipe. "Whoever they are, they're probably educated real high. Your guesthouse won't be good enough for them, no matter how much wallpaper you stick on the walls."

Adeline waggled her finger at him. "You can make fun of me if you want. But answer me this: Do you think Justina's friends will be all girls, or could there be a boyfriend along with them?"

Frank shook his head, his face solemn though his eyes twinkled. "You answer me this first. Is Tina going to have a baby boy or a girl?"

Adeline smiled. "*Na yo*, who can say?"

Chapter 60

Victor followed his niece Esther and her husband off the train a smile tugging at his lips. It was good to be in Dayspring again Good to see the sun glinting off its familiar buildings: hardware Co-op store, telephone office, livery barn. The wind off the flat lands smelled of sun-warmed grass and sagebrush. Victor had almost forgotten that smell, almost lost it in the salt-scented mists of Vancouver.

Esther put on her hat. "What a sweet little town," she said her eyes sparkling. "I can hardly wait to—"

"Victor!" Justina called, darting over from the station house

Victor dropped his suitcase and hurried to meet her. "Darling, it's great to see you." His voice rang with joy, the voice of a bridegroom. He kissed her, then turned to his relatives "Esther, Konrad, I'd like you to meet my fiancée, Justina."

Justina extended a small rosy hand. "I'm so glad you could come."

Victor's heart swelled with pride. Justina acted as confident as a duchess. A lot of girls—women—would have been nervous about meeting their fiancé's relatives. Not Justina. Not Adeline Epp's daughter. Not a shred of self-doubt.

"I parked in the shade," Justina said, gesturing toward the green Studebaker near the station house. She led the way and Esther fell into step beside her. As the men followed with the suitcases, Victor thought for the hundredth time how enterprising Justina was. Most girls wouldn't have the courage to buy a car, let alone paint it and teach themselves to drive it.

Esther linked her arm into Justina's, her light voice floating back to him. "Victor's parents said to tell you they're sorry they couldn't come."

"I understand," Justina said. "If Vic's dad's not feeling good, it's best to stay put. I'll meet them soon anyway."

Victor wondered what his parents would think of Justina. How could anyone help loving her? She was like a rose—not a hothouse rose, but a wild one, combining hardiness with her beauty.

On the other hand, how easily would Justina transplant? She'd never lived in a big city like Vancouver. But she'd be equal to it, he told himself, squaring his shoulders. More than equal.

The paint on Justina's car was peeling worse than Victor remembered. Oh well, he'd talk her into taking it to a body shop and getting it painted right.

He put the suitcases in the trunk, opened the back door for Esther and Konrad, and slid into the front seat beside Justina. As she tramped on the gas, powering the car out of town, Esther leaned into the front. "Justina, are you nervous about the wedding?"

She shrugged. "Everything's planned, I guess. As much as it can be without spilling the beans to my folks."

"I still don't know why you didn't tell them."

Justina shook her head. "Wait till you meet my mom. You'll know."

"Adeline means well," Victor said quickly. "But she's the type who likes to take over, and Justina wanted to plan our wedding her own way."

Justina grinned at him. "Vic's got Mom pegged all right."

Konrad tapped Victor on the shoulder. "What's that crop there?" he asked, pointing at the field on their right.

"That's the Hundebys' rye," Victor said. "It's coming nice, *nicht?*"

As they passed the Berndts' farm, then the Martens' and Stoeszes', Victor repeated the familiar names to himself, their sounds like poetry in his ears. He laid his hand on Justina's knee. "Darling, do you know what I sometimes wish?"

"What?"

"That you and I could live here instead of in Vancouver."

"That would be nice," Justina said. "We'd be near my family. But there are more opportunities in a big city." She glanced over her shoulder at Esther and Konrad. "Did Vic tell you he's thinking about studying to be a doctor?"

Victor lifted his hand off his fiancée's knee. "I told you Justina. We can't afford it. Besides, I'm too old already."

"We'll see about that. Mom would be thrilled. I can just hear her: 'My son-in-law the doctor.'"

Victor felt the blood drain from his face. "I hope you won't mention it to your mother." Adeline meant well but she was as persistent as a sawfly. If she thought there was the slightest chance of him going to medical school, she'd never let the idea rest.

Justina manoeuvred the Studebaker around a pothole in the road. "Of course I won't mention it. Us getting married will be a big enough surprise for Mom. I can hardly wait to see her face when we walk in together."

"Together?" Victor raised his eyebrows. "I thought we agreed. I'm going to stop at Frank and Tina's first."

"Why?"

"It would make a better surprise, *nicht?* Your folks will think Esther and Konrad are the only friends you brought. Then all of a sudden, I'll show up, strolling along the pasture fence just like old times."

Justina frowned. "I'd rather we surprised Mom together. Couldn't we visit the Warkentins later?"

Something told Victor he needed to win this argument, that it set a pattern for the future. "No, I've got to see them alone first. Once your mother gets in gear, I might not have a chance."

They passed the Fehr-Friesen corner, then the Coyote Junction School with its crumbling cement steps. As they approached Frank and Tina's driveway, Victor grew more and more nervous, wondering if Justina would stop.

What if she didn't? Would he reach over and step on the brake himself? He'd hate to embarrass himself in front of his relatives.

Moments later, to his relief, Justina jolted the car to a halt opposite the Warkentins' driveway. Victor climbed out and hurried around to the driver's side. "I'll be at your parents' place soon, Sweetheart. I promise." He leaned in and kissed her.

She sighed. "Make sure you're there in time for afternoon coffee. Mom has baked herself into a frenzy."

Chapter 61

Victor was surprised at how nostalgic he felt, sitting at Frank and Tina's kitchen table. He'd missed the uneasy familiarity he and the Warkentins had once enjoyed. Was it still here? Probably not. Frank and Tina had hardly said a word since he'd arrived.

Frank tossed a calendar onto the table, sat down, and frowned over the numbered squares. Was he still angry at Victor for "betraying" him with Tina? Or was he embarrassed, realizing his reaction had been too strong?

Tina stood at the ironing board, bulky in an orange maternity dress. She was ironing pillow cases, the smell clean and hot in the air.

A few tense moments later, she finished the last pillow case, washed her hands, and set some cookies on a plate. Coconut macaroons and spicy brown *paypanayt*. Victor was too nervous to eat. He'd better speak his piece before he lost his nerve altogether. He leaned across the table. "Frank?"

Frank grunted and jotted something near the bottom of the calendar. What was that about? Was it the day he hoped to start summer-fallowing? Maybe it was the day he and Tina expected the baby.

Victor cleared his throat and tried again. "Frank?"

Frank glanced up with narrowed eyes. "Yeah?"

"I want you to be my best man at the wedding."

Tina gasped.

"Me?" Frank barked out a laugh and pressed down so hard on his pencil that it broke. "Why not ask one of your friends?"

Victor winced.

Frank clumped over to the cupboard near the coal box and yanked open a drawer. "Or ask one of Justina's brothers." He grabbed a paring knife from the drawer.

"No." Victor lifted his chin. "I want you."

Frank returned to his chair and began sharpening the pencil, flicking shavings across the table at Victor. "People are still gossiping about how you and Tina made a fool of me." His voice was gritty, like sand in ball bearings.

Victor swallowed, feeling his Adam's apple bob. "That's why I want you to be my best man. When I marry Justina, everyone will see that I'm making a fresh start, *nicht*? Let them see you're making a—"

"Victor!" A little girl in a freshly ironed red dress darted into the kitchen, her curls flying. "You came back." She threw herself at him.

"Klara! How's the princess?" Victor asking, setting her on his lap. "You're getting so big, I don't think I can even swing you through the air anymore."

"Try, Victor, please." She jumped off his lap, bouncing on her bare brown feet.

"Okay, just a couple times." He rose from his chair. "But let's go outside. We don't want to break anything in here."

Tina held the plate of cookies out to him. "You didn't even try one of my *paypanayt*. Susie gave me the recipe. It's a new one from her aunt in Steinbach."

"Sorry, I gotta get to the Epps' place. New boss's orders." He grinned. "But the *paypanayt* will keep good in the cellar, *nicht*? Why don't you bring them for the wedding lunch?"

"Victor," Klara called, opening the door. "Are you coming?"

"Coming." Victor headed for the door, then stopped and searched Frank's face for some hint of the camaraderie they'd once enjoyed. It couldn't all have evaporated, could it? "Frank, I wish you'd forgive me. I've asked you more than once. What else can I do?"

"Just leave it." Frank rose and stomped to the stairway. "You better get over to the Epps'."

"Okay, okay, I'm going. As soon as I swing Klara through the air a couple times. But if you change your mind, just stand up with me at the wedding. Then everybody will know you're not mad at me and Tina anymore."

Chapter 62

Adeline stood in the cool quietness of her cellar admiring her shelves of homemade pickles — dilled cucumbers, sweet cucumbers, beets, mustard pickles. She'd polished the jars till they shone: green, red, yellow. This whole house was Dutch clean, even the attic. She'd be proud to show any part of the place to her daughter's fancy friends when they arrived.

She peered at the beams in the ceiling, looking for spider webs. Good; there were no new ones since she'd swept them down yesterday. Everything was ready. She smiled, smoothing the collar of her dress. She just wished Justina had told her more about the friends she was bringing home. It seemed strange to act so mysterious. Why hadn't Justina at least told her the friends' names? Were all three of them girls, or could there be a boyfriend among them?

Adeline heard tires crunch in the driveway, then Justina's car pulling up beside the house. She lifted the edge of her hairnet and fluffed up her curls under it. As she climbed the cellar stairs, she heard the kitchen door open.

"Mom, where are you?" Justina called. "Come and meet the Klippensteins."

Klippensteins? With a name like that, Justina's friends must be Mennonites. Adeline stepped up into the kitchen, smiling.

A young woman in a brown dirndl dress stood inside the kitchen door. Towering over her was a big-stomached man wearing a white shirt and black pants. Justina nudged the young woman toward Adeline. "Mom, I'd like you to meet Esther and Konrad Klippenstein."

Adeline shook Esther's hand, trying not to wince at its limp softness. It was a hand that had probably never plucked chickens, pitched hay, or even planted a garden.

Konrad's handshake felt firmer. "You've got a nice place here, Mrs. Epp. Very clean." His voice sounded like it came from a loudspeaker.

"Sit yourselves." Adeline gestured toward the bench behind the table. "Please sit yourselves."

"We've heard a lot about you," Konrad said, sliding onto the bench after Esther.

"I haven't heard nothing about you." Why had Justina been so close-mouthed about the Klippensteins? They seemed like ordinary people. In fact, they were sort of disappointing, even though they were Mennonites. Maybe the third friend would be more interesting.

Adeline smalled her eyes at Justina. "You said you were bringing three friends. Where's the other one?"

Justina pulled a chair out from the table and sat across from the Klippensteins. "My other friend had something else to do first. Should be here soon."

Adeline turned her gaze on Konrad. "Are you Esther's brother?" she asked, wondering if Konrad could be Justina's boyfriend. His stomach was bigger than Adeline liked to see in a man, but at least he was a Mennonite.

Esther smiled and leaned on Konrad's arm. "No, we're married."

Adeline couldn't help breathing a sigh of relief. Justina could find herself a better-looking man than Konrad. She was a smart, pretty girl.

"So how did you learn to know Justina?" Adeline asked. "Did you meet in church? Maybe you're missionaries." She had a vision of Justina planning to go to Africa or India as a missionary. Maybe she'd brought these friends home to help break the news to her family.

Konrad laughed. "No, we're not missionaries. I'm a fish inspector in—"

Justina jumped up from the table, making her chair wobble

on its legs. "Konrad, Esther, would you like some coffee? Or some tea? Lemonade?"

Esther yawned. "Not for me, thanks. I'd love to take a nap if that's okay. I didn't get much sleep on the train."

Konrad eased his stomach out from behind the table. "I wouldn't mind a little snooze myself."

Justina headed for the door. "Come on outside. Mom and I will show you the guesthouse. We'll have coffee later."

Adeline's heart lifted with pride as she led her daughter and the Klippensteins toward the guesthouse on the far side of the garden. The little blue building looked nice with its white curtains fluttering in the windows. So inviting. She followed the gravel path to the door, opened it, and led the way into the living room.

"What a sweet little cottage!" Esther exclaimed as she and Justina followed Adeline inside.

Konrad came in after them, went straight to the couch, and peered up at the Bible-verse plaques on the wall above it. Adeline was glad to see him take an interest. She'd bought those plaques at a church bazaar. Each one was decorated with a different flower. A red rose for *Jesus saves*. A white geranium for *Ye must be born again*. A sunflower for *Be not afraid, only believe*.

The sunflower plaque hung a little crooked. Adeline straightened it, then turned to Konrad. "Are you and your wife Bible-believing Christians?" They probably were, being Mennonites, but it never hurt to ask.

Konrad's grey eyes widened. "Of course. We attend the same church as . . . Justina's other friend."

"Mennonite," Adeline said with a smile.

"No, Baptist."

Adeline's smile sagged a little. "Well, Baptists are almost as good as Mennonites. We had a wonderful hired man last year, Victor Graf. He was a German Baptist, but we could hardly tell him from a Mennonite."

Konrad glanced at his wife. "Actually there are som important differences between Baptists and Mennonites—"

"My brother Wally made the table in the bedroom, Justina broke in. "Come and see."

Adeline beamed with pride. "That Wally, he's so smart. She opened the bedroom door. "Esther, you and Konrad ca sleep in here. Your other friend can sleep in the living room. have the sheets and pillows fixed ready."

Adeline's mouth dropped open. Somebody was standin outside the bedroom window grinning at her, the white curtain framing his red hair and freckled face. Victor Graf.

Why? What was Victor doing here?

"Hey, Adeline," he called. "What does a guy have to do t get a cup of coffee around here?"

Adeline's youngest son, Simon, bounced up and dow beside Victor, his face appearing and disappearing in the win dow. "Mom," the little boy called, "Victor says he's going to b my brother-in-law."

Adeline stared at the faces in the window, then at Justin and the Klippensteins. "Brother-in-law? What does that mean?"

Justina patted her mother's arm. "What do you think i means?"

"You?" Adeline gulped. "You and Victor, getting married?

Justina laughed. "Yup. We sure surprised you, right?"

Adeline clutched at her heart, which was almost splittin with joy. Her daughter was going to marry Victor Graf, one o her favourite people in the world.

Adeline's legs crumpled and the floor rose to meet her. Bu before it hit her, firm hands grasped her from behind, proppin her against something warm and bouncy. Konrad Klippenstein' stomach. It was good for something after all.

Chapter 63

Clutching her laundry stick, Adeline stood at the kitchen stove stirring the tablecloths she was simmering in the copper boiler. There were two of them, heavy white ones, swirling through the steaming water. Her daughter Justina was hanging five more on the clotheslines near the garden. That should be plenty for the wedding lunch.

What a pity she and Justina had needed to borrow some tablecloths from the neighbours. She would have made her own, nicer cloths, if Justina and Victor had told her sooner they were getting married. She could have organized everything better if she'd known sooner. Could have baked a fruitcake, ordered marzipan from Moose Jaw, and told Isaac and the boys to butcher a steer for roast beef. But it was too late for all that now. The wedding guests would have to make do with ham, cheese, buns, pickles, jellied salads, potato salads, and whatever kind of cake she and Justina managed to throw together.

Adeline heard her daughter whistling in the lean-to and turned from the boiler. "Justina?"

"Yeah?"

"We should have your wedding on Saturday, *nicht?*" The silly girl didn't want a proper Saturday wedding, just an add-on after Sunday morning church. That might work okay in old-style villages where most people were Mennonites, but it didn't suit a community where lots of English-speaking people lived. Many *Englische* attended every wedding, no matter who was getting married.

Justina stepped into the kitchen carrying the empty laundry basket. "I don't see any problem with holding the wedding on Sunday. It'll be simpler. Victor doesn't want much fuss."

"But it'll be so awkward." Adeline thrashed the tablecloth through the water with her stick, scowling at the idea of English-speaking people in a German church service. "The *Englische* won't understand a word of our Sunday service." Language wasn't the only problem with the *Englische*. They also lived by different rules. God didn't expect as much from them as he did from Mennonites. Mixing with the *Englische* could lead Mennonites into worldliness and worse.

"Ma, it'll work fine. You'll see. Preacher Schellenberg said—"

Justina jerked her head up as her brother Wally hurtled down the stairs buttoning his shirt over his muscular chest, his head smooth as a seal's with his hair slicked back. He glanced at the stove. "Any porridge left, Ma? Boiled eggs? Sausages?"

Adeline shook her head. "*Na yo*, my high-educated son. What's wrong with you, that you couldn't get up this morning? The rest of us ate breakfast already, even the Klippensteins." Victor's relatives were city folks; they usually slept late. But they'd gotten up early today because Victor wanted them to see the sunrise over the north pasture.

Justina gave her mother a sly smile. "I wonder if Myrtlemay McBride had anything to do with Wally sleeping in this morning."

Adeline turned on Wally, waving her laundry stick like a sword. "Myrtlemay McBride?" She jabbed the stick at her son's chest. "Myrtlemay's not even a Mennonite."

"Calm yourself, Ma." He twisted the stick out of her hand. "Just because she's not a Mennonite, that doesn't mean she's not a good person."

Adeline thumped herself down on a chair. "A person could die from such children like you."

"Cheer up, Ma." Wally dropped the stick on the table, went to the pantry, and returned with the box of cornflakes.

'Myrtlemay's okay," he said, pouring cornflakes into a bowl. "Anyway, I only gave her a ride home from the wiener roast. I'm not planning on marrying her or anything."

Tears gathered in Adeline's eyes. "Don't you know that mixing with the *Englische* brings heartaches? I pray the dear God will give you sense."

Wally retreated to the cellar and came back with the pitcher of milk. As he sloshed milk on his breakfast, Justina took the laundry stick and lifted a dripping tablecloth out of the boiler. "Don't worry, Ma. The wedding will be fine on Sunday. Preacher Schellenberg said he'd hold the service in English this time."

"English?" Adeline shrieked, clasping her hands to her cheeks. "We never had it in English before. Some of our Mennonite old people don't even know English."

Justina dropped the tablecloth into the tub of rinse water on the reservoir. "Some of our *Englische* friends don't know Jesus." Tears shone in the girl's grey eyes. "You want them to learn about him, don't you?"

Of course. Who could argue with that? But still—English in the pulpit of the Dayspring Mennonite church? Adeline's stomach churned with the wrongness of it.

Wally shovelled cornflakes into his mouth, chewed, and swallowed. "Have you got the worms, Justina?"

"Worms?" Adeline shot to her feet. "Worms?"

Wally grinned at her. "We're taking Victor and the Klippensteins fishing in Knutson Lake."

"Fishing! At a busy time like this?"

He shrugged. "Sure. Why don't you come along?"

Justina took her arm. "Come on, Ma, it'll be fun. We can just finish the tablecloths and go."

Adeline felt like a cake falling flat. "We can't go fishing. We have to shop and bake and cook for your wedding."

"Not necessary," Justina replied with an airy wave of her hand. "Last night at the wiener roast, all the Mennonite families said they'd bring food for the wedding lunch. Some of the *Englische* even offered."

"Don't worry," Wally said, his spoon clattering against the bowl. "There'll be plenty to eat."

Adeline clutched at her heart. "People will think we're beggars, lazybones, if we don't even put on our own wedding lunch." She went to the phone and grabbed the receiver off its hook. "Phone them." She shook the receiver at Justina. "Tell them we changed our minds. We'll make everything ourselves. Esther Klippenstein can help."

"Ma, there isn't time." Justina hung the receiver back on the hook. "It would be too much work for three people, making so much food so fast. We'd be worn out by Sunday."

"But what will the *Englische* bring? It could be anything—half-raw roast beef, horseradish, tuna casserole, frog-leg stew."

"I doubt it'll be frog-leg stew," Wally said, spooning up the last of his cornflakes.

"Maybe not, but we should at least bake a few dozen buns, *nicht?* And we'll cook some hams so we're sure we have enough decent food."

Justina sighed. "Ma, relax. That's exactly what I didn't want, you running around like a turkey with its head cut off. You can set the tables, and make coffee and tea. That's lots of work right there."

"What about the wedding cake?" Adeline wailed. "We should at least make our own wedding cake. If you'd told me sooner that you and Victor were getting married, I would have baked you such a fruitcake."

"Don't worry," Justina said. "I bought a nice cake in Moose Jaw. And last night Myrtlemay McBride said she and her mother would be happy to decorate it. I'm sure they'll make it look very nice."

Adeline gasped. "A person could die."

Wally scraped his chair back from the table. "Buck up, Ma."

Everything will turn out fine. Myrtlemay is going to write a nice Bible verse on the cake. With blue icing. The *Englische* aren't total heathens, you know."

Chapter 64

Tina lay wide-eyed in bed, listening to Frank snore in the spare room down the hall. She tried to copy his deep, steady breathing. She needed to get some sleep. Tomorrow was Victor's wedding day. She didn't want dark circles under her eyes.

The baby in her belly pressed against her spine, sending shooting pains into her hips. She rolled onto her right side. In that position, her hips didn't hurt as much, but her stomach needed support. She stuffed a pillow under it.

This baby felt bigger than Herbert had, though it didn't kick as hard. She'd be glad when she and Frank got to Calgary and saw the specialists his dad had found for them. They should know what to do if the baby got sick like Herbert. But what if they couldn't help? She shuddered at the thought of losing another baby.

Her lower belly hurt—a pressing, burning sensation. Of course she needed to go to the bathroom again. She could tinkle in the chamber pot, but maybe she'd take a walk to the back house instead. Sometimes a little walk helped her sleep.

Tina felt around in the dark for her shoes, put them on and trundled downstairs. She threw a coat over her nightgown and went out. The night air smelled of clover. From the barn came the fluted whinnying of an owl. High overhead, the stars glittered like peepholes into heaven.

Slim, the dog, trotted toward her, snuffling. She patted his rough head and he escorted her to the backhouse, a consoling companion. Slim waited outside the backhouse, accompanied her to the porch, and followed her up the steps, his toenails clicking on the wood.

Tina sank onto the porch bench and the dog lay down at her feet. She leaned back, gazing up at the stars. "God, are you there?" she whispered. She hadn't been able to pray since baby Herbert's death, not really. At first she'd been too angry, then too sad, then too bitter, and maybe just out of practice. But she needed the Lord tonight. "Can you hear me?" she asked.

A coyote howled in the pasture. A gust of wind ruffled Slim's coat. As it lifted Tina's hair off her forehead, Jesus seemed to speak to her. Not in words. More like flowers opening in her heart. I love you, he said. Do you believe that?

She thought for a moment. "I guess so," she said. "I grew up believing it."

I'd like to be closer to you. In fact, I want to come and live in your heart. I want to give you peace and joy, and take you to heaven when you die.

"I wish you would," Tina said.

But I can't. Your sins have built a wall between you and me.

"What sins, Lord?"

Holding onto your bitterness about Herbert. Daydreaming about Victor. Deceiving your husband. Complaining about him and the home I've given you.

"But Frank doesn't love me anymore. Not like he used to. At least he doesn't act like it."

Leave Frank to me. As for you, I want you to tell me you're sorry for your sins. I'll wash them away, then come and live in your heart.

"But Frank is so grouchy and unforgiving. He's not even a Christian. I'm surprised you don't scold me for marrying an unbeliever."

I said leave Frank to me.

"Yes, Jesus," she whispered. "And please forgive my sins. I'm sorry I offended you. Please come and live in my heart like you said."

I will. I am.

Tina waited a few more moments but the conversation seemed to be over. As she rose from the bench and walked into the house, she expected to feel something like holy fireworks in her heart. Instead she felt only a new orderliness, like her thoughts were sorting themselves into new file folders. She crossed the silent kitchen, climbed the stairs, and eased herself into bed.

The next morning while Frank was shaving, she told him what had happened during the night.

"I've heard all that before," he said, lathering his chin with shaving soap. "That sort of God-talk runs off me like water off an oil barrel, even when I try to understand it."

"I've heard it before, too," Tina said. "But Jesus means more to me now. He means the world to me. It's like somebody took a blindfold off my eyes."

Frank scrunched up his mouth to shave his chin. "Tell it to the preacher, Sweetie." His voice was muffled. "It sounds like preacher talk to me."

Chapter 65

Tina stood in the doorway of the Epps' living room, admiring the decorations Justina and her friends had put up. Vases of mauve and white zinnias lined the windowsills. A crock of pink delphiniums stood on the organ. Another stood beside the lace-covered table that Preacher Schellenberg would use as a pulpit. Pink and white streamers hung over the rows of chairs where people were gathering.

Tina smiled at familiar faces, then passed the English-speaking guests and seated herself among the Mennonite women.

She smoothed her black maternity smock over her stomach, wondering again why Justina had decided to get married after Sunday-morning church instead of on a Saturday. It was an Old Country custom that didn't seem modern enough for such a young bride. But it had one big advantage. It meant people who seldom attended church were here today. People like herself and Frank.

Her husband sat across the aisle from her, as handsome as the day she'd married him: broad shoulders, crow-black hair. But what was he thinking, plotting, planning behind those chocolate eyes? Would he take his place as Victor's best man, or was he still too angry with her and Vic for "hoodwinking" him?

Dear God, Tina prayed, don't let Frank make a scene.

Hilda Wiens, looking like a butterfly in her yellow dress, seated herself at the organ and pulled out several of its stops. She kicked off her shoes like she always did before she played. Preacher Schellenberg stepped up to the table and opened his hymn book. "Let's begin by singing hymn number 78," he said in English.

Tina was surprised. The preacher had always spoken High German in church before. Probably he was speaking English for the sake of the *Englische* visitors in the back rows.

Even when it came time for Holy Communion, Preacher Schellenberg continued in English. "All are welcome to share in the Lord's table, no matter what your denomination." The preacher craned his neck, scanning the visitors in the back. "But please don't partake unless you're in a right relationship with God."

A warm sense of peace filled Tina's heart. She was in a right relationship with God. Since last night she was. Dear Lord, she prayed, bowing her head, I'm so glad I can talk to you like a friend now. Could you please give Frank right thoughts and help him forgive Victor and me?

Tina raised her head as the ushers approached Preacher Schellenberg. He gave each of them a plate filled with tiny cubes of white bread, then nodded at Dave Friesen, the head usher. "Dave, would you please give thanks for the body of Christ, broken for us?"

The congregation bowed their heads for the prayer, and Tina peeked across the aisle at her husband. What was going through his mind?

He sat straight as a yardstick scowling at the back of Victor's head several rows ahead of him. That scowl probably meant Frank would refuse to go forward with Victor when the time came. Vic would be forced to call on his alternate best man. He'd get married with a heavy heart, knowing Frank still hadn't forgiven him.

Leave Frank to me, God told her. He'd said the same last night, Tina reminded herself, watching Dave and the other ushers proceed down the aisles.

They handed the plates to the people at the ends of the rows, who helped themselves and passed the plates along. Tina's heart was pounding by the time Dave approached the end of her row. She could hardly wait for the plate to reach her. Finally Dave handed it to her, and for the first time in almost two years, Tina helped herself to a cube of communion bread, almost dropping it in her eagerness.

With the same eagerness, she awaited the tray filled with tiny glasses of grape juice. Thank you, Jesus. Thank you for washing my sins away in your precious blood. The juice trickled down her throat, sharp and sweet as salvation. Tears of joy gathered in her eyes. She wiped them away with her handkerchief, not caring who saw her cry.

As the congregation rose for the closing hymn, a wave of generosity swept Tina to her feet. For the first time she thanked God for bringing Victor and Justina together. What a relief not to carry that load of jealousy anymore. It was a sinful attitude; she'd known that all along. Now God in his kindness had taken it away.

By the time the regular church service was over, the day was growing warm. Tina fanned herself with her handkerchief. Justina's brother Wally rose and opened a couple of windows.

Preacher Schellenberg gave his tie a little hitch, smoothed the tablecloth on his makeshift pulpit, and began arranging his notes for the wedding ceremony. Hilda readjusted the stops of the organ and propped up her sheet music. Whispers of anticipation rustled through the congregation. Tina turned with the others and watched the bride, Justina, slip off her pink flowered coat-dress, revealing a white muslin frock underneath. She unpinned the lacy veil of her hat, letting it fall, and her matron of honour, Esther, helped her arrange it around her shoulders. Then Justina turned and gestured to her father, who sat across the aisle from her.

He stepped into the aisle and offered her his brown-suited arm. Esther moved out ahead of them, and the three stood waiting for the groom and best man to make their way to the front.

Victor rose from his chair, his red hair flaming against his snowy collar and black suit. He looked over his shoulder at Frank, his designated best man.

Frank sat staring ahead like the sphinx.

Victor stepped into the aisle, raising his eyebrows at Frank.

Tina twisted her handkerchief in her hands, willing her husband to go forward with Victor.

A baby cried. Somebody coughed. The pendulum of the wall clock swung back and forth, ticking away the seconds.

Frank did nothing.

Victor stood motionless for several moments. Then, with sagging shoulders, he began trudging up toward Preacher Schellenberg.

God, where are you? Tina prayed. You could make Frank go. Why don't you?

Victor's substitute best man, Benno Fehr, rose from his chair in front of Frank's and moved into the aisle, sandy-haired and solemn. He took a step forward, glanced back at Frank, and took another. As Benno took a third step, Frank rose and bolted into the aisle. Frank's big brown hand grasped the back of Benno's jacket. "I'll go, Brother Fehr," he said in quite a loud voice.

Tina felt like iron chains were breaking inside her, one after the other. She could hardly believe this was happening, though she'd prayed for it.

Frank turned and grinned at her, giving her the V sign for victory. Then he strode up the aisle after Victor. Whispers rippled along the row of women sitting behind Tina.

"Who's the best man supposed to be anyway?"

"I thought it was Benno, but Frank—"

"That's odd. I thought Frank and Victor weren't friends anymore."

As Frank and Victor approached the table, the beaming Preacher Schellenberg stepped out from behind it and shook

their hands. Then the three men turned to face the congregation, and Preacher Schellenberg signalled Hilda to launch into
the wedding march.

Chapter 66

Frank stood in the spare room, humming as he removed his suit jacket. A meadowlark sang outside his window, brash as yellow paint. Frank felt like singing, too. He would have if Tina and Klara weren't napping in their rooms. He didn't want to wake them.

He slid his zipper down, removed his trousers, and stood grinning in his boxer shorts. He sure had surprised everybody in church today. His dramatic reconciliation with Victor had turned the wedding lunch into a near-revival meeting. Frank chuckled, remembering how the Mennonites had slapped him on the back, crying, praying, quoting Scripture verses. Some of them had paid more attention to him than to the bride and groom. Justina and Victor didn't seem to notice. They were too much in love.

The happy couple would be consummating their marriage soon, or maybe they already had. The thought stirred Frank's loins. Nothing had stirred them much lately. His bitterness had clogged up his juices. Well, he'd sluiced out the bitterness now, forgiving Victor and Tina. Dear God, it was good to feel alive again.

He stepped into the hallway, tiptoed to the door of Tina's room, and knocked. Three loud and two soft—their secret knock.

"Frank, is that you?" She sounded sleepy.

"Do you have room in your bed for a Gypsy fool?"

He heard a sharp in-suck of breath. Then footsteps padded to the door. Tina opened it, her eyes wide, her pregnant belly like a mountain under her rose-sprigged nightgown.

He threw his arms around her.

Tina kissed his ear and he groaned. He kicked the door shut, latched it, and led her to the bed.

Chapter 67

Frank leaned back on the bench he'd built for the porch, reading the paper and enjoying the evening chorus of crickets in the grass. Tina sat beside him knitting a bonnet for the baby, her thigh pressed against his like they were newlyweds. He felt like they were. Sex every night since Victor's wedding, five nights in a row. That must be some kind of a record, at least for Mennonites. It was a challenge, manoeuvring around Tina's big belly, but they managed. Love oiled their hinges.

The dog, Slim, trotted up the porch steps, sniffed at their feet, and rolled over. Frank scratched the dog's stomach with his boot, scanning the for-sale ads in the paper. A moment later he stopped scratching. "Tina, look at this." Frank handed her the newspaper, jabbing his finger at an ad halfway down the page.

She rested her knitting on her stomach and held the paper up to the fading light. "Prime farmland," she read aloud. "Quarter-section twelve miles east of Dayspring, Sask." She glanced at Frank. "That must be around here."

"It sure is."

Tina peered at the ad again. "Cultivated land. Asking $1400. Send inquiries to Mrs. Alvin Froese, 457 Home Street, Winnipeg, Man." Tina frowned down at the paper. "What's Fania thinking of, advertising her land without even telling you?"

"I'm not sure but I'm not surprised." His half-sister was okay in her own way, but she had a troublemaking streak inherited from his stepmother.

Tina handed Frank the paper. "Fania knew you were saving to buy that quarter-section. Why didn't she offer it to you first?"

"You tell me. You're the one she's in cahoots with."

Tina rolled her eyes. "In cahoots? With Fania? What are you saying? Your sister and I just enjoy writing to each other We have things in common. Knitting, painting, cooking—"

"Not being half-Gypsy." Frank waited for his wife's angry response.

It didn't come. Tina sat silent for several moments. When she spoke again, her voice was slow and steady. "I'm sorry your sister put that ad in the paper, but I had nothing to do with it." She laid her hand on his arm. "Please believe me. I hope you'll get Fania's land if you want it."

Frank pulled away from his wife. "You never liked this farm. You can't fool me. You probably hope I'll lose Fania's quarter so I'll get discouraged about living here. Then we can move to your precious farm by town."

Tina stared at him. "I wouldn't hatch a scheme like that. It would never occur to me. Why are you acting so suspicious again? I thought you'd decided to trust people more."

Frank grimaced. Tina was right. He'd turned over a new leaf at Victor's wedding and he'd felt happier since—freer in his body and mind. But this was different. This was—

Tina took his arm. "Instead of arguing, we should be deciding what to do. While we're wasting time, that ad's sitting there in the paper. Farmers are reading it, planning how to get the money to buy your sister's beautiful land. Can we do anything to save it?"

Frank's mind skidded over the possibilities. "We could start by asking Dave Friesen if Fania offered him that quarter. He's the renter. She should have given him a chance to buy before she advertised it."

"Why would Fania offer it to Dave and not to you, her own brother?"

Frank shrugged. "Maybe my stepmother put her up to it. Lottie never wanted me to do well, not really."

"Frank, could we pray about this? Together?"

Where had that come from? Tina had never suggested praying together except for saying grace at the table. "You go ahead and pray," he said, bolting off the bench. "I'll go talk to Dave."

Chapter 68

By the time Frank reached the Friesens' place, the moon was gliding high above their house. The clove-like smell of Nettie's petunias tickled his nostrils as he knocked on the door. Nettie opened it a few inches, wrapping a purple housecoat around her scrawny frame. "Frank! What are you doing here? It's late for dropping in."

He peered around the door. "Sorry, but I need to ask Dave something."

Dave's voice blared from the kitchen. "Yeah?"

Frank craned his neck around Nettie. Dave was sitting in a galvanized tub beside the kitchen stove, his shoulders like half-moons above the scribbles of hair on his chest.

Frank took a step backwards. "Sorry, Dave," he called, "I didn't know you were taking a bath. I'll drop back tomorrow."

"What did you want to talk about?" Dave bellowed. "If you wanna wait on the porch, I'll put some clothes on and—"

"No, don't bother. I just wanted to ask you one thing. Did my sister give you a chance on her land before she advertised it?"

"No, she didn't," Dave hollered past Nettie, who still stood guarding the door. "I told Fania last winter I didn't want to rent her land next year—or buy it. I'm dealing on other land."

Frank had heard something about the Friesens moving closer to town.

"But don't worry," Dave called. "Nobody around Dayspring will offer on Fania's land."

"Why not? It's one of the highest assessed quarters around here."

"Yeah, but it should stay in your family if you want it. Nobody will buy it out from under your *schnauz*."

"What if somebody does?"

"We'd freeze him out," Dave hollered. "People wouldn't have a thing to do with a guy like that. We wouldn't drink coffee with him, lend him our tools, let our kids play with his kids, or even give him the time of day."

"Is that so?"

"Of course it's so. I was in town today and everybody said the same. The guys at the Mennonite breakfast said so, too." Dave shifted in the tub, making the bathwater slosh. "But couldn't we discuss this later? I've got the little woman all primed up to wash my back, and you know what that could lead to."

Nettie's face flushed pink.

Frank felt his own face warm. "Sorry. Yeah. I'll talk to you later." He turned and retreated to his car.

He drove home slowly, thinking about his conversation with Dave. Brief though it was, it had opened a window in his mind. Maybe people around Dayspring thought more highly of him than he'd realized. Otherwise they wouldn't pass up beautiful land like that for his sake, would they?

He'd go to town tomorrow and phone Fania. He'd inform his sister that things had changed since she'd lived at Dayspring. Frank Herbert Warkentin wasn't a black sheep anymore. He was a respected man-about-the-municipality. Nobody else would buy her quarter-section if he wanted it. And he did want it. Maybe she'd accept part of the money from him now and the rest later.

While he was in town, he'd phone his dad and stepmother, too. He'd already bought the train tickets, so he could tell them when he and Tina were due to arrive in Calgary.

Chapter 69

Frank had forgotten how warm a summer afternoon in Calgary could be. His shirt stuck to his back as he and Tina trudged up the driveway to his parents' grey bungalow. His hand was slick with sweat on the handle of the suitcase.

Tina looked tired. She had dark circles under her eyes and her shoulders drooped. No wonder, lugging that big stomach around. Well, she'd be lighter in a few days and they'd have their baby. Frank hoped the doctors his dad had found could handle its health problems, if it had any.

The door of the bungalow burst open and Frank's dad hobbled out. "Children, children," he called, tottering across the porch on long bony legs. He trundled down the steps, threw an arm around each of them, and propelled them up to the door.

As Frank followed Tina inside, the aroma of roasting goose teased his nostrils. And was that raisin bread he smelled? His stepmother must have remembered how much Tina liked raisin bread with goose.

Frank's dad turned to Tina, his green eyes big and watery behind his glasses. "You must be tired. Is it too warm in here? We could sit in the back yard." He headed for the back door. "I'll go find the lawn chairs."

Frank's stepmother scurried out of the kitchen, a tiny ferret-faced woman in a grey dress. "I wouldn't call our little square of grass a back yard." She took Tina's arm. "How are you, my dear?"

Tina smiled. "Glad to be here instead of on the train."

"Lottie!" Frank extended his hand to his stepmother, trying to look pleased to see her. He never knew whether to shake her hand, kiss her powdery cheek, or just say hello. Whatever he did, it felt awkward.

Lottie shook his hand, then reached up and straightened the collar of his sweaty shirt. "It's good to see you, Frankie, but I wish you hadn't set your suitcase on my nice clean rug."

Had he done that? He hadn't noticed. Frank picked up the suitcase, mumbling an apology. Whenever he was around Lottie, he did the wrong thing. She made him feel as jumpy as a grasshopper.

Lottie rolled her eyes at Tina. "Frankie hasn't changed much. He always was an untidy boy, growing up."

"I don't find him untidy, *Muttachye*. Anyway our suitcase isn't that dirty. It's just been on the train."

Good for Tina, Frank thought, retreating to the spare bedroom with the suitcase. His wife had stuck up for him. At the same time she'd managed to flatter Lottie by calling her *Muttachye*—mother—not stepmother. *Shteefmuttachye* was an ugly word, though that wouldn't prevent him from using it. There was no point in pretending he and Lottie had ever had a good mother-son relationship.

The spare room smelled of carbolic soap. Its tarry odour always haunted this room. Frank opened the window, took a shirt from the suitcase, and changed from his sweaty one. He might as well do that before his stepmother nagged him into it.

As he rejoined his wife and stepmother, Lottie was calling out the back door, "Herbert, don't bother with those lawn chairs. They're too shaky. We'll sit in the living room."

Frank's dad raised his head as if to protest, then threw up his hands and doddered into the house.

"*Muttachye!*" Tina exclaimed as Lottie led the way into the living room. "You didn't tell us you'd redecorated in here." Frank followed his wife's gaze from the lace curtains, to the brown velvet couch, to the multi-coloured quilt that hung on the wall above it.

Tina went to the quilt like a bee to its hive. "This is

wonderful," she said, turning to Lottie with a smile. "You neve
made a picture quilt before, did you?"

Lottie shrugged. "It's just bits and pieces from over th
years."

"It looks nice," Frank admitted, moving closer to take a bet
ter look. The quilt was a patchwork of green, brown, black
beige, and blue pieces fitted together to look like a pasture seer
from a window. It was his west pasture at home, Frank realized
He recognized the rock pile in the distance, the road on the left
the patch of stinkweed on the right.

The scene looked realistic but too gloomy for Frank's taste
Too many dark patches. Typical Lottie. She hadn't put a sun ir
the picture or any flowers in the pasture, not even the sunflower
that grew along the fence.

"Children, sit down," Frank's dad said. He patted the couch

Tina gave the quilt a lingering look, then turned and easec
herself onto the couch, supporting her stomach with her hand
Frank's dad pulled a footstool from under a side table. "Here
Tina, put your feet up."

He quirked an eyebrow at his wife. "Lottie, do you think
we could have some coffee?"

Lottie wrinkled her nose. "You know coffee keeps you
awake at night. I made lemonade instead. It's healthier."

Frank's dad sighed and plopped himself down beside Tina

Poor old fellow, Frank thought, sitting on the other side of
his dad. Here in the city, he didn't even have a barn or machine
shed where he could escape from Lottie.

As she hurried into the kitchen, Frank's dad reached into
his pocket and pulled out a black and white tin of cough drops.
"This heat reminds me of my cousin Reuben Enns." He tossed
a black cough drop into his mouth. "Reuben said it was sure
hot in Turkey when he was there during The Great War."

Tina smiled at the old man. "What was your cousin doing
in Turkey?"

It was nice of her to act so interested, Frank thought. Tina knew as well as he did that his dad's storytelling was like a leaky faucet. Once it started running, it was almost impossible to turn off.

Frank's dad pocketed his tin of cough drops, pushing it in with two knobby fingers. "Reuben was an orderly taking care of the wounded soldiers."

Frank heard the clinking of glasses as Lottie bustled into the room with the lemonade on a tray.

Tina hauled herself to her feet. "Let me help you."

Frank's dad frowned at her. "Tina, sit down." The cough drop rattled against his teeth. "You're carrying a lot of weight in that stomach of yours."

"Dad, don't worry," Frank said with a grin. "My wife is tough." She wasn't really, though she was getting tougher.

"Anyway," Frank's dad continued as Tina took the tray from Lottie, "one day when it was so terribly hot, Reuben stood in a train tunnel to get out of the heat. But the tunnel was damp and he got some kind of a flu or fever from that. A Russian army doctor told Reuben, 'See those goats on the hill? They're eating wormwood. It's a very bitter herb. Buy some milk that comes from those goats and drink some every day. Or make wormwood tea and drink some every day. You'll get better.'"

"And did he?" Tina asked, handing Frank's dad a glass of lemonade.

"Oh, sure," Frank's dad said, setting his lemonade on the floor. "We have a picture of him after he got home from the war. Where would that photo album be, Lottie? The one with the red cover."

"All those old albums are in the trunk," Lottie said. She shook her head at Tina. "I keep telling Herbert, 'Build some book shelves like we had on the farm. Or hire the Hutterites to build some. They do good work.' But the old man never gets around to it. One of these days, I'll phone the Hutterites myself."

Lottie scurried into the hallway and returned a moment late
with the red photo album.

She plunked the album into her husband's lap. "I'll go se
how our goose is cooking."

Tina rose and followed her. "I'll help you."

"No, no," Lottie steered Tina back to the couch. "You sta
here and rest. My kitchen is so small, it's hard for two people t
even exist in there, let alone work." She let out a loud sigh. "I'
like to have some extra cupboards in the hallway. Herbert i
against it but one of these days I'll phone the Hutterites—" Sh
disappeared into the kitchen, her voice following her like a tail

Tina settled on the couch again, and Frank's dad flippe
through the photo album. "I'm sure Reuben's in here some
where. Must be—" The old man sucked in his breath.

Frank leaned forward to see what his dad was looking at
There, under a photo of the Mennonite clock factory in Rosen
thal, was a yellowed tintype of his father with his first wife
Morga. Frank's mother.

Seeing his mama so unexpectedly gave Frank a jolt. Sh
looked girlish in the photo, peering out from under her fring
of black curls. At the same time, there was a sureness in her dar
eyes, an awareness of her own beauty.

"I loved that girl," his dad murmured. "My cousin Abe said
'You can't marry Morga. She's just a Gypsy dancing girl. Hav
a little fun with her maybe, but don't marry her.'"

Frank had heard this story hundreds of times, but he neve
got tired of it.

The old man shifted his cough drop from one side of hi
mouth to the other. "My mother said, 'Why don't you marry
one of our Mennonite widows? What about Susie Wiebe? Sh
owns part of the flour mill.'" Frank's dad leaned over the photo
touching a gnarled finger to it. "But I wanted Morga." H
stroked her cheek. "And I married Morga, and I've never been
sorry." He glanced toward the kitchen, his voice dropping to a

whisper. "With Morga, love was a whole different thing than with Lottie. It was like Morga and I invented a love all our own. Something never known in the world before."

Tears stung Frank's eyes. His dad was just a bony shell of his former self. But he'd been a real *mensch*, ignoring other people's prejudices to follow his heart.

Frank watched Tina pat the old man's shoulder, and a warmth like sunshine washed through him. His wife was such a sympathetic person. He wished he loved her like his dad had loved his mama.

No, he thought with a sigh. A grand passion like his dad's and mama's was a rare gift. It came once in a lifetime or never. Theirs was a fiery love, blazing bright. But fire can burn out. His mama's love must have. Otherwise why would she have abandoned him and his dad?

He caught his wife's eye and gave her a long slow smile. His and Tina's love was a more gradual kind, a kind that improved over time. He and his wife weren't an ideal couple. They didn't have much in common. At least they hadn't had when they'd gotten married. But now, with seven years of shared experiences, they were piecing together a decent marriage. It had plenty of dark patches, like the quilt on the wall behind them, but there were bright patches, too. Maybe there'd be more bright ones in the future, especially once the new baby came. Frank reached around his dad to squeeze his wife's arm.

Chapter 70

The tarry aroma of carbolic soap wafted into Tina's nostrils as she and Frank retreated to the spare bedroom that evening. The smell seemed to come from the yellow trunk at the foot of the bed. Maybe she should ask Frank to move the trunk into the hall for the night.

No, she'd better not bother him about it, Tina decided. He was in a bad enough mood already.

"You look tired," she remarked, taking the bedspread off the bed.

He yanked the window blind down. "That stepmother of mine drains the energy right out of me."

"I know what you mean." Tina draped the bedspread over the trunk, trying to smother the carbolic smell. "She's not the most cheery person in the world."

"Lottie always was a complainer," Frank said, unbuttoning his shirt, "but she's gotten worse since she and Dad moved to Calgary. City life aggravates her." He lifted the edge of the window blind and peered out. "No wonder. When you look outside, all you see is another house and another house and another house. The wind can't even blow properly. I wouldn't live here if you paid me."

That night Tina lay awake a long time, thinking about her life and exercising her renewed ability to pray. Dear God, please help Frank get along better with Lottie. And bless our sweet little daughter. Help her to be a good girl and not get too lonesome at Dad and Mom's house. And please give me courage for the baby's birth.

Tina heaved herself onto her left side, and the infant responded with a couple of kicks. And help me to be more

satisfied with my lot in life. Please don't let me become a complainer like Lottie.

The next morning Tina put on her orange maternity dress,
combed her hair, and sat down on the bed. All she needed now
was shoes, but her stomach was too big to let her bend over to
put them on. She looked up as her husband returned from the
bathroom. "Frank, could you help me?"

He knelt on the rug in front of her, lithe and handsome in
his green shirt and black trousers. As Tina gazed down at his
dark head, her love for him welled up inside, almost choking
her. She clasped her arms around his head.

"Hey." Frank's voice was muffled. "What're you trying to
do? Smother me? Squash my brains?"

She leaned as close to Frank's ear as she could, her stomach a hump between them. "I need to tell you something."

"Yeah?"

"I'm sorry for every time I complained about our farm."

Frank dropped her shoe. "What brought this on?"

"Lottie complaining. It made me realize I've been wishing
my life away—wishing our lives away, always dreaming about
living near Dayspring or in Vancouver."

Frank heaved himself to his feet. "I guess it's just human
nature," he said, sitting on the bed beside her. "Always thinking
the clover's greener on the other side of the fence."

"It's more than that," Tina said. "I feel like I've been skidding through our whole marriage with my brakes on."

"Why? Do you think we made a mistake, getting married?"

Where had that come from all of a sudden? "No, please,
I'm not saying it was a mistake." She grabbed his arm. "You
don't think so, do you?"

"I guess not." He didn't sound sure. "But I sometimes wonder if I'm the marrying kind at all. I realize I haven't been an
ideal husband to you."

No, Tina had to admit, Frank wasn't an ideal husband. On

the other hand, she wasn't an ideal wife. But they were learning to accept each other as they were. And despite their weaknesses there was always that quicksilver connection between them: the fleeting joys and flashes of humour that shone through all the disappointments and frustrations. She elbowed him in the ribs "You're right," she said with a laugh. "You're a terrible husband. Do you know that?"

Frank jerked his head up. "What did you say?"

"I said you're a terrible husband. You're indecisive, grouchy, sacrilegious, unreliable, and restless."

He grinned and pretended to bite her shoulder. "And you're a terrible wife. Do you know that? You're sanctimonious, two-faced, dissatisfied, lazy. And shrewish."

"Anything else?"

He lay back on the bed, crossing his arms under his head. "That's pretty well all your faults I can think of right now. But there must be more. I'll let you know."

"You do that." She lay down beside him. "You're a terrible husband and I'm a terrible wife. We're agreed on that, so what do we do? Get a divorce?"

"Nope. As far as I'm concerned, you and I are stuck with each other. Like two burrs under a roping saddle."

Tina nuzzled his ear. "That's one of the nicest things you've ever said to me. You know, I still get nightmares about you not proposing to me. Letting me grow old and grey on my uncle and aunt's veranda."

Frank kissed her cheek. "You might have been better off staying in Vancouver."

"For years I kept one foot there—" Tina fell silent, hearing the tapping of Lottie's little shoes outside the bedroom door.

"Are you two almost ready for breakfast?" Lottie called through the door. "Tina needs to be at Doctor Kovak's office by ten o'clock. Kovak always keeps people waiting, but—"

"We're coming, *Shteefmuttachye*," Frank said, rolling off

the bed. "As soon as we finish our true confessions here."

"Shhhh." Tina laid her finger on her lips. "You're embarrassing me." She waited till Lottie's footsteps had retreated, then looked up at Frank. "Now that we're being honest with each other, there's something else I want to say."

"Yeah?" He knelt on the floor and started easing her feet into her shoes.

"I think we should name the baby after your mother, if it's a girl."

Frank frowned. "You mean name the baby *Shteefmuttachye?*"

"Of course not. You know what I mean."

"You mean name her Lottie? What if he's a boy? Will we call him Lot like in the Bible?"

"No, I mean name the baby after your real mother, Morga. She meant the world to your dad. It would be a wonderful thing to do for him. And for yourself."

Chapter 71

Frank manoeuvred the Hudson along the gravel road toward his in-laws' house, careful to avoid the potholes. He didn't want to wake Tina and the baby, who dozed on the seat beside him.

It was good to hear the crackle of Dayspring gravel under his tires again. After three weeks in Calgary, it was good to see the wide Saskatchewan sky, the clean horizon.

Actually the horizon wasn't quite clean. The trees on his in-laws' farm mucked it up, but that was okay, sort of. Trees had their uses. A guy could hang a children's swing on a tree, for example. Maybe he'd plant some trees of his own now that Tina had quit nagging about moving closer to town. He wouldn't choose evergreens though. He'd never understood his in-laws' craze for them. Evergreens were tricky to grow around Dayspring and they blocked the light, summer and winter.

Frank passed the Lutheran graveyard with its iron gate, then the pond-like slough where the rosebushes grew. As he turned the car into his in-laws' driveway, he noticed a row of spruce seedlings running along the edge of the garden. Those hadn't been there before; Rachel and Obrom must have just planted them. Klara was darting in and out among the tiny trees, looking like an oriole in her orange dress. Frank honked the horn. She wheeled around, her face splitting into a grin. "Daddy!"

She ran to him and he tramped on the brake. "How's my princess?" He turned off the ignition, got out of the car, and scooped Klara up in his arms. "I sure missed you." He kissed her and carried her around to the passenger side.

As he opened the passenger door, Klara threw herself at her mother, jostling the blanket-wrapped bundle in Tina's arms. "You brought the baby. Is it okay?"

"Sure, Sweetie." Tina hugged her daughter. "The baby's fine."

Frank gathered the infant into his arms and helped Tina out of the car. Klara stood on tiptoes, bouncing with excitement as Frank turned the blanket back to let her see the baby.

He hiccupped, his mouth forming a moist pink O.

Klara touched one of his tiny hands. "Hello, little girl."

Tina put her arm around Klara. "I know you wanted a sister, but you got a sweet little brother instead. Don't you remember what Daddy told Grandpa on the phone?"

Klara sighed.

Frank took her hand. "Come on. Let's go show Grandpa and Grandma."

As they headed for the house, Klara tripped along between her parents, tugging at Frank's hand. "We've got cake, Daddy. Aunt Adeline's here and she brought rhubarb cake."

"I could use some cake," Frank said. "Even sour rhubarb." He puckered his mouth at the baby in his arms.

In the kitchen Adeline cut the cake and put it on plates while Tina's parents exclaimed over the baby. Rachel poured the coffee, then took the infant from Frank. "He looks like a sturdy little fellow," she said, seating herself at the table with the others.

The baby scrunched up his nose like he was going to sneeze. Tina reached over and stroked his cheek. "Well, he had trouble with his blood at the beginning, but the doctors managed to help him, thank God."

Klara slid off her chair and stood over the baby, peering down into his face. "What's his name again?"

"Morgan," Frank said. "We named him after his Grandma Morga."

Adeline sniffed. "That suits him. He looks like a Gypsy. Look how brown his ears are already. He's going to be as dark as Klara, maybe darker."

Tina frowned. "Please, Adeline, I wish you wouldn't say things like that. We don't want Klara growing up feeling bad about how she looks."

Obrom cleared his throat. "That baby looks fine to me. He looks perfect, just like his sister." He grinned and snapped his fingers at Klara.

"Of course he does," Adeline said, her face flushing. "I just meant—Morgan and Klara both have such nice . . ." Her voice trailed off.

Obrom coughed, breaking the silence. "Let's pray." He glanced around the table. "We didn't give thanks for the cake yet, so I'll do it now." He bowed his head. "Dear God, thank you for this food and for the hands that have prepared it." He smothered a sneeze. As he fumbled for his handkerchief, Frank noticed that Adeline was clenching and unclenching her hands. Did she regret her rudeness or was she just embarrassed because Tina had stood up to her?

Obrom blew his nose. "And Lord," he said, "I want to thank you especially for Frank."

What? The old man had never prayed that before.

Obrom flicked his handkerchief across the end of his nose. "Thank you for bringing Frank into our family, and for the two beautiful children you've given him and Tina. Klara and baby Morgan." His voice grew louder. "Morgan. A good strong name."

Frank seemed to have something in his eyes. He blinked. Blinked again.

"And Lord," Obrom continued, "we ask you to bless this whole family. And bless Adeline and her family. Wash away our sins in Jesus' precious blood. Help us to live in a way that pleases you." He paused. "And bring us all safe to heaven when we die. In Jesus' name, Amen."

Frank shook his head. Obrom made religion sound so straightforward, even easy. It wasn't, of course. Or maybe it was for people who swallowed it whole without thinking much about it.

What about a hardened sceptic like himself? Could he ever overcome his doubts and take a chance on the Father, Son, and Holy Ghost—three guys he couldn't even see? He doubted it. Too scary and embarrassing.

Chapter 72

Tina watched Adeline's car disappear along the dusty road, then turned and trudged toward the Hudson with her parents. Fatigue dragged at her arms and legs. When was the last time she'd had a good night's sleep? Probably the night before her labour had started.

If only she could borrow some of Frank's energy. He was striding ahead with the baby, Klara skipping along beside him.

Tina's eyes drifted shut, then flew open as she stumbled over her own feet. Had she ever been this tired before? Probably not. But exhausted as she was, she felt a deep contentment. Baby Morgan was healthy, she was back at Dayspring with her family, and Frank was a real sweetheart. He'd been so kind and patient in the hospital, bringing her yellow chrysanthemums and holding her hand through five hours of labour, refusing to leave till the nurses chased him out.

Tina's mother nudged her arm. "Here we are."

The car loomed through Tina's fatigue. Frank helped her into the passenger seat, then settled the baby in her lap. As he shut the door, Tina's mom caught his arm. "Frank, I almost forgot. We've got some extra spruce seedlings. Do you want to plant them at your place? We could bring them out in a few days."

Tina held her breath. Whenever she'd suggested to Frank that they plant trees on their farm, the result had been an argument. This time she wouldn't say a word. She was too tired to fight.

"Sorry, Rachel." Frank's voice rumbled through the open window. "I'm not much of a tree man. I doubt if I could get spruce trees to grow."

Tina sighed. It was the same old story. Her husband didn't want trees mucking up his precious horizon. Trees made him feel trapped. That was his excuse. Probably he just didn't want to bother with trees.

Frank went around to the driver's side, then leaned over the car roof toward her mom. "I guess you could bring us some maples or poplars if you want. It wouldn't hurt to have a few around the place now that Tina's putting down roots."

Tina closed her eyes. Frank's words were like a kiss from God. She leaned into it, savouring its sweetness.

Chapter 73

Tina sat on the grassy hillside among the Dayspring Mennonites, fanning her face with her gloves. Her eyes hurt from squinting down the hill at the sparkling blue water of Knutson Lake, their "baptismal font."

Today's service had been long. Preacher Schellenberg had baptized four young people and preached for over an hour. Now the congregation was singing *"Christ unser Herr zum Jordan kam."* Christ our Lord came to the Jordan River.

Tina didn't have the energy to sing. She was exhausted from feeding baby Morgan, bathing him, soothing him, washing piles of diapers. The extra chores were a privilege of course. It was a blessing to have a healthy son. She just wished she wasn't so tired.

The baby stirred in his sleep and Tina loosened the blanket in his bassinet to free his feet. What was he dreaming behind those dark lashes? She stroked his cheek, watching his lips curve into a smile like Frank's.

Klara fidgeted on the purple quilt beside Tina, jostling first against her, then against Agatha Gunther. Across the weedy aisle separating the women from the men, Frank sat on a red quilt beside Bill Schmidt in his wheelchair, holding a hymn book up for Bill to see.

The wind blew the last notes of the hymn away, and Preacher Schellenberg stepped onto the flat, high rock near the water's edge. He looked like a frog in his grey-green suit. "Are there any announcements?" the preacher asked, smoothing his hair over his bald spot.

Dave Friesen rose and strolled down the hill toward the rock where Preacher Schellenberg stood. As he approached it,

Tina noticed a horsefly landing on baby Morgan's cheek. She shooed the insect away, and Morgan's eyelashes flickered open. He smacked his little lips, making sucking sounds. He must be hungry. Dear God, Tina prayed, watching Dave step onto the rock, please let the announcement be short.

Dave cleared his throat and scanned the congregation. "The Lutheran pastor, Nordstrom, asked me to remind everybody about the Lutheran Bible camp next week. All are welcome to attend. The evening services start at seven-thirty."

"All right, thank you," Preacher Schellenberg said. "I believe they have a special speaker coming from Minnesota." He straightened his necktie. "Are there other announcements?" He waited a few moments. "If not, we'll take our special collection for the Mennonite missions."

Tina rocked the baby's bassinet, trying to soothe him to sleep, wondering if this service would ever end. As the ushers began passing the collection plates, she felt a quick movement beside her. She turned and saw Klara leaning forward to tickle Agatha with a stalk of grass. Tina caught her daughter's arm. "I told you not to bother other people."

Klara sighed and flopped back on the quilt. "I'm bored, Mommy."

"We'll leave in a few minutes." Tina smoothed her daughter's hair off her sweaty forehead. Klara had been a good girl considering the length of the service. Was she grown up enough to go to Bible camp? She'd be five soon. Some of the Lutherans brought children younger than that. Maybe Frank would agree to let Klara stay with her grandparents so they could take her to the beginners' classes.

Tina wished she could take Klara to camp herself, but it was too far to drive every day. Life would be much simpler if she and Frank lived near town. But she wasn't going to start nagging about that again, especially now that he'd managed to buy his sister's land. Tina reminded herself that she'd resolved to be happy—try to be happy—always remembering to thank God for his blessings.

If only Frank would give his heart to Jesus. Then the two of them could pray and read the Bible together. He could help her raise their children as Christians. The Warkentin family could become a real part of the Mennonite community, not just occasional drop-ins at church. Would Frank ever commit himself to the Lord? It was hard to say; he'd been a doubter for so long. Maybe doubt had taken up permanent residence in his soul.

When the ushers had finished taking the collection, Preacher Schellenberg raised a bony hand. "Before we close, I want to give an opportunity for those who'd like to rededicate their lives to the Lord." He flipped through his hymn book. "If you feel moved in that direction, please come forward and we'll pray together. Or if you've never accepted Jesus as your Saviour, why not come and partake of the eternal life he offers to all who believe? While you're responding, we'll sing hymn number 9, 'Wer da will, der komme.' Whosoever will may come."

As the hymn gained momentum, Benno Fehr rose, strode down to the rock where Preacher Schellenberg stood, and knelt in front of it. Moments later his wife, Susie, followed. Then Adeline Epp shepherded her son Manfred to the rock. Other members of the congregation followed. Tina glanced across the aisle at Frank. Her husband's head was bowed, his eyes closed, though he still held the hymn book for Bill. Was Frank praying?

Tina's heartbeat quickened with hope. She rose, stepped across the weedy aisle, and touched his shoulder.

His eyes opened, murky with thoughts she could only guess at.

"Shall we go down to the preacher?" Tina asked.

Frank shook his head no. He wasn't smiling but he wasn't frowning either.

Tina sighed and returned to the children. She'd hoped for too much.

The baby whimpered, clenching his tiny hands into fists. Tina lifted him out of the bassinet. As she rocked him in her arms, she noticed Bill swaying in his wheelchair, his chin shiny with saliva, his face scrunching like it did when he tried to say something.

Frank leaned toward the young man, his hand resting on the arm of the wheelchair. A moment later Frank heaved himself to his feet.

What was going on? Tina watched her husband back the chair off the rocks that anchored it. He rolled it into the aisle, the wheels making long tracks in the weeds.

Maybe Bill had asked Frank to take him down to the preacher for prayer. She sucked in a breath. Once her husband was down among all those praying people, he might change his mind about accepting Jesus.

Tina watched Frank manoeuvre the wheelchair down the hill. Several people glanced up from their hymn books. Some smiled and gave little waves of encouragement. A few moments later, Tina saw the wheelchair jolt to a halt several yards short of the preacher on the rock.

She scrambled to her feet, craning her neck over the baby to see what was happening. The front wheels of the wheelchair seemed to be caught in a patch of weeds. She watched Frank yank at a handful of them. He grabbed more. Then Dave Friesen hurried into the aisle to help him.

Tina watched Frank and Dave tilt the wheelchair back and then roll it forward, pulling it free. As the front wheels settled on the ground again, hope revived in her heart. In a few moments Frank would be down at the rock.

Oh, no. Was he turning back? With a staggering heart, she watched him wave to Bill and Dave, then start tramping back up the hill.

Dave called to him.

Frank stopped and looked over his shoulder.

Tina held her breath, hoping, praying.

Frank shook his head and continued up the slope. H returned to the red quilt and sat down, not meeting her eyes.

Tina's heart ached as she watched Dave and Bill approacl the rock. She shouldn't have dared to hope Frank would mak. a decision for Christ. It was silly to get excited about somethin; that had so little chance of happening. She might as well returi to the car. "Come on, Klara," she said, propping baby Morgar against her shoulder.

Klara fluttered her hands in the air. "Mommy, what abou the quilt? What about the bassinet?"

"Daddy will bring them. He'll be coming soon."

Morgan began to wail and Tina cuddled him against he chest. With her free hand, she grasped Klara's small one. A: Tina plodded toward the parking lot with her children, the future stretched ahead of her like a patchwork of grey. So dreary There'd be bright patches, of course, and flashes of joy anc humour. But Frank's refusal to believe would overshadow then all.

She shook her head. No, that wasn't right. If her husband didn't believe, he didn't believe. He was still her Frank. She should appreciate and enjoy him for who he was—and keer praying for him. Maybe someday things would change.

APPENDIX
MENNONITE TIMELINE

1525   A new religious movement, Anabaptism, began in the highlands of Europe, namely Switzerland and southern Germany. Anabaptists stressed that the Christian church is, or should be, a body of believers. Since babies cannot believe, Anabaptists felt that infant baptism was not baptism at all. Instead, they baptized only adults who professed faith in Jesus Christ. Most of these adults had already been baptized in the Catholic or Lutheran tradition, so the new group came to be called Rebaptizers, or Anabaptists.

1530s Anabaptist beliefs arose in the lowlands of Europe, namely the Netherlands, Belgium, Luxembourg, and northern Germany.

1536   Menno Simons, a Dutch Roman Catholic priest, left the priesthood and joined the Anabaptists in the European lowlands. He organized them. These are some of the teachings that Menno Simons and his followers stressed:
- Being personally converted to faith in Christ
- Reading and knowing the Bible
- Living as disciples of Christ
- Being directly led by the Holy Spirit rather than by a central church authority
- Living a holy life separate from the wickedness of the world
- Keeping the church separate from the state

- Loving one's neighbours
- Working for peace and not bearing arms

1540s Lowlands Anabaptists began calling themselves Mennonites after their leader, Menno Simons. However, many Anabaptists in the Netherlands preferred the name *Doopsgezinde*, meaning "baptism minded." Persecution drove some lowlands Anabaptists to the Danzig area, which was a free state under Polish lordship. (Danzig was a port on the Baltic Sea, now called Gdansk.)

1562 and following years More lowlands Mennonites moved to the Danzig area. The majority were Dutch, many from the province of Friesland in the Netherlands. In the Danzig area, Mennonites enjoyed quite a lot of freedom, especially at the beginning. They became known for their simple, hard-working, thrifty way of life. For about 200 years, they held their church services in the Dutch language.

1600s Most highlands (Swiss and southern German) Anabaptists also began calling themselves Mennonites after Menno Simons. Persecution drove a number of Swiss Mennonites to relocate in the Netherlands, southern Germany, and elsewhere.

1683 German Mennonites, invited by William Penn, founder of Pennsylvania, started North America's first lasting Mennonite settlement. It was Germantown, later part of Philadelphia. In following years many German and Swiss Mennonites settled in the United States, first in Pennsylvania and then in Virginia, Ohio, and elsewhere.

688   Germantown Mennonites became one of the first groups to formally protest against slavery.

Late 1600s Danzig-area Mennonites still held their church services in Dutch. In daily life, however, most spoke a Low German dialect called *Plaut Dietsch*. This was a mixture of two forms of Low German. One was Netherlands Low German, which the Mennonites had brought with them from the Netherlands. The other was the Low German they had learned from their neighbours in and around Danzig. Mennonites in the Danzig area developed their own blend of these two dialects.

1693   Swiss Mennonite elder Jakob Ammann broke with the church over matters of discipline. The ultra-conservative Ammann and his followers started what became known as the Amish or Amish Mennonite Church.

1700s As Polish rule weakened, Mennonites in the Danzig area increasingly became subjects of the powerful German state of Prussia. Responding to Prussian pressure, the Mennonites gradually stopped using Dutch in their churches, schools, correspondence, and business dealings. They switched to High German, the official language of the Prussians. However, in casual conversation, many Mennonites still spoke their own special dialect of Low German.

1720s, 1730s A number of Amish people settled in Pennsylvania.

1775-1783 American Revolution. Americans threw off British rule.

1780s Some American Mennonites, desiring to stay loyal to Britain, moved north to the British colony that later became the province of Ontario, Canada.

1786   Empress Catherine II of Russia wanted to develop a newly acquired area, south Russia. Its fertile plains ha few settled inhabitants and almost no farms. Catherin II offered free land to German-speaking settlers willin to relocate there. She also offered them freedom from military service, as well as control of their own churches, schools, and many other aspects of their community life.

Fall 1786 The Danzig-area Mennonites sent two deputies to south Russia. They were Jacob Hoeppner and Johann Bartsch. The deputies inspected the land and discussed Catherine II's offer with Russian officials.

1789   A group of Danzig-area Mennonites, encouraged by Hoeppner and Bartsch, packed up and moved to south Russia. They started its first Mennonite settlement, Chortitza (pronounced *HOR-tee-tsa*), in the province of Jekaterinoslav. Like most later Mennonite settlements, Chortitza was composed of a number of farming villages. Many settlers started with sheep and other livestock, later also raising wheat and other crops.

1804   Mennonites from the Danzig area started south Russia's second Mennonite settlement. It was Molotschna (pronounced *muh-LUCH-na*). Molotschna was located southeast of Chortitza in the province of Taurida. In following years both Chortitza and Molotschna started a number of daughter settlements nearby and in more distant parts of Russia.

Mennonites became known as some of the best farmers in the country.

1800s A number of Mennonites from Switzerland and southern Germany settled in Ohio, Indiana, and other states westward to Missouri.

About 1851 Since not all Mennonites had left the Netherlands, the Mennonite, or *Doopsgezinde*, church continued there. Over the years it stayed in touch with Mennonites in other parts of the world. About 1851 Dutch Mennonites sent their first missionary to Java. Learning of this Dutch mission work, Russian, Prussian, and American Mennonites sent support.

1862 The last large group of Danzig-area Mennonites moved to Russia.

1870s The Russian government broke some of its promises regarding letting Mennonites control their own lives. For example, it threatened compulsory military service and began forcing Mennonite schools to teach the Russian language. In response to such pressures, a third of all Russia's Mennonites left. Many moved to the province of Manitoba, Canada. Others moved to Kansas, Nebraska, and the Dakota Territory of the United States.

1870s, 1880s Swiss Mennonites and Amish Mennonites who had lived in Volhynia, Russia, moved to Kansas and the Dakota Territory of the United States.

1890s The first Mennonite settlements started in what were to become the Canadian provinces of Saskatchewan and Alberta.

1899 North American Mennonites started sending missionaries to India.

1901 North American Mennonites began sending missionaries to China and Nigeria.

1914 World War I broke out. The government of Russia made life even more difficult for Mennonites living in that country. Russia was at war with Germany and the Mennonites were seen as Germans, i.e., enemies. Some Russian, North American, and other Mennonites—not believing in bearing arms—performed medical and other government-approved non-combative military service. Some did forestry or other alternative service. Some were exempted from service because they were farming, raising food to help support the war effort.

1916 A delegation of Russian Mennonites travelled to the Russian capital, Petrograd, and tried to prove to government officials that Mennonites were Dutch, not German.

1917 The Russian (Communist) Revolution began. Russian Mennonite settlements experienced a reign of terror.

1918 World War I ended.

1918-1920 Russian Civil War. Bolsheviks (Communists) and anti-Bolsheviks fought for control of the country.

1920 Years of war had driven a number of Russian Mennonites from their homes. The refugees' lack of shelter, food, clothing, and medical aid led American Mennonites to form the Mennonite Central

Committee (MCC) to address these needs. Later, the MCC became known for helping not only Mennonites but needy people around the world.

1920s World War I had all but halted immigration to the US and Canada. However, immigration began again in 1923. A number of Russian Mennonites settled in Canada's prairie provinces, namely Manitoba, Saskatchewan, and Alberta.

1928 Mennonites started their first settlement in the province of British Columbia. It was at Yarrow near Abbotsford in the Fraser Valley.

1939-1945 World War II. As Mennonites had during World War I, some performed medical and other non-combative government-approved military service. Some did forestry or other alternative service. Some were exempted from service because they were farming, raising food to support the war effort. Despite the Mennonites' traditional opposition to war, some participated in armed combat.

1946-1950s World War II had driven many Russian and other European Mennonites from their homes. Sadly, international relief agencies didn't want to help them. Most saw Mennonites as Germans, and Germany had been the enemy. The Mennonite Central Committee insisted that Mennonites were neither German nor Russian. In the MCC's words, Mennonites had their own "culture, language (their special dialect of Low German), tradition, and a distinct way of life." Relief agencies became partly convinced. In post-war years they and the MCC helped displaced Russian and other European Mennonites emigrate to Canada, the United States, Paraguay, Uruguay, and elsewhere.

1970s and 1980s A number of Mennonites moved from Russia to Germany, settling in the Bonn, Cologne, and Hanover areas and elsewhere.

Today Significant numbers of Mennonites live in Canada, the United States, Germany, the Democratic Republic of the Congo, Ethiopia, India, Indonesia, Tanzania, Zimbabwe, Southeast Asia, Kenya, Paraguay, Mexico, Nigeria, and Bolivia. Some Mennonites, or *Doopsgezinde*, still live in the Netherlands, which was a cradle of the church 500 years ago.

Study Guide

1. Who is your favourite character in the novel? What do you like about him or her?

2. What is your favourite part of the novel? Why do you like it?

3. In a museum, you might see a washboard like the one Tina uses for laundry, or a fanning mill like the one Frank uses to clean seed wheat, or a coal- and wood-burning stove like the one they use for cooking. What do such items indicate about rural life in Canada in the 1940s? Was it harder or easier than life today?

4. The novel's first two chapters are written in Tina's point of view. The next three are in Frank's. These two characters' viewpoints keep alternating throughout the novel, with a few exceptions. What does the author accomplish by writing in alternating viewpoints? Have you read other stories written like this?

5. In Vancouver, Tina enjoys her view of English Bay. On the farm, she looks out at flat prairie with a horizon like a distant wedding ring. In what other ways does her Vancouver setting differ from the farm?

6. Why does Tina leave Vancouver? Would you have done the same in her situation? Why or why not?

7. What if Frank had married his neighbour Dorrie Harms? How might his life have turned out?

8. What if Tina had married the carpenter Victor Graf? How might her life have turned out?

9. What is the purpose of marriage? What makes a good one?

10. Dorrie Harms and Roland Fast seem mismatched yet their marriage turns out well. Can you suggest reasons?

11. Frank lost his mother as a boy. How does this loss affect his relationships with Tina and others?

12. To what extent does the Coyote Mennonite community meet Frank's need for acceptance and a sense of belonging? Can you suggest reasons?

13. Why does Frank prefer to associate with local Scandinavian and British people rather than Mennonites?

14. The Mennonites are a minority in the municipality of Coyote. How might their lives be different if they were a majority?

15. Before marriage, Tina looks forward to life on Frank's farm. After their marriage, why does she long to move closer to the village of Dayspring? Why does Frank resist moving?

16. How can disagreement about where to live affect a couple's relationship? Can you suggest ways of dealing with it?

17. Before marriage, Tina tries to convince herself that Frank shares her Christian faith though she probably knows he doesn't. Can you suggest reasons? How does she try to lead him to faith after their marriage?

18. How important is it for a couple to have the same or similar religious beliefs? In what ways might they deal with any differences?

19. Why is Frank disappointed when his and Tina's first child is a girl? What do you think of his attitude? In what way does Frank's attitude change as the story continues?

20. Do you know someone like Adeline Epp? How would you relate to her if she were your neighbour?

21. Why does Tina turn away from her faith after baby Herbert dies? How does Frank react to her loss of faith? Does his reaction surprise you?

22. Frank says he'd be helping the war effort by working in the Montana gold mine. Is this his strongest motive? What else motivates him?

23. How does Victor Graf's idealistic approach to life affect his attitude toward the war and his service as a hospital corpsman?

24. Why does the author convey some information through letters written by the characters? What can letters accomplish that other forms of narrative can't? If a similar story happened in the present day, what other methods of long-distance communication might the characters use?

25. If you were Victor, would you have accepted Frank's offer of a job on the farm? Was his decision a wise one?

26. What does Tina's attitude toward Victor tell you about her?

27. Why is Frank suspicious of other people's motives and actions? How and why does his suspicious outlook change near the end of the story?

28. Why does Adeline disapprove of using English instead of German in a Mennonite church service? What do you think of her attitude?

29. Who changes more during the course of the story, Tina or Frank? In what ways do they change?

30. What do you think Tina and Frank might be doing ten years after the story ends? How might they feel about each other?